Look at the Harlequins!

'The variety, force and richness of Nabokov's perceptions have not even the palest rival in modern fiction . . . the nearest thing to pure sensual pleasure that prose can offer' Martin Amis

'He did us all an honour by electing to use, and transform, our language' Anthony Burgess

'The power of the imagination is not apt soon to find another champion of such vigour' John Updike

'He has moulded and manipulated the language with greater dexterity, wit and invention than any author since Shakespeare' *Daily Mail*

'A real magician' Paul Bailey

'The butterflies of his mind made earthworks of his contemporaries' *Sunday Times*

'One of the most original and creative ɪ   ʳime' *Financial Times*

'He has mastered all the technical triʿ invented a few of his own' Peter Ackʲ

'Besides his gift of translating a subjeʲ Nabokov has also an extravagant seɲ absurd behind the tragic' *Observer*

Vladimir Nabokov was born in St Petersburg in 1899, the elder son of an aristocratic, cultured, politically liberal family. When the Bolsheviks seized power the family left Russia and moved first to London, then to Berlin, where Nabokov rejoined them in 1922, after having completed his studies at Trinity College, Cambridge. Between 1923 and 1940 he published novels, short stories, plays, poems and translations in the Russian language and was recognized as one of the outstanding writers of the emigration. In 1940 he and his wife and son moved to America, where he was a lecturer at Wellesley College from 1941 to 1948. He was then Professor of Russian Literature at Cornell University until he retired from teaching in 1959. His first novel written in English, *The Real Life of Sebastian Knight*, was published in 1941 and his best-known novel, *Lolita*, brought him worldwide fame. In 1973 he was awarded the American National Medal for Literature. He died in 1977 in Montreux, Switzerland.

His works include, from the Russian novels, *The Luzhin Defense* and *The Gift*; from the English novels, *Lolita, Pnin, Pale Fire* and *Ada or Ardor*; the autobiographical *Speak, Memory*; translations of *Alice in Wonderland* into Russian and *Eugene Onegin* into English; and lectures on literature. All of the fiction and *Speak, Memory* are published in Penguin.

Nabokov is one of the great writers of the twentieth century. As Martin Amis has written, 'the variety, force and richness of Nabokov's perceptions have not even the palest rival in modern fiction. To read him in full flight is to experience stimulation that is at once intellectual, imaginative and aesthetic, the nearest thing to pure sensual pleasure that prose can offer.'

VLADIMIR NABOKOV

Look at the Harlequins!

PENGUIN BOOKS

PENGUIN CLASSICS

Published by the Penguin Group
Penguin Books Ltd, 80 Strand, London WC2R ORL, England
Penguin Group (USA) Inc., 375 Hudson Street, New York, New York 10014, USA
Penguin Group (Canada), 90 Eglinton Avenue East, Suite 700, Toronto, Ontario, Canada M4P 2Y3
(a division of Pearson Penguin Canada Inc.)
Penguin Ireland, 25 St Stephen's Green, Dublin 2, Ireland (a division of Penguin Books Ltd)
Penguin Group (Australia), 250 Camberwell Road, Camberwell, Victoria 3124, Australia
(a division of Pearson Australia Group Pty Ltd)
Penguin Books India Pvt Ltd, 11 Community Centre, Panchsheel Park, New Delhi – 110 017, India
Penguin Group (NZ), 67 Apollo Drive, Rosedale, North Shore 0632, New Zealand
(a division of Pearson New Zealand Ltd)
Penguin Books (South Africa) (Pty) Ltd, 24 Sturdee Avenue, Rosebank, Johannesburg 2196, South Africa

Penguin Books Ltd, Registered Offices: 80 Strand, London WC2R ORL, England

www.penguin.com

First published by McGraw-Hill International Inc. 1974
Reissued in Penguin Classics 2011
1

Set in 10.5/13 pt Monotype Dante
Typeset by Ellipsis Books Limited, Glasgow
Printed in England by Clays Ltd, St Ives plc

978–0–141–198033

www.greenpenguin.co.uk

To Véra

I. Other Books by the Narrator

In Russian:

Tamara   1925
Pawn Takes Queen   1927
Plenilune   1929
Camera Lucida (Slaughter in the Sun)   1931
The Red Top Hat   1934
The Dare   1950

In English:

See under Real   1939
Esmeralda and Her Parandrus   1941
Dr. Olga Repnin   1946
Exile from Mayda   1947
A Kingdom by the Sea   1962
Ardis   1970

PART ONE

I

I met the first of my three or four successive wives in somewhat odd circumstances, the development of which resembled a clumsy conspiracy, with nonsensical details and a main plotter who not only knew nothing of its real object but insisted on making inept moves that seemed to preclude the slightest possibility of success. Yet out of those very mistakes he unwittingly wove a web, in which a set of reciprocal blunders on my part caused me to get involved and fulfill the destiny that was the only aim of the plot.

Some time during the Easter Term of my last Cambridge year (1922) I happened to be consulted, 'as a Russian,' on certain niceties of make-up in an English version of Gogol's *Inspector* which the Glowworm Group, directed by Ivor Black, a fine amateur actor, intended to stage. He and I had the same tutor at Trinity, and he drove me to distraction with his tedious miming of the old man's mincing ways – a performance he kept up throughout most of our lunch at the Pitt. The brief business part turned out to be even less pleasant. Ivor Black wanted Gogol's Town Mayor to wear a dressing gown because 'wasn't it merely the old rascal's nightmare and didn't *Revizor*, its Russian title, actually come from the French for "dream," *rêve?*' I said I thought it a ghastly idea.

If there were any rehearsals, they took place without me. In fact, it occurs to me now that I do not really know if his project ever saw the footlights.

Shortly after that, I met Ivor Black a second time – at some party or other, in the course of which he invited me and five other men to spend the summer at a Côte d'Azur villa he had just inherited, he said, from an old aunt. He was very drunk at the moment and seemed surprised when a week or so later on the eve of his departure I reminded him of his exuberant invitation, which, it so happened, I alone had accepted. We both were unpopular orphans, and should, I remarked, band together.

Illness detained me in England for another month and it was only at the beginning of July that I sent Ivor Black a polite postcard advising him that I might arrive in Cannes or Nice some time next week. I am virtually sure I mentioned Saturday afternoon as the likeliest date.

Attempts to telephone from the station proved futile: the line remained busy, and I am not one to persevere in a struggle with faulty abstractions of space. But my afternoon was poisoned, and the afternoon is my favorite item of time. I had been coaxing myself into believing, at the start of my long journey, that I felt fairly fit; by now I felt terrible. The day was unseasonably dull and damp. Palm trees are all right only in mirages. For some reason, taxis, as in a bad dream, were unobtainable. Finally I boarded a small smelly bus of blue tin. Up a winding road, with as many turns as 'stops by request,' the contraption reached my destination in twenty minutes – about as long as it would have taken me to get there on foot from the coast by using an easy shortcut that I was to learn by heart, stone by stone, broom by brush, in the course of that magic summer. It appeared anything but magic during that dismal drive! The main reason I had agreed to come was the hope of treating in the 'brilliant brine' (Bennett? Barbellion?) a nervous complaint that skirted insanity. The left side of my head was now a bowling alley of pain. On the other side an inane baby was staring at me across its mother's shoulder over the back of the seat in front of me. I sat next to a warty woman in solid black and pitted nausea against the lurches between green sea and gray rockwall. By the time we finally made it to the village of Carnavaux (mottled plane trunks, picturesque hovels, a post office, a church) all my senses had converged into one golden image; the bottle of whisky which I was bringing Ivor in my portmanteau and which I swore to sample even before he glimpsed it. The driver ignored the question I put to him, but a tortoise-like little priest with tremendous feet who was getting off before me indicated, without looking at me, a transverse avenue. The Villa Iris, he said, was at three minutes of march. As I prepared to carry my two bags up that lane toward a triangle of sudden sunlight my presumptive host appeared on the opposite pavement. I remember – after the passing of half a century! – that I wondered fleetingly if I had packed the right clothes. He wore plus fours and brogues but was incongruously stockingless, and the inch of shin he showed looked painfully pink. He was heading, or feigned to be heading, for the post office to send me a telegram suggesting I put off my visit till August when a job he now had in Cannice would no longer threaten to interfere with our frolics. He hoped, furthermore, that Sebastian – whoever that was – might still be coming for the grape season or lavender gala. Muttering thus under his breath, he relieved me of the smaller of my bags – the one with the toilet things, medical supplies, and an almost finished garland of sonnets (which would eventually go to a Russian *émigré* magazine in Paris). Then he also grabbed my portmanteau that I had set down in order to fill my pipe. Such lavishness in the registration of trivialities is due, I suppose, to their being accidentally caught in the advance light of a great event. Ivor broke the silence to add, frowning, that he was delighted to welcome me as a house guest, but that he should warn me of something he ought to have told me about in Cambridge. I might get frightfully bored by the end of a week or so because of one melancholy fact. Miss Grunt, his former governess, a heartless but clever person, liked to repeat that his little sister would never break the rule of 'children should not be heard' and, indeed, would never hear it said to anybody. The melancholy fact was that his sister – but, perhaps, he had better postpone the explanation of her case till we and the bags were installed more or less.

2

'What kind of childhood did *you* have, McNab' (as Ivor insisted on calling me because I looked, he thought, like the haggard yet handsome young actor who adopted that name in the last years of his life or at least fame)?

Atrocious, intolerable. There should be a natural, internatural, law against such inhuman beginnings. Had my morbid terrors not been replaced at the age of nine or ten by more abstract and trite anxieties (problems of infinity, eternity, identity, and so forth), I would have lost my reason long before finding my rhymes. It was not a matter of dark rooms, or one-winged agonizing angels, or long corridors, or nightmare mirrors with reflections overflowing in messy pools on the floor – it was not *that* bedchamber of horrors, but simply, and far more horribly, a certain insidious and relentless connection with other states of being which were not exactly 'previous' or 'future,' but definitely out of bounds, mortally speaking. I was to learn more, much more about those aching links only several decades later, so 'let us not anticipate' as the condemned man said when rejecting the filthy old blindfold.

The delights of puberty granted me temporary relief. I was spared the morose phase of self-initiation. Blest be my first sweet love, a child in an orchard, games of exploration – and her outspread five fingers dripping with pearls of surprise. A house tutor let me share with him the ingénue in my grand-uncle's private theater. Two lewd young ladies rigged me up once in a lacy chemise and a Lorelei wig and laid me to sleep between them, 'a shy little cousin,' as in a ribald novella, while their husbands snored in the next room after the boar hunt. The great houses of various relatives with whom I dwelt on and off in my early teens under the pale summer skies of this or that province of old Russia offered me as many compliant handmaids and fashionable flirts as might have done closets and bowers a couple of centuries earlier. In a word, if the years of my infancy might have provided the subject for the kind of learned thesis upon which a paedopsychologist founds a lifetime of fame, my teens, on the other hand, could have yielded, and in fact did yield, quite a number of erotic passages scattered like rotting plums and brown pears throughout an aging novelist's books. Indeed, the present memoir derives much of its value from its being a *catalogue raisonné* of the roots and origins and amusing birth canals of many images in my Russian and especially English fiction.

I saw my parents infrequently. They divorced and remarried and redivorced at such a rapid rate that had the custodians of my fortune been less alert, I might have been auctioned out finally to a pair of strangers of Swedish or Scottish descent, with sad bags under hungry eyes. An extraordinary grand-aunt, Baroness Bredow, born Tolstoy, amply replaced closer blood. As a child of seven or eight, already harboring the secrets of a confirmed madman, I seemed even to her (who also was far from normal) unduly sulky and indolent; actually, of course, I kept daydreaming in a most outrageous fashion.

'Stop moping!' she would cry: 'Look at the harlequins!'

'What harlequins? Where?'

'Oh, everywhere. All around you. Trees are harlequins, words are harlequins. So are situations and sums. Put two things together – jokes, images – and you get a triple harlequin. Come on! Play! Invent the world! Invent reality!'

I did. By Jove, I did. I invented my grand-aunt in honor of my first daydreams, and now, down the marble steps of memory's front porch, here she slowly comes, sideways, sideways, the poor lame lady, touching each step edge with the rubber tip of her black cane.

(When she cried out those four words, they came out in a breathless dactylic line with a swift lispy lilt, as if it were 'lookaty,' assonating with 'lickety' and introducing tenderly, ingratiatingly those 'harlequins' who arrived with festive force, the 'har' richly stressed in a burst of inspired persuasion followed by a liquid fall of sequin-like syllables.)

I was eighteen when the Bolshevist revolution struck – a strong and anomalous verb, I concede, used here solely for the sake of narrative rhythm. The recurrence of my childhood's disarray kept me in the Imperial Sanatorium at Tsarskoe for most of the next winter and spring. In July, 1918, I found myself recuperating in the castle of a Polish landowner, a distant relation of mine, Mstislav Charnetski (1880–1919?). One autumn evening poor Mstislav's young mistress showed me a fairy-tale path winding through a great forest where a last aurochs had been speared by a first Charnetski under John III (Sobieski). I followed that path with a knapsack on my back and – why not confess – a tremor of remorse and anxiety in my young heart. Was I right in abandoning my cousin in the blackest hour of Russia's black history? Did I know how to exist alone in strange lands? Was the diploma I had received after being examined by a special committee (presided over by Mstislav's father, a venerable and corrupt mathematician) in all the subjects of an ideal lyceum, which I had never attended bodily, sufficient for Cambridge without some infernal entrance test? I trudged all night, through a labyrinth of moonlight, imagining the rustlings of extinct animals. Dawn at last miniated my ancient map. I thought I had crossed the frontier when a bare-headed Red Army soldier with a Mongol face who was picking whortleberries near the trail challenged me: 'And whither,' he asked picking up his cap from a stump, 'may you be rolling (*kotishsya*), little apple (*yablochko*)? *Pokazyvay-ka dokumentiki* (Let me see your papers).'

I groped in my pockets, fished out what I needed, and shot him dead, as he lunged at me; then he fell on his face, as if sunstruck on the parade ground, at the feet of his king. None of the serried tree trunks looked his way, and I fled, still clutching Dagmara's lovely little revolver. Only half an hour later, when I reached at last another part of the forest in a more or less conventional republic, only then did my calves cease to quake.

After a period of loafing through unremembered German and Dutch towns, I crossed over to England. The Rembrandt, a little hotel in London, was my next address. The two or three small diamonds that I kept in a chamois pouch melted away faster than hailstones. On the gray eve of poverty, the author, then a self-exiled youth (I transcribe from an old diary), discovered an unexpected patron in the person of Count Starov, a grave old-fashioned Mason who had graced several great Embassies during a spacious span of international inter-course, and who since 1913 had resided in London. He spoke his mother tongue with pedantic precision, yet did not spurn rotund folksy expressions. He had no sense of humor whatever. His man was a young Maltese (I loathe tea but dared not call for brandy). Nikifor Nikodimovich, to use his tongue-twisterish Christian name *cum* patronymic, was rumored to have been for years on end an admirer of my beautiful and bizarre mother, whom I knew mainly from stock phrases in an anonymous memoir. A *grande passion* can be a conven-ient mask, but on the other hand, a gentlemanly devotion to her memory can alone explain his paying for my education in England and leaving me, after his death in 1927, a modest subsidy (the Bolshevist *coup* had ruined him as it had all our clan). I must admit, however, that I felt embarrassed by the sudden live glances of his otherwise dead eyes set in a large, pasty, dignified face, of the sort that Russian writers used to call 'carefully shaven' (*tshchatel'no vybritoe*), no doubt because the ghosts of patriarchal beards had to be laid, in the pre-sumed imagination of readers (long dead by now). I did my best to put down those interrogatory flashes to a search for some traits of the exquisite woman whom once upon a time he had handed into a *calèche*, and whom, after waiting for her to settle down and open her parasol, he would heavily join in the springy vehicle; but at the same time I could not help wondering if my old *grandee* had escaped a perversion that was current in so-called circles of high diplomacy. N.N. sat in his easy chair as in a voluminous novel, one pudgy hand on the elbow-rest griffin, the other, signet-ringed, fingering on the Turkish table beside him what looked like a silver snuffbox but contained, in fact, a small supply of bead-like cough drops or rather droplets, colored lilac, green, and, I believe, coral. I should add that some information obtained later showed me to be detestably wrong in conjecturing on his part anything but a quasi-paternal interest in me, as well as in another youth, the son of a notorious St. Petersburg courtesan who preferred an electric brougham to a *calèche*; but enough of those edible beads.

3

To return to Carnavaux, to my luggage, to Ivor Black carrying it, with a big show of travail, and muttering comedy stuff in some rudimentary role.

The sun had regained full control, when we entered a garden, separated from the road by a stone wall and a row of cypresses. Emblematic irises surrounded a green pondlet presided over by a bronze frog. From under a curly holm oak a graveled path ran between two orange trees. At one end of the lawn a eucalypt cast its striate shade across the canvas of a lounge chair. This is not the arrogance of total recall but an attempt at fond reconstruction based on old snapshots in an old bonbon box with a fleur-de-lis on its lid.

It was no use ascending the three steps of the front entrance, 'hauling two tons of stones,' said Ivor Black: he had forgotten the spare key, had no servants to answer bells on Saturday afternoons, and as he had explained earlier could not communicate by normal means with his sister though she had to be somewhere inside, almost certainly crying in her bedroom as she usually would whenever guests were expected, especially weekenders who might be around at all hours, well into Tuesday. So we walked round the house, skirting prickly-pear shrubs that caught at the raincoat over my arm. I suddenly heard a horrible subhuman sound and glanced at Ivor, but the cur only grinned.

It was a large, lemon-breasted, indigo-blue ara with striped white cheeks squawking intermittently on its bleak back-porch perch. Ivor had dubbed it Mata Hari partly because of its accent but chiefly by reason of its political past. His late aunt, Lady Wimberg, when already a little gaga, around Nineteen Fourteen or Fifteen, had been kind to that tragic old bird, said to have been abandoned by a shady stranger with a scarred face and a monocle. It could say *allô*, Otto, and pa-pa, a modest vocabulary, somehow suggestive of a small anxious family in a hot country far from home. Sometimes when I work too late and the spies of thought cease to relay messages, a wrong word in motion feels somehow like the dry biscuit that a parrot holds in its great slow hand.

I do not remember seeing Iris before dinner (or perhaps I glimpsed her standing at a stained window on the stairs with her back to me as I popped back from the *salle d'eau* and its hesitations to my ascetic room across the landing). Ivor had taken care to inform me that she was a deaf-mute and such a shy one, too, that even now, at twenty-one, she could not make herself learn to read male lips. That sounded odd. I had always thought that the infirmity in question confined the patient in an absolutely safe shell as limpid and strong as shatterproof glass, within which no shame or sham could exist. Brother and sister conversed in sign language using an alphabet which they had invented in childhood and which had gone through several revised editions. The present one consisted of preposterously elaborate gestures in the low relief of a pantomime that mimicked things rather than symbolized them. I barged in with some grotesque contribution of my own but Ivor asked me sternly not to play the fool, she easily got offended. The whole affair (with a sullen maid, an old Cannicoise slapping down plates in the margin of the scene) belonged to another life, to another book, to a world of vaguely incestuous games that I had not yet consciously invented.

Both were small, but exquisitely formed, young people, and the family likeness between them could not escape one though Ivor was quite plain looking, with sandy hair and freckles, and she a suntanned beauty with a black bob and eyes like clear honey. I do not recall the dress she wore at our first meeting, but I know that her thin arms were bare and stung my senses at every palm grove and medusa-infested island that she outlined in the air while her brother translated for me her patterns in idiotic asides. I had my revenge after dinner. Ivor had gone to fetch my whisky. Iris and I stood on the terrace in the saintly dusk. I was lighting my pipe while Iris nudged the balustrade with her hip and pointed out with mermaid undulations – supposed to imitate waves – the shimmer of seaside lights in a parting of the india-ink hills. At that moment the telephone rang in the drawing room behind us, and she quickly turned around – but with admirable presence of mind transformed her dash into a nonchalant shawl dance. In the meantime Ivor had already skated phoneward across the parquetry to hear what Nina Lecerf or some other neighbor wanted. We liked to recall, Iris and I, in our later intimacy that revelation scene with Ivor bringing us drinks to toast her fairy-tale recovery and she, without minding his presence, putting her light hand on my knuckles: I stood gripping the balustrade in exaggerated resentment and was not prompt enough, poor dupe, to acknowledge her apology by a Continental hand kiss.

4

A familiar symptom of my complaint, not its gravest one but the toughest to get rid of after every relapse, belongs to what Moody, the London specialist, was the first to term the 'numerical nimbus' syndrome. His account of my case has been recently reprinted in his collected works. It teems with ludicrous inaccuracies. That 'nimbus' means nothing. 'Mr. N., a Russian nobleman' did *not* display any 'signs of degeneracy.' He was not '32' but 22 when he consulted that fatuous celebrity. Worst of all, Moody lumps me with a Mr. V.S. who is less of a postscriptum to the abridged description of *my* 'nimbus' than an intruder whose sensations are mixed with mine throughout that learned paper. True, the symptom in question is not easy to describe, but I think I can do better than either Professor Moody or my vulgar and voluble fellow sufferer.

At its worst it went like this: An hour or so after falling asleep (generally well after midnight and with the humble assistance of a little Old Mead or Chartreuse) I would wake up (or rather 'wake in') momentarily mad. The hideous pang in my brain was triggered by some hint of faint light in the line of my sight, for no matter how carefully I might have topped the well-meaning efforts of a servant by my own struggles with blinds and purblinds, there always remained some damned slit, some atom or dimmet of artificial streetlight or natural moonlight that signaled inexpressible peril when I raised my head with a gasp above the level of a choking dream. Along the dim slit brighter points traveled with dreadful meaningful intervals between them. Those dots corresponded, perhaps, to my rapid heart-beats or were connected optically with the blinking of wet eyelashes but the rationale of it is inessential; its dreadful part was my realizing in helpless panic that the event had been stupidly unforeseen, yet had been bound to happen and was the representation of a fatidic problem which had to be solved lest I perish and indeed might have been solved now if I had given it some forethought or had been less sleepy and weak-witted at this all-important moment. The problem itself was of a calculatory order: certain relations between the twinkling points had to be measured or, in my case, guessed, since my torpor prevented me from counting them properly, let alone recalling what the *safe* number should be. Error meant instant retribution – beheading by a giant or worse; the right guess, per contra, would allow me to escape into an enchanting region situated just beyond the gap I had to wriggle through in the thorny riddle, a region resembling in its idyllic abstraction those little landscapes engraved as suggestive vignettes – a brook, a *bosquet* – next to capital letters of weird, ferocious shape such as a Gothic *B* beginning a chapter in old books for easily frightened children. But how could I know in my torpor and panic that *this* was the simple solution, that the brook and the boughs and the beauty of the Beyond all began with the initial of Being?

There were nights, of course, when my reason returned at once and I rearranged the curtains and presently slept. But at other, more critical times, when I was far from well yet and would experience that nobleman's nimbus, it took me up to several hours to abolish the optical spasm which even the light of day could not overcome. My first night in any new place never fails to be hideous and is followed by a dismal day. I was racked with neuralgia, I was jumpy and pustulous, and unshaven, and I refused to accompany the Blacks to a seaside party to which I had been, or was told I had been, also invited. In fact, those first days at Villa Iris are so badly distorted in my diary, and so blurred in my mind, that I am not sure if, perhaps, Iris and Ivor were not absent till the middle of the week. I remember, however, that they were kind enough to arrange an appointment for me with a doctor in Cannice. This presented itself as a splendid opportunity to check the incompetence of my London luminary against that of a local one.

The appointment was with Professor Junker, a double personage, consisting of husband and wife. They had been practicing as a team for thirty years now, and every Sunday, in a secluded, though consequently rather dirty, corner of the beach, the two analyzed each other. They were supposed by their patients to be particularly alert on Mondays, but I was not, having got frightfully tight in one or two pubs before reaching the mean quarter where the Junkers and other doctors lived, as I seemed to have gathered. The front entrance was all right being among the flowers and fruit of a market place, but wait till you see the back. I was received by the female partner, a squat old thing wearing trousers, which was delightfully daring in 1922. That theme was continued immediately outside the casement of the W.C. (where I had to fill an absurd vial large enough for a doctor's purpose but not for mine) by the performance that a breeze was giving above a street sufficiently narrow for three pairs of long drawers to cross over on a string in as many strides or leaps. I commented on this and on a stained-glass window in the consulting room featuring a mauve lady exactly similar to the one on the stairs of Villa Iris. Mrs. Junker asked me if I liked boys or girls, and I looked around saying guardedly that I did not know what she had to offer. She did not laugh. The consultation was not a success. Before diagnosing neuralgia of the jaw, she wanted me to see a dentist when sober. It was right across, she said. I know she rang him up to arrange my visit but do not remember if I went there the same afternoon or the next. His name was Molnar with that *n* like a grain in a cavity; I used him some forty years later in *A Kingdom by the Sea*.

A girl whom I took to be the dentist's assistant (which, however, she was much too holidayish in dress to be) sat cross-legged talking on the phone in the hallway and merely directed me to a door with the cigarette she was holding without otherwise interrupting her occupation. I found myself in a banal and silent room. The best seats had been taken. A large conventional oil, above a cluttered bookshelf, depicted an alpine torrent with a fallen tree lying across it. From the shelf a few magazines had already wandered at some earlier consultation hour onto an oval table which supported its own modest array of things, such as an empty flower vase and a watch-size *casse-tête*. This was a wee circular labyrinth, with five silvery peas inside that had to be coaxed by judicious turns of the wrist into the center of the helix. For waiting children.

None were present. A corner armchair contained a fat fellow with a nosegay of carnations across his lap. Two elderly ladies were seated on a brown sofa – strangers to each other, if one took into account the urbane interval between them. Leagues away from them, on a cushioned stool, a cultured-looking young man, possibly a novelist, sat holding a small memoranda book in which he kept penciling separate items – possibly the description of various objects his eyes roved over in between notes – the ceiling, the wallpaper, the picture, and the hairy nape of a man who stood by the window, with his hands clasped behind him, and gazed idly, beyond flapping underwear, beyond the mauve casement of the Junkers' W.C., beyond the roofs and foothills, at a distant range of mountains where, I idly thought, there still might exist that withered pine bridging the painted torrent.

Presently a door at the end of the room flew open with a laughing sound, and the dentist entered, ruddy-faced, bow-tied, in an ill-fitting suit of festive gray with a rather jaunty black armband. Handshakes and congratulations followed. I started reminding him of our appointment, but a dignified old lady in whom I recognized Madame Junker interrupted me saying it was her mistake. In the meantime Miranda, the daughter of the house whom I had seen a moment ago, inserted the long pale stems of her uncle's carnations into a tight vase on the table which by now was miraculously draped. A soubrette placed upon it, amid much applause, a great sunset-pink cake with '50' in calligraphic cream. 'What a charming attention!' exclaimed the widower. Tea was served and several groups sat down, others stood, glass in hand. I heard Iris warning me in a warm whisper that it was spiced apple juice, not liquor, so with raised hands I recoiled from the tray proffered by Miranda's fiancé, the person whom I had caught using a spare moment to check certain details of the dowry. 'We were not expecting you to turn up,' said Iris, giving the show away, for this could not be the *partie de plaisir* to which I had been invited ('They have a lovely place on a rock'). No, I believe that much of the confused impressions listed here in connection with doctors and dentists must be classed as an oneiric experience during a drunken siesta. This is corroborated scriptorially. Glancing through my oldest notes in pocket diaries, with telephone numbers and names elbowing their way among reports on events, factual or more or less fictional, I notice that dreams and other distortions of 'reality' are written down in a special left-slanted hand – at least in the earlier entries, before I gave up following accepted distinctions. A lot of the pre-Cantabrigian stuff displays that script (but the soldier really did collapse in the path of the fugitive king).

5

I know I have been called a solemn owl but I do detest practical jokes and am bored stiff ('Only humorless people use that phrase,' according to Ivor) by a constant flow of facetious insults and vulgar puns ('A stiff borer is better than a limp one' – Ivor again). He was a good chap, however, and it was not really respite from his banter that made me welcome his regular week-day absences. He worked in a travel agency run by his Aunt Betty's former *homme d'affaires*, an eccentric in his own right, who had promised Ivor a bonus in the form of an Icarus phaeton if he was good.

My health and handwriting very soon reverted to normal, and I began to enjoy the South. Iris and I lounged for hours (she wearing a black swimsuit, I flannels and blazer) in the garden, which I preferred at first, before the inevitable seduction of seabathing, to the flesh of the *plage*. I translated for her several short poems by Pushkin and Lermontov, paraphrasing and touching them up for better effect. I told her in dramatic detail of my escape from my country. I mentioned great exiles of old. She listened to me like Desdemona.

'I'd love to learn Russian,' she said with the polite wistfulness which goes with that confession. 'My aunt was practically born in Kiev and at seventy-five still remembered a few Russian and Rumanian words, but I am a rotten linguist. How do you say "eucalypt" in your language?'

'*Evkalipt.*'

'Oh, that would make a nice name for a man in a short story. "F. Clipton." Wells has a "Mr. Snooks" that turns out to derive from "Seven Oaks." I adore Wells, don't you?'

I said that he was the greatest romancer and magician of our time, but that I could not stand his sociological stuff.

Nor could she. And did I remember what Stephen said in *The Passionate Friends* when he left the room – the neutral room – where he had been allowed to see his mistress for the very last time?

'I can answer that. The furniture there was slipcovered, and he said, "It's because of the flies." '

'Yes! Isn't that marvelous! Just blurting out something so as not to cry. It makes one think of the housefly an old Master would paint on a sitter's hand to show that the person had died in the meantime.'

I said I always preferred the literal meaning of a description to the symbol behind it. She nodded thoughtfully but did not seem convinced.

And who was our favorite modern poet? How about Housman?

I had seen him many times from afar and once, plain. It was in the Trinity Library. He stood holding an open book but looking at the ceiling as if trying to remember something – perhaps, the way another author had translated that line.

She said she would have been 'terribly thrilled.' She uttered those words thrusting forward her earnest little face and vibrating it, the face, with its sleek bangs, rapidly.

'You ought to be thrilled *now*! After all, I'm *here*, this is the summer of 1922, this is your brother's house –'

'It is not,' she said, sidestepping the issue (and at the twist of her speech I felt a sudden overlap in the texture of time as if this had happened before or would happen again); 'It is *my* house, Aunt Betty left it to *me* as well as some money, but Ivor is too stupid or proud to let me pay his appalling debts.'

The shadow of my rebuke was more than a shadow. I actually believed even then, in my early twenties, that by mid-century I would be a famous and free author, living in a free, universally respected Russia, on the English quay of the Neva or on one of my splendid estates in the country, and writing there prose and poetry in the infinitely plastic tongue of my ancestors: among them I counted one of Tolstoy's grand-aunts and two of Pushkin's boon companions. The forefeel of fame was as heady as the old wines of nostalgia.

It was remembrance in reverse, a great lakeside oak reflected so picturesquely in such clear waters that its mirrored branches looked like glorified roots. I felt this future fame in my toes, in the tips of my fingers, in the hair of my head, as one feels the shiver caused by an electric storm, by the dying beauty of a singer's dark voice just before the thunder, or by one line in *King Lear*. Why do tears blur my glasses when I invoke that phantasm of fame as it tempted and tortured me then, five decades ago? Its image was innocent, its image was genuine, its difference from what actually was to be breaks my heart like the pangs of separation.

No ambition, no honors tainted the fanciful future. The President of the Russian Academy advanced toward me to the sound of slow music with a wreath on the cushion he held – and had to retreat growling as I shook my graying head. I saw myself correcting the page proof of a new novel which was to change the destiny of Russian literary style as a matter of course – *my* course (with no self-love, no smugness, no surprise on my part) – and reworking so much of it in the margin – where inspiration finds its sweetest clover – that the whole had to be set anew. When the book made its belated appearance, as I gently aged, I might enjoy entertaining a few dear sycophantic friends in the arbor of my favorite manor of Marevo (where I had first 'looked at the harlequins') with its alley of fountains and its shimmering view of a virgin bit of Volgan steppeland. It *had* to be that way.

From my cold bed in Cambridge I surveyed a whole period of new Russian literature. I looked forward to the refreshing presence of inimical but courteous critics who would chide me in the St. Petersburg literary reviews for my pathological indifference to politics, major ideas in minor minds, and such vital problems as overpopulation in urban centers. No less amusing was it to envisage the inevitable pack of crooks and ninnies abusing the smiling marble, and ill with envy, maddened by their own mediocrity, rushing in pattering hordes to the lemming's doom but presently all running back from the opposite side of the stage, having missed not only the point of my book but also their rodential Gadara.

The poems I started composing after I met Iris were meant to deal with her actual, unique traits – the way her forehead wrinkled when she raised her eyebrows, waiting for me to see the point of her joke, or the way it developed a totally different set of soft folds as she frowned over the Tauchnitz in which she searched for the passage she wanted to share with me. My instrument, however, was still too blunt and immature; it could not express the divine detail, and *her* eyes, *her* hair became hopelessly generalized in my otherwise well-shaped strophes.

None of those descriptive and, let us be frank, banal pieces, were good enough (particularly when nakedly Englished without rhyme or treason) to be shown to Iris; and, besides, an odd shyness – which I had never felt before when courting a girl in the brisk preliminaries of my carnal youth – kept me back from submitting to Iris a tabulation of her charms. On the night of July 20, however, I composed a more oblique, more metaphysical little poem which I decided to show her at breakfast in a literal translation that took me longer to write than the original. The title, under which it appeared in an *émigré* daily in Paris (October 8, 1922, after several reminders on my part and one please-return request) was, and is, in the various anthologies and collections that were to reprint it in the course of the next fifty years, *Vlyublyonnost'*, which puts in a golden nutshell what English needs three words to express.

> *My zabyváem chto vlyublyónnost'*
> *Ne prósto povorót litsá,*
> *A pod kupávami bezdónnost',*
> *Nochnáya pánika plovtsá.*
>
> *Pokúda snítsya, snís', vlyublyónnost',*
> *No probuzhdéniem ne múch',*
> *I lúchshe nedogovoryónnost'*
> *Chem éta shchél' i étot lúch.*
>
> *Napomináyu chto vlyublyónnost'*
> *Ne yáv', chto métiny ne té,*
> *Chto mózhet-byt' potustorónnost'*
> *Priotvorílas' v temnoté.*

'Lovely,' said Iris. 'Sounds like an incantation. What does it mean?'

'I have it here on the back. It goes like this. We forget – or rather tend to forget – that being in love (*vlyublyonnost'*) does not depend on the facial angle of the loved one, but is a bottomless spot under the nenuphars, *a swimmer's panic in the night* (here the iambic tetrameter happens to be rendered – last line of the first stanza, *nochnáya pánika plovtsá*). Next stanza: While the dreaming is good – in the sense of "while the going is good" – do keep appearing to us in our dreams, *vlyublyonnost'*, but do not torment us by waking us up or telling too much: reticence is better than that chink and that moonbeam. Now comes the last stanza of this philosophical love poem.'

'This what?'

'Philosophical love poem. *Napominágu*, I remind you, that *vlyublyonnost'* is not wide-awake reality, that the markings are not the same (a moon-striped ceiling, *polosatyy ot luny potolok*, is, for instance, not the same kind of reality as a ceiling by day), and that, maybe, the hereafter stands slightly ajar in the dark. *Voilà.*'

'Your girl,' remarked Iris, 'must be having a jolly good time in your company. Ah, here comes our breadwinner. *Bonjour*, Ives. The toast is all gone, I'm afraid. We thought you'd left hours ago.'

She fitted her palm for a moment to the cheek of the teapot. And it went into *Ardis*, it all went into *Ardis*, my poor dead love.

6

After fifty summers, or ten thousand hours, of sunbathing in various countries, on beaches, benches, roofs, rocks, decks, ledges, lawns, boards, and balconies, I might have been unable to recall my novitiate in sensory detail had not there been those old notes of mine which are such a solace to a pedantic memoirist throughout the account of his illnesses, marriages, and literary life. Enormous amounts of Shaker's Cold Cream were rubbed by kneeling and cooing Iris into my back as I lay prone on a rough towel in the blaze of the *plage*. Beneath my shut eyelids pressed to my forearm swam purple photomatic shapes: 'Through the prose of sun blisters came the poetry of her touch –,' thus in my pocket diary, but I can improve upon my young preciosity. Through the itch of my skin, and in fact seasoned by that itch to an exquisite degree of rather ridiculous enjoyment, the touch of her hand on my shoulder blades and along my spine resembled too closely a deliberate caress not to be deliberate mimicry, and I could not curb a hidden response to those nimble fingers when in a final gratuitous flutter they traveled down to my very coccyx, before fading away.

'There,' said Iris with exactly the same intonation as that used, at the end of a more special kind of treatment, by one of my Cambridge sweethearts, Violet McD., an experienced and compassionate virgin.

She, Iris, had had several lovers, and as I opened my eyes and turned to her, and saw her, and the dancing diamonds in the blue-green inward of every advancing, every tumbling wave, and the wet black pebbles on the sleek fore-beach with dead foam waiting for live foam – and, oh, there it comes, the crested wave line, trotting again like white circus ponies abreast, I understood, as I perceived her against that backdrop, how much adulation, how many lovers had helped form and perfect my Iris, with that impeccable complexion of hers, that absence of any uncertainty in the profile of her high cheekbone, the elegance of the hollow beneath it, the *accroche-coeur* of a sleek little flirt.

'By the way,' said Iris as she changed from a kneeling to a half-recumbent position, her legs curled under her, 'by the way, I have not apologized yet for my dismal remark about that poem. I now have reread your 'Valley Blondies' (*vlyublyonnost'*) a hundred times, both the English for the matter and the Russian for the music. I think it's an absolutely divine piece. Do you forgive me?'

I pursed my lips to kiss the brown iridescent knee near me but her hand, as if measuring a child's fever, palmed my forehead and stopped its advance.

'We are watched,' she said, 'by a number of eyes which seem to look everywhere except in our direction. The two nice English schoolteachers on my right – say, twenty paces away – have already told me that your resemblance to the naked-neck photo of Rupert Brooke is *a-houri-sang* – they know a little French. If you ever try to kiss me, or my leg, again, I'll beg you to leave. I've been sufficiently hurt in my life.'

A pause ensued. The iridescence came from atoms of quartz. When a girl starts to speak like a novelette, all you need is a little patience.

Had I posted the poem to that *émigré* paper? Not yet; my garland of sonnets had had to be sent first. The two people (lowering my voice) on my left were fellow expatriates, judging by certain small indices. 'Yes,' agreed Iris, 'they practically got up to stand at attention when you started to recite that Pushkin thing about waves lying down in adoration at her feet. What other signs?'

'He kept stroking his beard very slowly from top to tip as he looked at the horizon and she smoked a cigarette with a cardboard mouth-piece.'

There was also a child of ten or so cradling a large yellow beach ball in her bare arms. She seemed to be wearing nothing but a kind of frilly harness and a very short pleated skirt revealing her trim thighs. She was what in a later era amateurs were to call a 'nymphet.' As she caught my glance she gave me, over our sunny globe, a sweet lewd smile from under her auburn fringe.

'At eleven or twelve,' said Iris, 'I was as pretty as that French orphan. That's her grandmother all in black sitting on a spread Cannice-Matin with her knitting. I let smelly gentlemen fondle me. I played indecent games with Ivor – oh nothing very unusual, and anyway he now prefers dons to donnas – at least that's what he says.'

She talked a little about her parents who by a fascinating coincidence had died on the same day, she at seven A.M. in New York, he at noon in London, only two years ago. They had separated soon after the war. She was American and horrible. You don't speak like that of your mother but she was really horrible. Dad was Vice President of the Samuels Cement Company when he died. He came from a respectable family and had 'good connections.' I asked what grudge exactly did Ivor bear to 'society' and vice versa? She vaguely replied he disliked the 'fox-hunting set' and the 'yachting crowd.' I said those were abominable clichés used only by Philistines. In my set, in my world, in the opulent Russia of my boyhood we stood so far above any concept of 'class' that we only laughed or yawned when reading about 'Japanese Barons' or 'New England Patricians.' Yet strangely enough Ivor stopped clowning and became a normal serious individual only when he straddled his old, dappled, bald hobbyhorse and started reviling the English 'upper classes' – especially their pronunciation. It was, I remonstrated, a speech superior in quality to the best Parisian French, and even to a Petersburgan's Russian; a delightfully modulated whinny, which both he and Iris were rather successfully, though no doubt unconsciously, imitating in their every-day intercourse, when not making protracted fun of a harmless foreigner's stilted or outdated English. By the way what was the nationality of the bronzed old man with the hoary chest hair who was wading out of the low surf preceded by his bedrabbled dog – I thought I knew his face.

It was, she said, Kanner, the great pianist and butterfly hunter, his face and name were on all the Morris columns. She was getting tickets for at least two of his concerts; and there, right there, where his dog was shaking itself, the P. family (exalted old name) had basked in June when the place was practically empty, and cut Ivor, though he knew young L.P. at Trinity. They'd now moved down there. Even more select. See that orange dot? That's their cabana. Foot of the Mirana Palace. I said nothing but I too knew young P. and disliked him.

Same day. Ran into him in the Mirana Men's Room. Was effusively welcomed. Would I care to meet his sister, tomorrow is what? Saturday. Suggested they stroll over tomorrow afternoon to the foot of the Victoria. Sort of cove to your right. I'm there with friends. Of course you know Ivor Black. Young P. duly turned up, with lovely, long-limbed sister. Ivor – frightfully rude. Rise, Iris, you forget we are having tea with Rapallovich and Chicherini. That sort of stuff. Idiotic feuds. Lydia P. screamed with laughter.

Upon discovering the effect of that miracle cream, at my boiled-lobster stage, I switched from a conservative *caleçon de bain* to a briefer variety (still banned at the time in stricter paradises). The delayed change resulted in a bizarre stratification of tan. I recall sneaking into Iris's room to contemplate myself in a full-length looking glass – the only one in the house – on a morning she had chosen for a visit to a beauty salon, which I called up to make sure she was there and not in the arms of a lover. Except for a Provençal boy polishing the banisters, there was nobody around, thus allowing me to indulge in one of my oldest and naughtiest pleasures: circulating stark naked all over a strange house.

The full-length portrait was not altogether a success, or rather contained an element of levity not improper to mirrors and medieval pictures of exotic beasts. My face was brown, my torso and arms caramel, a carmine equatorial belt undermargined the caramel, then came a white, more or less triangular, southward pointed space edged with the redundant carmine on both sides, and (owing to my wearing shorts all day) my legs were as brown as my face. Apically, the white of the abdomen, brought out in frightening *repoussé*, with an ugliness never noticed before, a man's portable zoo, a symmetrical mass of animal attributes, the elephant proboscis, the twin sea urchins, the baby gorilla, clinging to my underbelly with its back to the public.

A warning spasm shot through my nervous system. The fiends of my incurable ailment, 'flayed consciousness,' were shoving aside my harlequins. I sought first-aid distraction in the baubles of my love's lavender-scented bedroom: a Teddy bear dyed violet, a curious French novel (*Du côté de chez Swann*) that I had bought for her, a trim pile of freshly laundered linen in a Moïse basket, a color photograph of two girls in a fancy frame, obliquely inscribed as 'The Lady Cressida and thy sweet Nell, Cambridge 1919'; I mistook the former for Iris herself in a golden wig and a pink make-up; a closer inspection, however, showed it to be Ivor in the part of that highly irritating girl bobbing in and out of Shakespeare's flawed farce. But, then, Mnemosyne's chromodiascope can also become a bore.

In the music room the boy was now cacophonically dusting the keys of the Bechstein as with less zest I resumed my nudist rambles. He asked me what sounded like '*Hora?*,' and I demonstrated my wrist turning it this way and that to reveal only a pale ghost of watch and watch bracelet. He completely misinterpreted my gesture and turned away shaking his stupid head. It was a morning of errors and failures.

I made my way to the pantry for a glass or two of wine, the best breakfast in times of distress. In the passage I trod on a shard of crockery (we had heard the crash on the eve) and danced on one foot with a curse as I tried to examine the imaginary gash in the middle of my pale sole.

The litre of *rouge* I had visualized was there all right, but I could not find a corkscrew in any of the drawers. Between bangs the macaw could be heard crying out something crude and dreary. The postman had come and gone. The editor of *The New Aurora* (*Novaya Zarya*) was afraid (dreadful poltroons, those editors) that his 'modest *émigré* venture (*nachinanie*)' could not etc. – a crumpled 'etc.' that flew into the garbage pail. Wineless, wrathful, with Ivor's *Times* under my arm, I slapped up the back stairs to my stuffy room. The rioting in my brain had now started.

It was then that I resolved, sobbing horribly into my pillow, to preface tomorrow's proposal of marriage with a confession that might make it unacceptable to my Iris.

7

If one looked from our garden gate down the asphalted avenue leading through leopard shade to the village some two hundred paces east, one saw the pink cube of the little post office, its green bench in front, its flag above, all this limned with the numb brightness of a color transparency, between the last two plane trees of the twin files marching on both sides of the road.

On the right (south) side of the avenue, across a marginal ditch, overhung with brambles, the intervals between the mottled trunks disclosed patches of lavender or lucerne and, farther away, the low white wall of a cemetery running parallel to our lane as those things are apt to do. On the left (north) side, through analogous intervals, one glimpsed an expanse of rising ground, a vineyard, a distant farm, pine groves, and the outline of mountains. On the penult tree trunk of that side somebody had pasted, and somebody else partly scraped off, an incoherent notice.

We walked down that avenue nearly every morning, Iris and I, on our way to the village square and – from there by lovely shortcuts – to Cannice and the sea. Now and then she liked to return on foot, being one of those small but strong lassies who can hurdle, and play hockey, and climb rocks, and then shimmy till any pale mad hour ('*do bezúmnogo blédnogo chása*' – to quote from my first direct poem to her). She usually wore her 'Indian' frock, a kind of translucent wrap, over her skimpy swimsuit, and as I followed close behind, and sensed the solitude, the security, the all-permitting dream, I had trouble walking in my bestial state. Fortunately it was not the none-so-very-secure solitude that held me back but a moral decision to confess something very grave before I made love to her.

As seen from those escarpments, the sea far below spread in majestic wrinkles, and, owing to distance and height, the recurrent line of foam arrived in rather droll slow motion because we knew it was sure, as we had been sure, of its strapping pace, and now that restraint, that stateliness . . .

Suddenly there came from somewhere within the natural jumble of our surroundings a roar of unearthly ecstasy.

'Goodness,' said Iris, 'I do hope that's not a happy escapee from Kanner's Circus.' (No relation – at least, so it seemed – to the pianist.)

We walked on, now side by side: after the first of the half-dozen times it crossed the looping main road, our path grew wider. That day as usual I argued with Iris about the English names of the few plants I could identify – rock roses and griselda in bloom, agaves (which she called 'centuries'), broom and spurge, myrtle and arbutus. Speckled butterflies came and went like quick sun flecks in the occasional tunnels of foliage, and once a tremendous olive-green fellow, with a rosy flush somewhere beneath, settled on a thistlehead for an instant. I know nothing about butterflies, and indeed do not care for the fluffier night-flying ones, and would hate any of them to touch me: even the prettiest gives me a nasty shiver like some floating spider web or that bathroom pest on the Riviera, the silver louse.

On the day now in focus, memorable for a more important matter but carrying all kinds of synchronous trivia attached to it like burrs or incrustated like marine parasites, we noticed a butterfly net moving among the beflowered rocks, and presently old Kanner appeared, his panama swinging on its vest-button string, his white locks flying around his scarlet brow, and the whole of his person still radiating ecstasy, an echo of which we no doubt had heard a minute ago.

Upon Iris immediately describing to him the spectacular green thing, Kanner dismissed it as *eine* 'Pandora' (at least that's what I find jotted down), a common southern *Falter* (butterfly). '*Aber* (but),' he thundered, raising his index, 'when you wish to look at a real rarity, never before observed west of Nieder-Österreich, then I will show what I have just caught.'

He leant his net against a rock (it fell at once, Iris picked it up reverently) and, with profuse thanks (to Psyche? Baalzebub? Iris?) that trailed away accompanimentally, produced from a compartment in his satchel a little stamp envelope and shook out of it very gently a folded butterfly onto the palm of his hand.

After one glance Iris told him it was merely a tiny, very young Cabbage White. (She had a theory that houseflies, for instance, *grow*.)

'Now look with attention,' said Kanner ignoring her quaint remark and pointing with compressed tweezers at the triangular insect. 'What you see is the inferior side – the under white of the left *Vorderflügel* ('fore wing') and the under yellow of the left *Hinterflügel* ('hind wing'). I will not open the wings but I think you can believe what I'm going to tell you. On the upper side, which you can't see, this species shares with its nearest allies – the Small White and Mann's White, both common here – the typical little spots of the fore wing, namely a black full stop in the male and a black *Doppelpunkt* ('colon') in the female. In those allies the punctuation is reproduced on the underside, and only in the species of which you see a folded specimen on the flat of my hand is the wing blank beneath – a typographical caprice of Nature! *Ergo* it is an Ergane.'

One of the legs of the reclining butterfly twitched.

'Oh, it's alive!' cried Iris.

'No, it can't fly away – one pinch was enough,' rejoined Kanner soothingly, as he slipped the specimen back into its pellucid hell; and presently, brandishing his arms and net in triumphant farewells, he was continuing his climb.

'The brute!' wailed Iris. She brooded over the thousand little creatures he had tortured, but a few days later, when Ivor took us to the man's concert (a most poetical rendition of Grünberg's suite *Les Châteaux*) she derived some consolation from her brother's contemptuous remark: 'All that butterfly business is only a publicity stunt.' Alas, as a fellow madman I knew better.

All I had to do when we reached our stretch of *plage* in order to absorb the sun was to shed shirt, shorts, and sneakers. Iris shrugged off her wrap and lay down, bare limbed, on the towel next to mine. I was rehearsing in my head the speech I had prepared. The pianist's dog was today in the company of a handsome old lady, his fourth wife. The nymphet was being buried in hot sand by two young oafs. The Russian lady was reading an *émigré* newspaper. Her husband was contemplating the horizon. The two English women were bobbing in the dazzling sea. A large French family of slightly flushed albinos was trying to inflate a rubber dolphin.

'I'm ready for a dip,' said Iris.

She took out of the beach bag (kept for her by the Victoria concierge) her yellow swim bonnet, and we transferred our towels and things to the comparative quiet of an obsolete wharf of sorts upon which she liked to dry afterwards.

Already twice in my young life a fit of *total* cramp – the physical counterpart of lightning insanity – had all but overpowered me in the panic and blackness of bottomless water. I see myself as a lad of fifteen swimming at dusk across a narrow but deep river with an athletic cousin. He is beginning to leave me behind when a special effort I make results in a sense of ineffable euphoria which promises miracles of propulsion, dream prizes on dream shelves – but which, at its satanic climax, is replaced by an intolerable spasm first in one leg, then in the other, then in the ribs and both arms. I have often attempted to explain, in later years, to learned and ironical doctors, the strange, hideous, *segmental* quality of those pulsating pangs that made a huge worm of me with limbs transformed into successive coils of agony. By some fantastic fluke a third swimmer, a stranger, was right behind me and helped to pull me out of an abysmal tangle of water-lily stems.

The second time was a year later, on the West-Caucasian coast. I had been drinking with a dozen older companions at the birthday party of the district governor's son and, around midnight, a dashing young Englishman, Allan Andoverton (who was to be, around 1939, my first British publisher!) had suggested a moonlight swim. As long as I did not venture too far in the sea, the experience seemed quite enjoyable. The water was warm; the moon shone benevolently on the starched shirt of my first evening clothes spread on the shingly shore. I could hear merry voices around me; Allan, I remember, had not bothered to strip and was fooling with a champagne bottle in the dappled swell; but presently a cloud engulfed everything, a great wave lifted and rolled me, and soon I was too upset in all senses to tell whether I was heading for Yalta or Tuapse. Abject fear set loose instantly the pain I already knew, and I would have drowned there and then had not the next billow given me a boost and deposited me near my own trousers.

The shadow of those repellent and rather colorless recollections (mortal peril is colorless) remained always present in my 'dips' and 'splashes' (another word of hers) with Iris. She got used to my habit of staying in comfortable contact with the bed of shallows, while she executed 'crawls' (if that is what those overarm strokes were called in the Nineteen-Twenties) at quite a distance away; but that morning I nearly did a very stupid thing.

I was gently floating to and fro in line with the shore and sinking a probing toe every now and then to ascertain if I could still feel the oozy bottom with its unappetizing to the touch, but on the whole friendly, vegetables, when I noticed that the seascape had changed. In the middle distance a brown motorboat manned by a young fellow in whom I recognized L.P. had described a foamy half-circle and stopped beside Iris. She clung to the bright brim, and he spoke to her, and then made as if to drag her into his boat, but she flipped free, and he sped away, laughing.

It all must have lasted a couple of minutes, but had the rascal with his hawkish profile and white cable-stitched sweater stayed a few seconds longer or had my girl been abducted by her new beau in the thunder and spray, I would have perished; for while the scene endured, some virile instinct rather than one of self-preservation had caused me to swim toward them a few insensible yards, and now when I assumed a perpendicular position to regain my breath I found underfoot nothing but water. I turned and started swimming landward – and already felt the ominous foreglow, the strange, never yet described aura of total cramp creeping over me and forming its deadly pact with gravity. Suddenly my knee struck blessed sand, and in a mild undertow I crawled on all fours onto the beach.

8

'I have a confession to make, Iris, concerning my mental health.'

'Wait a minute. Must peel this horrid thing off – as far down – as far down as it can decently go.'

We were lying, I supine, she prone, on the wharf. She had torn off her cap and was struggling to shrug off the shoulder straps of her wet swimsuit, so as to expose her entire back to the sun; a secondary struggle was taking place on the near side, in the vicinity of her sable armpit, in her unsuccessful efforts not to show the white of a small breast at its tender juncture with her ribs. As soon as she had wriggled into a satisfactory state of decorum, she half-reared, holding her black bodice to her bosom, while her other hand conducted that delightful rapid monkey-scratching search a girl performs when groping for something in her bag – in this instance a mauve package of cheap Salammbôs and an expensive lighter; whereupon she again pressed her bosom to the spread towel. Her earlobe burned red through her black liberated 'Medusa,' as that type of bob was called in the young twenties. The moldings of her brown back, with a patch-size beauty spot below the left shoulder blade and a long spinal hollow, which redeemed all the errors of animal evolution, distracted me painfully from the decision I had taken to preface my proposal with a special, tremendously important confession. A few aquamarines of water still glistened on the underside of her brown thighs and on her strong brown calves, and a few grains of wet gravel had stuck to her rose-brown ankles. If I have described so often in my American novels (*A Kingdom by the Sea*, *Ardis*) the unbearable magic of a girl's back, it is mainly because of my having loved Iris. Her compact little nates, the most agonizing, the fullest, and sweetest bloom of her puerile prettiness, were as yet unwrapped surprises under the Christmas tree.

Upon resettling in the waiting sun after this little flurry, Iris protruded her fat underlip as she exhaled smoke and presently remarked: 'Your mental health is jolly good, I think. You are sometimes strange and somber, and often silly, but that's in character with *ce qu'on appelle* genius.'

'What do *you* call "genius"?'

'Well, seeing things others don't see. Or rather the invisible links between things.'

'I am speaking, then, of a humble morbid condition which has nothing to do with genius. We shall start with a specific example and an authentic decor. Please close your eyes for a moment. Now visualize the avenue that goes from the post office to your villa. You see the plane trees converging in perspective and the garden gate between the last two?'

'No,' said Iris, 'the last one on the right is replaced by a lamppost – you can't make it out very clearly from the village square – but it is really a lamppost in a coat of ivy.'

'Well, no matter. The main thing is to imagine we're looking from the village *here* toward the garden gate *there*. We must be very careful about our here's and there's in this problem. For the present "there" is the quadrangle of green sunlight in the half-opened gate. We now start to walk up the avenue. On the second tree trunk of the right-side file we notice traces of some local proclamation –'

'It was Ivor's proclamation. He proclaimed that things had changed and Aunt Betty's protégés should stop making their weekly calls.'

'Splendid. We continue to walk toward the garden gate. Intervals of landscape can be made out between the plane trees on both sides. On your right – please, close your eyes, you will see better – on your right there's a vineyard; on your left, a churchyard – you can distinguish its long, low, very low, wall –'

'You make it sound rather creepy. And I want to add something. Among the blackberries, Ivor and I discovered a crooked old tombstone with the inscription *Dors, Médor!* and only the date of death, 1889; a found dog, no doubt. It's just before the last tree on the left side.'

'So now we reach the garden gate. We are about to enter – but you stop all of a sudden: you've forgotten to buy those nice new stamps for your album. We decide to go back to the post office.'

'Can I open my eyes? Because I'm afraid I'm going to fall asleep.'

'On the contrary: now is the moment to shut your eyes tight and concentrate. I want you to imagine yourself turning on your heel so that "right" instantly becomes "left," and you instantly see the "here" as a "there," with the lamppost now on your left and dead Médor now on your right, and the plane trees converging toward the post office. Can you do that?'

'Done,' said Iris. 'About-face executed. I now stand facing a sunny hole with a little pink house inside it and a bit of blue sky. Shall we start walking back?'

'*You* may, I can't! This is the point of the experiment. In actual, physical life I can turn as simply and swiftly as anyone. But mentally, with my eyes closed and my body immobile, I am unable to switch from one direction to the other. Some swivel cell in my brain does not work. I can cheat, of course, by setting aside the mental snapshot of one vista and leisurely selecting the opposite view for my walk back to my starting point. But if I do not cheat, some kind of atrocious obstacle, which would drive me mad if I persevered, prevents me from imagining the twist which transforms one direction into another, directly opposite. I am crushed, I am carrying the whole world on my back in the process of trying to visualize my turning around and making myself see in terms of "right" what I saw in terms of "left" and vice versa.'

I thought she had fallen asleep, but before I could entertain the thought that she had not heard, not understood anything of what was destroying me, she moved, rearranged her shoulder straps, and sat up.

'First of all, we shall agree,' she said, 'to cancel all such experiments. Secondly, we shall tell ourselves that what we had been trying to do was to solve a stupid philosophical riddle – on the lines of what does "right" and "left" *mean* in our absence, when nobody is looking, in pure space, and what, anyway, is space; when I was a child I thought space was the inside of a nought, any nought, chalked on a slate and perhaps not quite tidy, but still a good clean zero. I don't want you to go mad or to drive me mad, because those perplexities are catching, and so we'll drop the whole business of revolving avenues altogether. I would like to seal our pact with a kiss, but we shall have to postpone that. Ivor is coming in a few minutes to take us for a spin in his new car, but perhaps you do not care to come, and so I propose we meet in the garden, for a minute or two, just before dinner, while he is taking his bath.'

I asked what Bob (L.P.) had been telling her in my dream. 'It was not a dream,' she said. 'He just wanted to know if his sister had phoned about a dance they wanted us all three to come to. If she had, nobody was at home.'

We repaired for a snack and a drink to the Victoria bar, and presently Ivor joined us. He said, nonsense, he could dance and fence beautifully on the stage but was a regular bear at private affairs and would hate to have his innocent sister pawed by all the *rastaquouères* of the Côte.

'Incidentally,' he added, 'I don't much care for P.'s obsession with moneylenders. He practically ruined the best one in Cambridge but has nothing but conventional evil to repeat about them.'

'My brother is a funny person,' said Iris, turning to me as in play. 'He conceals our ancestry like a dark treasure, yet will flare up publicly if someone calls someone a Shylock.'

Ivor prattled on: 'Old Maurice (his employer) is dining with us tonight. Cold cuts and a *macédoine au* kitchen rum. I'll also get some tinned asparagus at the English shop; it's much better than the stuff they grow here. The car is not exactly a Royce, but it rolls. Sorry Vivian is too queasy to come. I saw Madge Titheridge this morning and she said French reporters pronounce her family name *"Si c'est riche."* Nobody's laughing today.'

9

Being too excited to take my usual siesta, I spent most of the afternoon working on a love poem (and this is the last entry in my 1922 pocket diary – exactly one month after my arrival in Carnavaux). In those days I seemed to have had two muses: the essential, hysterical, genuine one, who tortured me with elusive snatches of imagery and wrung her hands over my inability to appropriate the magic and madness offered me; and her apprentice, her palette girl and stand-in, a little logician, who stuffed the torn gaps left by her mistress with explanatory or meter-mending fillers which became more and more numerous the further I moved away from the initial, evanescent, savage perfection. The treacherous music of Russian rhythms came to my specious rescue like those demons who break the black silence of an artist's hell with imitations of Greek poets and prehistorical birds. Another and final deception would come with the Fair Copy in which, for a short while, calligraphy, vellum paper, and India ink beautified a dead doggerel. And to think that for almost five years I kept trying and kept getting caught – until I fired that painted, pregnant, meek, miserable little assistant!

I dressed and went downstairs. The french window giving on the terrace was open. Old Maurice, Iris, and Ivor sat enjoying Martinis in the orchestra seats of a marvelous sunset. Ivor was in the act of mimicking someone, with bizarre intonations and extravagant gestures. The marvelous sunset has not only remained as a backdrop of a life-transforming evening, but endured, perhaps, behind the suggestion I made to my British publishers, many years later, to bring out a coffee-table album of auroras and sunsets, in the truest possible shades, a collection that would also be of scientific value, since some learned celestiologist might be hired to discuss samples from various countries and analyze the striking and never before discussed differences between the color schemes of evening and dawn. The album came out eventually, the price was high and the pictorial part passable; but the text was supplied by a luckless female whose pretty prose and borrowed poetry botched the book (Allan and Overton, London, 1949).

For a couple of moments, while idly attending to Ivor's strident performance, I stood watching the huge sunset. Its wash was of a classical light-orange tint with an oblique bluish-black shark crossing it. What glorified the combination was a series of ember-bright cloudlets riding along, tattered and hooded, above the red sun which had assumed the shape of a pawn or a baluster. 'Look at the sabbath witches!' I was about to cry, but then I saw Iris rise and heard her say: 'That will do, Ives. Maurice has never met the person, it's all lost on him.'

'Not at all,' retorted her brother, 'he will meet him in a minute and *recognize* him (the verb was an artist's snarl), that's the point!'

Iris left the terrace via the garden steps, and Ivor did not continue his skit, which a swift playback that now burst on my consciousness identified as a clever burlesque of my voice and manner. I had the odd sensation of a piece of myself being ripped off and tossed overboard, of my being separated from my own self, of flying forward and at the same time turning away. The second action prevailed, and presently, under the holm oak, I joined Iris.

The crickets were stridulating, dusk had filled the pool, a ray of the outside lamp glistened on two parked cars. I kissed her lips, her neck, her necklace, her neck, her lips. Her response dispelled my ill humor; but I told her what I thought of the idiot before she ran back to the festively lit villa.

Ivor personally brought up my supper, right to my bedside table, with well-concealed dismay at being balked of his art's reward and charming apologies for having offended me, and 'had I run out of pyjamas'? to which I replied that, on the contrary, I felt rather flattered, and in fact always slept naked in summer, but preferred not to come down lest a slight headache prevent me from not living up to that splendid impersonation.

I slept fitfully, and only in the small hours glided into a deeper spell (illustrated for no reason at all with the image of my first little inamorata in the grass of an orchard) from which I was rudely roused by the spattering sounds of a motor. I slipped on a shirt and leant out of the window, sending a flock of sparrows whirring out of the jasmin, whose luxuriant growth reached up to the second floor, and saw, with a sensual start, Ivor putting a suitcase and a fishing rod into his car which stood, throbbing, practically in the garden. It was a Sunday, and I had been expecting to have him around all day, but there he was getting behind the wheel and slamming the door after him. The gardener was giving tactical directions with both arms; his pretty little boy was also there, holding a yellow and blue feather duster. And then I heard her lovely English voice bidding her brother have a good time. I had to lean out a little more to see her; she stood on a patch of cool clean turf, barefooted, barecalved, in an ample-sleeved peignoir, repeating her joyful farewell, which he could no longer hear.

I dashed to the W.C. across the landing. A few moments later, as I left my gurgling and gulping retreat, I noticed her on the other side of the staircase. She was entering my room. My polo shirt, a very short, salmon-colored affair, could not hide my salient impatience.

'I hate to see the stunned look on the face of a clock that has stopped,' she said, as she stretched a slender brown arm up to the shelf where I had relegated an old egg timer lent me in lieu of a regular alarm. As her wide sleeve fell back I kissed the dark perfumed hollow I had longed to kiss since our first day in the sun.

The door key would not work, that I knew; still I tried, and was rewarded by the silly semblance of recurrent clicks that did not lock anything. Whose step, whose sick young cough came from the stairs? Yes of course that was Jacquot, the gardener's boy who rubbed and dusted things every morning. He might butt in, I said, already speaking with difficulty. To polish, for instance, that candlestick. Oh, what does it matter, she whispered, he's only a conscientious child, a poor foundling, as all our dogs and parrots are. Your tum, she said, is still as pink as your shirt. And please do not forget, darling, to clear out before it's too late.

How far, how bright, how unchanged by eternity, how disfigured by time! There were bread crumbs and even a bit of orange peel in the bed. The young cough was now muted, but I could distinctly hear creakings, controlled footfalls, the hum in an ear pressed to the door. I must have been eleven or twelve when the nephew of my grand-uncle visited the Moscow country house where I was spending that hot and hideous summer. He had brought his passionate bride with him – straight from the wedding feast. Next day at the siesta hour, in a frenzy of curiosity and fancy, I crept to a secret spot under the second-floor guest-room window where a gardener's ladder stood rooted in a jungle of jasmin. It reached only to the top of the closed first-floor shutters, and though I found a foothold above them, on an ornamental projection, I could only just grip the sill of a half-open window from which confused sounds issued. I recognized the jangle of bedsprings and the rhythmic tinkle of a fruit knife on a plate near the bed, one post of which I could make out by stretching my neck to the utmost; but what fascinated me most were the manly moans coming from the invisible part of the bed. A superhuman effort afforded me the sight of a salmon-pink shirt over the back of a chair. He, the enraptured beast, doomed to die one day as so many are, was now repeating her name with ever increasing urgency, and by the time my foot slipped he was in full cry, thus drowning the noise of my sudden descent into a crackle of twigs and a snowstorm of petals.

10

Just before Ivor returned from his fishing trip, I moved to the Victoria, where she visited me daily. That was not enough; but in the autumn Ivor migrated to Los Angeles to join his half-brother in directing the Amenic film company (for which, thirty years later, long after Ivor's death over Dover, I was to write the script of *Pawn Takes Queen*, my most popular at the time, but far from best, novel), and we returned to our beloved villa, in the really quite nice blue Icarus, Ivor's thoughtful wedding present.

Sometime in October my benefactor, now in the last stage of majestic senility, came for his annual visit to Mentone, and, without warning, Iris and I dropped in to see him. His villa was incomparably grander than ours. He staggered to his feet to take between his wax-pale palms Iris's hand and stare at her with blue bleary eyes for at least five seconds (a little eternity, socially) in a kind of ritual silence, after which he embraced me with a slow triple cross-kiss in the awful Russian tradition.

'Your bride,' he said, using, I knew, the word in the sense of *fiancée* (and speaking an English which Iris said later was exactly like mine in Ivor's unforgettable version) 'is as beautiful as your wife will be!'

I quickly told him – in Russian – that the *maire* of Cannice had married us a month ago in a brisk ceremony. Nikifor Nikodimovich gave Iris another stare and finally kissed her hand, which I was glad to see she raised in the proper fashion (coached, no doubt, by Ivor who used to take every opportunity to paw his sister).

'I misunderstood the rumors,' he said, 'but all the same I am happy to make the acquaintance of such a charming young lady. And where, pray, in what church, will the vow be sanctified?'

'In the temple we shall build, Sir,' said Iris – a trifle insolently, I thought.

Count Starov 'chewed his lips,' as old men are wont to do in Russian novels. Miss Vrode-Vorodin, the elderly cousin who kept house for him, made a timely entrance and led Iris to an adjacent alcove (illuminated by a resplendent portrait by Serov, 1896, of the notorious beauty, Mme. de Blagidze, in Caucasian costume) for a nice cup of tea. The Count wished to talk business with me and had only ten minutes 'before his injection.'

What was my wife's maiden name?

I told him. He thought it over and shook his head. What was her mother's name?

I told him that, too. Same reaction. What about the financial aspect of the marriage?

I said she had a house, a parrot, a car, and a small income – I didn't know exactly how much.

After another minute's thought, he asked me if I would like a permanent job in the White Cross? It had nothing to do with Switzerland. It was an organization that helped Russian Christians all over the world. The job would involve travel, interesting connections, promotion to important posts.

I declined so emphatically that he dropped the silver pill box he was holding and a number of innocent gum drops were spilled all over the table at his elbow. He swept them onto the carpet with a gesture of peevish dismissal.

What then was I intending to do?

I said I'd go on with my literary dreams and nightmares. We would spend most of the year in Paris. Paris was becoming the center of émigré culture and destitution.

How much did I think I could earn?

Well, as N.N. knew, currencies were losing their identities in the whirlpool of inflation, but Boris Morozov, a distinguished author, whose fame had preceded his exile, had given me some illuminating 'examples of existence' when I met him quite recently in Cannice where he had lectured on Baratynski at the local *literaturnyy* circle. In his case, four lines of verse would pay for a *bifsteck pommes*, while a couple of essays in the *Novosti emigratsii* assured a month's rent for a cheap *chambre garnie*. There were also readings, in large auditoriums, at least twice a year, which might bring him each time the equivalent of, say, one hundred dollars.

My benefactor thought this over and said that as long as he lived I would receive a check for half that amount every first of the month, and that he would bequeath me a certain sum in his testament. He named the sum. Its paltriness took me aback. This was a foretaste of the disappointing advances publishers were to offer me after a long, promising, pencil-tapping pause.

We rented a two-room apartment in the 16th *arrondissement*, rue Despréaux, 23. The hallway connecting the rooms led, on the front side, to a bathroom and kitchenette. Being a solitary sleeper by principle and inclination, I relinquished the double bed to Iris, and slept on the couch in the parlor. The concierge's daughter came to clean up and cook. Her culinary capacities were limited, so we often broke the monotony of vegetable soups and boiled meat by eating at a Russian *restoranchik*. We were to spend seven winters in that little flat.

Owing to the foresight of my dear guardian and benefactor (1850?–1927), an old-fashioned cosmopolitan with a lot of influence in the right quarters, I had become by the time of my marriage the subject of a snug foreign country and thus was spared the indignity of a *nansenskiy pasport* (a pauper's permit, really), as well as the vulgar obsession with 'documents,' which provoked such evil glee among the Bolshevist rulers, who perceived some similarity between red tape and Red rule and a certain affinity between the civil plight of a hobbled expatriate and the political immobilization of a Soviet slave. I could, therefore, take my wife to any vacational resort in the world without waiting several weeks for a visa, and then being refused, perhaps, a return visa to our accidental country of residence, in this case France, because of some flaw in our precious and despicable papers. Nowadays (1970), when my British passport has been superseded by a no less potent American one, I still treasure that 1922 photo of the mysterious young man I then was, with the mysteriously smiling eyes and the striped tie and the wavy hair. I remember spring trips to Malta and Andalusia, but every summer, around the first of July, we drove to Carnavaux and stayed there for a month or two. The parrot died in 1925, the footboy vanished in 1927. Ivor visited us twice in Paris, and I think she saw him also in London where she went at least once a year to spend a few days with 'friends,' whom I did not know, but who sounded harmless – at least to a certain point.

I should have been happier. I had *planned* to be happier. My health continued patchy with ominous shapes showing through its flimsier edges. Faith in my work never wavered, but despite her touching intentions to participate in it, Iris remained on its outside, and the better it grew the more alien it became to her. She took desultory lessons in Russian, interrupting them regularly, for long periods, and finished by developing a dull habitual aversion to the language. I soon noticed that she had ceased trying to look attentive and bright when Russian, and Russian only, was spoken in her presence (after some primitive French had been kept up for the first minute or two of the party in polite concession to her disability).

This was, at best, annoying; at worst, heartrending; it did not, however, affect my sanity as something else threatened to do.

Jealousy, a masked giant never encountered before in the frivolous affairs of my early youth, now stood with folded arms, confronting me at every corner. Certain little sexual quirks in my sweet, docile, tender Iris, inflections of lovemaking, felicities of fondling, the easy accuracy with which she adapted her flexible frame to every pattern of passion, seemed to presuppose a wealth of experience. Before starting to suspect the present, I felt compelled to get my fill of suspecting her past. During the examinations to which I subjected her on my worst nights, she dismissed her former romances as totally insignificant, without realizing that this reticence left more to my imagination than would the most luridly overstated truth.

The three lovers (a figure I wrested from her with the fierceness of Pushkin's mad gambler and with even less luck) whom she had had in her teens remained nameless, and therefore spectral; devoid of any individual traits, and therefore identical. They performed their sketchy *pas* in the back of her lone act like the lowliest members of the *corps de ballet*, in a display of mawkish gymnastics rather than dance, and it was clear that none of them would ever become the male star of the troupe. She, the ballerina, on the other hand, was a dim diamond with all the facets of talent ready to blaze, but under the pressure of the nonsense around her had, for the moment, to limit her steps and gestures to an expression of cold coquetry, of flirtatious evasion – waiting as she was for the tremendous leap of the marble-thighed athlete in shining tights who was to erupt from the wings after a decent prelude. We thought I had been chosen for that part but we were mistaken.

Only by projecting thus on the screen of my mind those stylized images, could I allay the anguish of carnal jealousy centered on specters. Yet not seldom I chose to succumb to it. The french window of my studio in Villa Iris gave on the same red-tiled balcony as my wife's bedroom did, and could be set half-open at such an angle as to provide two different views melting into one another. It caught obliquely, through the monastic archway leading from room to room, part of her bed and of her – her hair, a shoulder – which otherwise I could not see from the old-fashioned lectern at which I wrote; but the glass also held, at arm's length as it were, the green reality of the garden with a peregrination of cypresses along its sidewall. So half in bed and half in the pale hot sky, she would recline, writing a letter that was crucified on my second-best chessboard. I knew that if I asked, the answer would be 'Oh, to an old schoolmate,' or 'To Ivor,' or 'To old Miss Kupalov,' and I also knew that in one way or another the letter would reach the post office at the end of the plane-tree avenue without my seeing the name on the envelope. And still I let her write as she comfortably floated in the life belt of her pillow, above the cypresses and the garden wall, while all the time I gauged – grimly, recklessly – to what depths of dark pigment the tentacled ache would go.

II

Most of those Russian lessons consisted of her taking one of my poems or essays to this or that Russian lady, Miss Kupalov or Mrs. Lapukov (neither of whom had much English) and having it paraphrased orally for her in a kind of makeshift Volapük. On my pointing out to Iris that she was losing her time at this hit-and-miss task, she cast around for some other alchemic method which might enable her to read everything I wrote. I had begun by then (1925) my first novel (*Tamara*) and she coaxed me into letting her have a copy of the first chapter, which I had just typed out. This she carried to an agency that dealt in translations into French of utilitarian texts such as applications and supplications addressed by Russian refugees to various rats in the ratholes of various *commissariats*. The person who agreed to supply her with the 'literal version,' which she paid for in *valuta*, kept the typescript for two months and warned her when delivering it that my 'article' had presented almost insurmountable difficulties, 'being written in an idiom and style utterly unfamiliar to the ordinary reader.' Thus an anonymous imbecile in a shabby, cluttered, clattering office became my first critic and my first translator.

I knew nothing of that venture, until I found her one day bending her brown curls over sheets of foolscap almost perforated by the violence of the violet characters that covered it without any semblance of margin. I was, in those days, naively opposed to any kind of translation, partly because my attempts to turn two or three of my first compositions into my own English had resulted in a feeling of morbid revolt – and in maddening headaches. Iris, her cheek on her fist and her eyes rolling in languid doubt, looked up at me rather sheepishly, but with that gleam of humor that never left her in the most absurd or trying circumstances. I noticed a blunder in the first line, a boo-boo in the next, and without bothering to read any further, tore up the whole thing – which provoked no reaction, save a neutral sigh, on the part of my thwarted darling.

In compensation for being debarred from my writings, she decided to become a writer herself. Beginning with the middle Twenties and to the end of her short, squandered, uncharmed life, my Iris kept working on a detective novel in two, three, four successive versions, in which the plot, the people, the setting, everything kept changing in bewildering bursts of frantic deletions – everything except the names (none of which I remember).

Not only did she lack all literary talent, but she had not even the knack of imitating the small number of gifted authors among the prosperous but ephemeral purveyors of 'crime fiction' which she consumed with the indiscriminate zest of a model prisoner. How, then, did my Iris know why this had to be altered, that rejected? What instinct of genius ordered her to destroy the whole heap of her drafts on the eve, practically on the eve, of her sudden death? All the odd girl could ever visualize, with startling lucidity, was the crimson cover of the final, ideal paperback on which the villain's hairy fist would be shown pointing a pistol-shaped cigarette lighter at the reader – who was not supposed to guess until everybody in the book had died that it was, in fact, a pistol.

Let me pick out several fatidic points, cleverly disguised at the time, within the embroidery of our seven winters.

During a lull in a magnificent concert for which we had not been able to obtain adjacent seats, I noticed Iris eagerly welcoming a melancholy-looking woman with drab hair and thin lips; I certainly had met her, somewhere, quite recently, but the very insignificance of her appearance canceled the pursuit of a vague recollection, and I never asked Iris about it. She was to become my wife's last teacher.

Every author believes, when his first book is published, that those that acclaim it are his personal friends or impersonal peers, while its revilers can only be envious rogues and nonentities. No doubt I might have had similar illusions about the way *Tamara* was reviewed in the Russian-language periodicals of Paris, Berlin, Prague, Riga, and other cities; but by that time I was already engrossed in my second novel, *Pawn Takes Queen*, and my first one had dwindled to a pinch of colored dust in my mind.

The editor of *Patria*, the *émigré* monthly in which *Pawn Takes Queen* had begun to be serialized, invited 'Irida Osipovna' and me to a literary samovar. I mention it only because this was one of the few salons that my unsociability deigned to frequent. Iris helped with the sand-wiches. I smoked my pipe and observed the feeding habits of two major novelists, three minor ones, one major poet, five minor ones of both sexes, one major critic (Demian Basilevski), and nine minor ones, including the inimitable 'Prostakov-Skotinin,' a Russian comedy name (meaning 'simpleton and brute') applied to him by his archrival Hristofor Boyarski.

The major poet, Boris Morozov, an amiable grizzly bear of a man, was asked how his reading in Berlin had gone, and he said: '*Nichevo*' (a 'so-so' tinged with a 'well enough') and then told a funny but not memorable story about the new President of the Union of *Emigré* Writers in Germany. The lady next to me informed me she had adored that treacherous conversation between the Pawn and the Queen about the husband and would they really defenestrate the poor chess player? I said they would but not in the next issue, and not for good: he would live forever in the games he had played and in the multiple exclamation marks of future annotators. I also heard – my hearing is almost on a par with my sight – snatches of general talk such as an explanatory, 'She is an Englishwoman,' murmured from behind a hand five chairs away by one guest to another.

All that would have been much too trivial to record unless meant to serve as the commonplace background, at any such meeting of exiles, against which a certain reminder flickered now and then, between the shoptalk and the tattle – a line of Tyutchev or Blok, which was cited in passing, as well as an everlasting presence, with the familiarity of devotion and as the secret height of art, and which ornamented sad lives with a sudden cadenza coming from some celestial elsewhere, a glory, a sweetness, the patch of rainbow cast on the wall by a crystal paperweight we cannot locate. That was what my Iris was missing.

To return to the trivia: I recall regaling the company with one of the howlers I had noticed in the 'translation' of *Tamara*. The sentence *vidnelos' neskol'ko barok* ('several barges could be seen') had become *la vue était assez baroque*. The eminent critic Basilevski, a stocky, fair-haired old fellow in a rumpled brown suit, shook with abdominal mirth – but then his expression changed to one of suspicion and displeasure. After tea he accosted me and insisted gruffly that I had made up that example of mistranslation. I remember answering that, if so, he, too, might well be an invention of mine.

As we strolled home, Iris complained she would never learn to cloud a glass of tea with a spoonful of cloying raspberry jam. I said I was ready to put up with her deliberate insularity but implored her to cease announcing *à la ronde:* 'Please, don't mind me: I love the sound of Russian.' *That* was an insult, like telling an author his book was unreadable but beautifully printed.

'I am going to make reparations,' she gaily replied. 'I've never been able to find a proper teacher, I always believed you were the only one – and you refused to teach me, because you were busy, because you were tired, because it bored you, because it was bad for your nerves. I've discovered at last someone who speaks both languages, yours and mine, as two natives in one, and can make all the edges fit. I am thinking of Nadia Starov. In fact it's her own suggestion.'

Nadezhda Gordonovna Starov was the wife of a *leytenant* Starov (Christian name unimportant), who had served under General Wrangel and now had some office job in the White Cross. I had met him in London recently, as fellow pallbearer at the funeral of the old Count, whose bastard or 'adopted nephew' (whatever that meant), he was said to be. He was a dark-eyed, dark-complexioned man, three or four years my senior; I thought him rather handsome in a brooding, gloomy way. A head wound received in the civil war had left him with a terrifying tic that caused his face to change suddenly, at variable intervals, as if a paper bag were being crumpled by an invisible hand. Nadezhda Starov, a quiet, plain woman with an indefinable Quakerish look about her, clocked those intervals for some reason, no doubt of a medical nature, the man himself being unconscious of his 'fireworks' unless he happened to see them in a mirror. He had a macabre sense of humor, beautiful hands, and a velvety voice.

I realized now that it was Nadezhda Gordonovna whom Iris had been talking to in that concert hall. I cannot say exactly when the lessons began or how long that fad lasted; a month or two months at the most. They took place either in Mrs. Starov's lodgings or in one of the Russian tearooms both ladies frequented. I kept a little list of telephone numbers so that Iris might be warned that I could always make sure of her whereabouts if, say, I felt on the brink of losing my mind or wanted her to buy on the way home a tin of my favorite Brown Prune tobacco. She did *not* know, on the other hand, that I would never have dared ring her up, lest her not being where she said she would be cause me even a few minutes of an agony that I could not face.

Sometime around Christmas, 1929, she casually told me that those lessons had been discontinued quite a while ago: Mrs. Starov had left for England, and it was rumored that she would not return to her husband. The lieutenant, it seemed, was quite a dasher.

12

At a certain mysterious point toward the end of our last winter in Paris something in our relationship changed for the better. A wave of new warmth, new intimacy, new tenderness, swelled and swept away all the delusions of distance – tiffs, silences, suspicions, retreats into castles of *amour-propre* and the like – which had obstructed our love and of which I alone was guilty. A more amiable, merrier mate I could not have imagined. Endearments, love names (based in my case on Russian forms) reentered our customary exchanges. I broke the monastic rules of work on my novella in verse *Polnolunie* (Plenilune) by riding with her in the Bois or dutifully escorting her to fashion-show teases and exhibitions of *avant-garde* frauds. I surmounted my contempt for the 'serious' cinema (depicting heartrending problems with a political twist), which she preferred to American buffoonery and the trick photography of Germanic horror films. I even gave a talk on my Cambridge days at a rather pathetic English Ladies Club, to which she belonged. And to top the treat, I told her the plot of my next novel (*Camera Lucida*).

One afternoon, in March or early April, 1930, she peeped into my room and, being admitted, handed me the duplicate of a typewritten sheet, numbered 444. It was, she said, a tentative episode in her interminable tale, which would soon display more deletions than insertions. She was stuck, she said. Diana Vane, an incidental but on the whole nice girl, sojourning in Paris, happened to meet, at a riding school, a strange Frenchman, of Corsican, or perhaps Algerian, origin, passionate, brutal, unbalanced. He mistook Diana – and kept on mistaking her despite her amused remonstrations – for his former sweetheart, also an English girl, whom he had last seen ages ago. We had here, said the author, a sort of hallucination, an obsessive fancy, which Diana, a delightful flirt with a keen sense of humor, allowed Jules to entertain during some twenty riding lessons; but then his attentions grew more realistic, and she stopped seeing him. There had been nothing between them, and yet he simply could not be dissuaded from confusing her with the girl he once had possessed or thought he had, for that girl, too, might well have been only the afterimage of a still earlier romance or remembered delirium. It was a very bizarre situation.

Now this page was supposed to be a last ominous letter written by that Frenchman in a foreigner's English to Diana. I was to read it as if it were a real letter and suggest, as an experienced writer, what might be the next development or disaster.

Beloved!

I am not capable to represent to myself that you really desire to tear up any connection with me. God sees, I love you more than life – more than two lives, your and my, together taken. Are you not ill? Or maybe you have found another? Another lover, yes? Another victim of your attraction? No, no, this thought is too horrible, too humiliating for us both.

My supplication is modest and just. Give only one more interview to me! One interview! I am prepared to meet with you it does not matter where – on the street, in some café, in the Forest of Boulogne – but I must see you, must speak with you and open to you many mysteries before I will die. Oh, this is no threat! I swear that if our interview will lead to a positive result, if, otherwise speaking, you will permit me to hope, only to hope, then, oh then, I will consent to wait a little. But you must reply to me without retardment, my cruel, stupid, adored little girl!

Your Jules

'There's one thing,' I said, carefully folding the sheet and pocketing it for later study, 'one thing the little girl should know. This is not a romantic Corsican writing a *crime passionnel* letter; it is a Russian blackmailer knowing just enough English to translate into it the stalest Russian locutions. What puzzles me is how did you, with your three or four words of Russian – *kak pozhivaete* and *do svidaniya* – how did you, the author, manage to think up those subtle turns, and imitate the mistakes in English that only a Russian would make? Impersonation, I know, runs in the family, but still –'

Iris replied (with that quaint *non sequitur* that I was to give to the heroine of my *Ardis* forty years later) that, yes, indeed, I was right, she must have had too many muddled lessons in Russian and she would certainly correct that extraordinary impression by simply giving the whole letter in French – from which, she had been told, incidentally, Russian *had* borrowed a lot of clichés.

'But that's beside the point,' she added. 'You don't understand – the point is what should happen next – I mean, logically? What should my poor girl do about that bore, that brute? She is uncomfortable, she is perplexed, she is frightened. Should this situation end in slapstick or tragedy?'

'In the wastepaper basket,' I whispered, interrupting my work to gather her small form onto my lap as I often did, the Lord be thanked, in that fatal spring of 1930.

'Give me back that scrap,' she begged gently, trying to thrust her hand into the pocket of my dressing gown, but I shook my head and embraced her closer.

My latent jealousy should have been fanned up to a furnace roar by the surmise that my wife had been transcribing an authentic letter – received, say, from one of the wretched, unwashed *émigré* poeticules, with smooth glossy hair and eloquent liquid eyes, whom she used to meet in the salons of exile. But after reexamining the thing, I decided that it just might be her own composition with some of the planted faults, borrowed from the French (*supplication, sans tarder*), while others could be subliminal echoes of the Volapük she had been exposed to, during sessions with Russian teachers, through bilingual or trilingual exercises in tawdry textbooks. Thus, instead of losing myself in a jungle of evil conjectures, all I did was preserve that thin sheet with its unevenly margined lines so characteristic of her typing in the faded and cracked briefcase before me, among other mementos, other deaths.

13

On the morning of April 23, 1930, the shrill peal of the hallway telephone caught me in the act of stepping into my bathwater.

Ivor! He had just arrived in Paris from New York for an important conference, would be busy all afternoon, was leaving tomorrow, would like to –

Here intervened naked Iris, who delicately, unhurriedly, with a radiant smile, appropriated the monologizing receiver. A minute later (her brother with all his defects was a mercifully concise phoner), she, still beaming, embraced me, and we moved to her bedroom for our last '*fairelamourir*' as she called it in her tender aberrant French.

Ivor was to fetch us at seven P.M. I had already put on my old dinner jacket; Iris stood sideways to the hallway mirror (the best and brightest in the whole flat) veering gently as she tried to catch a clear view of the back of her silky dark bob in the hand glass she held at head level.

'If you're ready,' she said, 'I'd like you to buy some olives. He'll be coming here after dinner, and he likes them with his "postbrandy." '

So I went downstairs and crossed the street and shivered (it was a raw cheerless night) and pushed open the door of the little delicatessen shop opposite, and a man behind me stopped it from closing with a strong hand. He wore a trench coat and a beret, his dark face was twitching. I recognized Lieutenant Starov.

'Ah!' he said. 'A whole century we did not meet!'

The cloud of his breath gave off an odd chemical smell. I had once tried sniffing cocaine (which only made me throw up), but this was some other drug.

He removed a black glove for one of those circumstantial handshakes my compatriots think proper to use at every entry and exit, and the liberated door hit him between the shoulder blades.

'Pleasant meeting!' he went on in his curious English (not parading it as might have seemed but using it by unconscious association). 'I see you are in a *smoking*. Banquet?'

I bought my olives, replying the while, in Russian, that, yes, my wife and I were dining out. Then I skipped a farewell handshake, by taking advantage of the shopgirl's turning to him for the next transaction.

'What a shame,' exclaimed Iris – 'I wanted the black ones, not the green!'

I told her I refused to go back for them because I did not want to run into Starov again.

'Oh, that's a detestable person,' she said. 'I'm sure he'll try now to come and see us, hoping for some *vaw-dutch-ka*. I'm sorry you spoke to him.'

She flung the window open and leant out just as Ivor was emerging from his taxi. She blew him an exuberant kiss and shouted, with illustrative gestures, that we were coming down.

'How nice it would be,' she said as we hurried downstairs, 'if you'd be wearing an opera cloak. You could wrap it around both of us as the Siamese twins do in your story. Now, quick!'

She dashed into Ivor's arms, and was the next moment in the safety of the cab.

'Paon d'Or,' Ivor told the driver. 'Good to see you, old boy,' he said to me, with a distinct American intonation (which I shyly imitated at dinner until he growled: 'Very funny').

The Paon d'Or no longer exists. Although not quite tops, it was a nice clean place, much patronized by American tourists, who called it 'Pander' or 'Pandora' and always ordered its 'putty saw-lay,' and that, I guess, is what we had. I remember more clearly a glazed case hanging on the gold-figured wall next to our table: it displayed four Morpho butterflies, two huge ones similar in harsh sheen but differently shaped, and two smaller ones beneath them, the left of a sweeter blue with white stripes and the right gleaming like silvery satin. According to the headwaiter, they had been caught by a convict in South America.

'And how's my friend Mata Hari?' inquired Ivor turning to us again, his spread hand still flat on the table as he had placed it when swinging toward the 'bugs' under discussion.

We told him the poor ara sickened and had to be destroyed. And what about his automobile, was she still running? She jolly well was –

'In fact,' Iris continued, touching my wrist, 'we've decided to set off tomorrow for Cannice. Pity you can't join us, Ives, but perhaps you might come later.'

I did not want to object, though I had never heard of that decision.

Ivor said that if ever we wanted to sell Villa Iris he knew someone who would snap it up any time. Iris, he said, knew him too: David Geller, the actor. 'He was (turning to me) her first beau before you blundered in. She must still have somewhere that photo of him and me in *Troilus and Cressida* ten years ago. He's Helen of Troy in it, I'm Cressida.'

'Lies, lies,' murmured Iris.

Ivor described his own house in Los Angeles. He proposed discussing with me after dinner a script he wished me to prepare based on Gogol's *Inspector* (we were back at the start, so to speak). Iris asked for another helping of whatever it was we were eating.

'You will die,' said Ivor. 'It's monstrously rich. Remember what Miss Grunt (a former governess to whom he would assign all kinds of gruesome apothegms) used to say: "The white worms lie in wait for the glutton." '

'That's why I want to be burned when I die,' remarked Iris.

He ordered a second or third bottle of the indifferent white wine I had had the polite weakness to praise. We drank to his last film – I forget its title – which was to be shown tomorrow in London, and later in Paris, he hoped.

Ivor did not look either very well or very happy; he had developed a sizable bald spot, freckled. I had never noticed before that his eyelids were so heavy and his lashes so coarse and pale. Our neighbors, three harmless Americans, hearty, flushed, vociferous, were, perhaps, not particularly pleasant, but neither Iris nor I thought Ivor's threat 'to make those Bronxonians pipe down' justified, seeing that he, too, was talking in fairly resonant tones. I rather looked forward to the end of the dinner – and to coffee at home – but Iris on the contrary seemed inclined to enjoy every morsel and drop. She wore a very open, jet-black frock and the long onyx earrings I had once given her. Her cheeks and arms, without their summer tan, had the mat whiteness that I was to distribute – perhaps too generously – among the girls of my future books. Ivor's roving eyes, while he talked, tended to appraise her bare shoulders, but by the simple trick of breaking in with some question, I managed to keep confusing the trajectory of his gaze.

At last the ordeal came to a close. Iris said she would be back in a minute; her brother suggested we 'repair for a leak.' I declined – not because I did not need it – I did – but because I knew by experience that a talkative neighbor and the sight of his immediate stream would inevitably afflict me with urinary impotence. As I sat smoking in the lounge of the restaurant I pondered the wisdom of suddenly transferring the established habit of work on *Camera Lucida* to other surroundings, another desk, another lighting, another pressure of outside calls and smells – and I saw my pages and notes flash past like the bright windows of an express train that did not stop at my station. I had decided to talk Iris out of her plan when brother and sister appeared from opposite sides of the stage, beaming at one another. She had less than fifteen minutes of life left.

Numbers are bleary along rue Despréaux, and the taxi-man missed our front porch by a couple of house lengths. He suggested reversing his cab, but impatient Iris had already alighted, and I scrambled out after her, leaving Ivor to pay the taxi. She cast a look around her; then started to walk so fast toward our house that I had trouble catching up with her. As I was about to cup her elbow, I heard Ivor's voice behind me, calling out that he had not enough change. I abandoned Iris and ran back to Ivor, and just as I reached the two palm readers, they and I heard Iris cry out something loud and brave, as if she were driving away a fierce hound. By the light of a streetlamp we glimpsed the figure of a mackintoshed man stride up to her from the opposite sidewalk and fire at such close range that he seemed to prod her with his large pistol. By now our taxi-man, followed by Ivor and me, had come near enough to see the killer stumble over her collapsed and curled up body. Yet he did not try to escape. Instead he knelt down, took off his beret, threw back his shoulders, and in this ghastly and ludicrous attitude lifted his pistol to his shaved head.

The story that appeared among other *faits-divers* in the Paris dailies after an investigation by the police – whom Ivor and I contrived to mislead thoroughly – amounted to what follows – I translate: a White Russian, Wladimir Blagidze, *alias* Starov, who was subject to paroxysms of insanity, ran amuck Friday night in the middle of a calm street, opened fire at random, and after killing with one pistol shot an English tourist Mrs. [name garbled], who chanced to be passing by, blew his brains out beside her. Actually he did not die there and then, but retained in his remarkably tough brainpan fragments of consciousness and somehow lingered on well into May, which was unusually hot that year. Out of some perverse dream-like curiosity, Ivor visited him at the very special hospital of the renowned Dr. Lazareff, a very round, mercilessly round, building on the top of a hill, thickly covered with horse chestnut, wild rose, and other poignant plants. The hole in Blagidze's mind had caused a complete set of recent memories to escape; but the patient remembered quite clearly (according to a Russian male nurse good at decoding the tales of the tortured) how at six years of age he was taken to a pleasure park in Italy where a miniature train consisting of three open cars, each seating six silent children, with a battery-operated green engine that emitted at realistic intervals puffs of imitation smoke, pursued a circular course through a brambly picturesque nightmare grove whose dizzy flowers nodded continuous assent to all the horrors of childhood and hell.

From somewhere in the Orkneys, Nadezhda Gordonovna and a clerical friend arrived in Paris only after her husband's burial. Moved by a false sense of duty, she attempted to see me so as to tell me 'everything.' I evaded all contact with her, but she managed to locate Ivor in London before he left for the States. I never asked him, and the dear funny fellow never revealed to me what that 'everything' was; I refuse to believe that it could have amounted to much – and I knew enough, anyway. By nature I am not vindictive; yet I like to dwell in fancy on the image of that little green train, running on, round and round, forever.

PART TWO

I

A curious form of self-preservation moves us to get rid, instantly, irrevocably, of all that belonged to the loved one we lost. Otherwise, the things she touched every day and kept in their proper context by the act of handling them start to become bloated with an awful mad life of their own. Her dresses now wear their own selves, her books leaf through their own pages. We suffocate in the tightening circle of those monsters that are misplaced and misshapen because she is not there to tend them. And even the bravest among us cannot meet the gaze of her mirror.

How to get rid of them is another problem. I could not drown them like kittens; in fact, I could not drown a kitten, let alone her brush or bag. Nor could I watch a stranger collect them, take them away, come back for more. Therefore, I simply abandoned the flat, telling the maid to dispose in any manner she chose of all those unwanted things. Unwanted! At the moment of parting they appeared quite normal and harmless; I would even say they looked taken aback.

At first I tried putting up in a third-rate hotel in the center of Paris. I would fight terror and solitude by working all day. I completed one novel, began another, wrote forty poems (all robbers and brothers under their motley skin), a dozen short stories, seven essays, three devastating reviews, one parody. The business of not losing my mind during the night was taken care of by swallowing an especially potent pill or buying a bedmate.

I remember a dangerous dawn in May (1931? or 1932?); all the birds (mostly sparrows) were singing as in Heine's month of May, with demonic monotonous force – that's why I know it must have been a wonderful May morning. I lay with my face to the wall and in a muddled ominous way considered the question should 'we' not drive earlier than usual to Villa Iris. An obstacle, however, kept preventing me from undertaking that journey: the car and the house had been sold, so Iris had told me herself at the Protestant cemetery, because the masters of her faith and fate interdicted cremation. I turned in bed from the wall to the window, and Iris was lying with her dark head to me on the window side of the bed. I kicked off the bedclothes. She was naked, save for her black-stockinged legs (which was strange but at the same time recalled something from a parallel world, for my mind stood astride on two circus horses). In an erotic footnote, I reminded myself for the ten thousandth time to mention somewhere that there is nothing more seductive than a girl's back with the profiled rise of the haunch accentuated by her lying sidelong, one leg slightly bent. *'J'ai froid,'* said the girl as I touched her shoulder.

The Russian term for any kind of betrayal, faithlessness, breach of trust, is the snaky, watered-silk word *izmena* which is based on the idea of change, shift, transformation. This derivation had never occurred to me in my constant thoughts about Iris, but now it struck me as the revelation of a bewitchment, of a nymph's turning into a whore – and this called for an immediate and vociferous protest. One neighbor thumped the wall, another rattled the door. The frightened girl, snatching up her handbag and my raincoat, bolted out of the room, and a bearded individual entered instead, farcically clad in a nightshirt and wearing rubbers on his bare feet. The crescendo of my cries, cries of rage and distress, ended in a hysterical fit. I think some attempt was made to whisk me off to a hospital. In any case, I had to find another home *sans tarder*, a phrase I cannot hear without a spasm of anguish by mental association with her lover's letter.

A small patch of countryside kept floating before my eyes like some photic illusion. I let my index finger stray at random over a map of northern France; the point of its nail stopped at the town of Petiver or Petit Ver, a small worm or verse, which sounded idyllic. An autobus took me to a road station not very far from Orléans, I believe. All I remember of my abode is its oddly slanting floor which corresponded to a slant in the ceiling of the café under my room. I also remember a pastel-green park to the east of the town, and an old castle. The

summer I spent there is a mere smudge of color on the dull glass of
my mind; but I did write a few poems – at least one of which, about
a company of acrobats staging a show on the church square, has been
reprinted a number of times in the course of forty years.

When I returned to Paris I found that my kind friend Stepan
Ivanovich Stepanov, a prominent journalist of independent means
(he was one of those very few lucky Russians who had happened to
transfer themselves and their money abroad before the Bolshevik
coup), had not only organized my second or third public reading
(*vecher*, 'evening,' was the Russian term consecrated to that kind of
performance) but wanted me to stay in one of the ten rooms of his
spacious old-fashioned house (Avenue Koch? Roche? It abuts, or
abutted, on the statue of a general whose name escapes me but surely
lurks somewhere among my old notes).

Its residents were at the moment old Mr. and Mrs. Stepanov, their
married daughter Baroness Borg, her eleven-year-old child (the Baron,
a businessman, had been sent by his firm to England), and Grigoriy
Reich (1899–1942?), a gentle, melancholy, lean, young poet, of no talent
whatever, who under the pen name of Lunin contributed a weekly
elegy to the *Novosti* and acted as Stepanov's secretary.

I could not avoid coming down in the evenings to join the frequent
gatherings of literary and political personages in the ornate salon or
in the dining room with its huge oblong table and the oil portrait *en
pied* of the Stepanovs' young son who had died in 1920 while trying
to save a drowning schoolmate. Nearsighted, gruffly jovial Alexander
Kerenski would usually be there, brusquely raising his eyeglass to
stare at a stranger or greeting an old friend with a ready quip in that
rasping voice of his, most of its strength lost years ago in the roar of
the Revolution. Ivan Shipogradov, eminent novelist and recent Nobel
Prize winner, would also be present, radiating talent and charm, and
– after a few jiggers of vodka – delighting his intimates with the kind
of Russian bawdy tale that depends for its artistry on the rustic gusto
and fond respect with which it treats our most private organs. A far
less engaging figure was I. A. Shipogradov's old rival, a fragile little
man in a sloppy suit, Vasiliy Sokolovski (oddly nicknamed 'Jeremy'
by I.A.), who since the dawn of the century had been devoting volume

after volume to the mystical and social history of a Ukrainian clan that had started as a humble family of three in the sixteenth century but by volume six (1920) had become a whole village, replete with folklore and myth. It was good to see old Morozov's rough-hewn clever face with its shock of dingy hair and bright frosty eyes; and for a special reason I closely observed podgy dour Basilevski – not because he had just had or was about to have a row with his young mistress, a feline beauty who wrote doggerel verse and vulgarly flirted with me, but because I hoped he had already seen the fun I had made of him in the last issue of a literary review in which we both collaborated. Although his English was inadequate for the interpretation of, say, Keats (whom he defined as 'a pre-Wildean aesthete in the beginning of the Industrial Era') Basilevski was fond of attempting just that. In discussing recently the 'not altogether displeasing preciosity' of my own stuff, he had imprudently quoted a popular line from Keats, rendering it as:

> *Vsegda nas raduet krasivaya veshchitsa*

which in retranslation gives:

> 'A pretty bauble always gladdens us.'

Our conversation, however, turned out to be much too brief to disclose whether or not he had appreciated my amusing lesson. He asked me what I thought of the new book he was telling Morozov (a monolinguist) about – namely Maurois' 'impressive work on Byron,' and upon my answering that I had found it to be impressive trash, my austere critic muttered, 'I don't think you have read it,' and went on educating the serene old poet.

I would steal away long before the party broke up. The sounds of farewells usually reached me as I glided into insomnia.

I spent most of the day working, ensconced in a deep armchair, with my implements conveniently resting before me on a special writing board provided by my host, a great lover of handy knick-knacks. Somehow or other I had started to gain weight since my bereavement and by now had to make two or three lurching efforts in order to leave my overaffectionate seat. Only one little person visited me; for her I kept my door slightly ajar. The board's proximal edge had a thoughtful incurvature to accommodate an author's abdomen, and the distal side was equipped with clamps and rubber-bands to hold papers and pencils in place; I got so used to those comforts that I regretted ungratefully the absence of toilet fixtures – such as one of those hollow canes said to be used by Orientals.

Every afternoon, at the same hour, a silent push opened the door wider, and the granddaughter of the Stepanovs brought in a tray with a large glass of strong tea and a plate of ascetic zwiebacks. She advanced, eyes bent, moving carefully her white-socked, blue-sneakered feet; coming to a near stop when the tea tossed; and advancing again with the slow steps of a clockwork doll. She had flaxen hair and a freckled nose, and I chose the gingham frock with the glossy black belt for her to wear when I had her continue her mysterious progress right into the book I was writing, *The Red Top Hat*, in which she becomes graceful little Amy, the condemned man's ambiguous consoler.

Those were nice, nice interludes! One could hear the Baroness and her mother playing *à quatre mains* in the salon downstairs as they had played and replayed, no doubt, for the last fifteen years. I had a box of chocolate-coated biscuits to supplement the zwiebacks and tempt my little visitor. The writing board was put aside and replaced by her folded limbs. She spoke Russian fluently but with Parisian interjections and interrogatory sounds, and those bird notes lent something eerie to the responses I obtained, as she dangled one leg and bit her biscuit, to the ordinary questions one puts to a child; and then quite suddenly in the midst of our chat, she would wriggle out of my arms and make for the door as if somebody were summoning her, though actually the piano kept stumbling on and on in the homely course of a family happiness in which I had no part and which, in fact, I had never known.

My stay at the Stepanovs' had been supposed to last a couple of weeks; it lasted two months. At first I felt comparatively well, or at least comfortable and refreshed, but a new sleeping pill which had worked so well at its beguiling stage began refusing to cope with certain reveries which, as suggested subsequently by an incredible sequel, I should have succumbed to like a man and got done with no matter how; instead of that I took advantage of Dolly's removal to England to find a new dwelling for my miserable carcass. This was a bed-sitting-room in a shabby but quiet tenement house on the Left Bank, 'at the corner of rue St. Supplice,' says my pocket diary with grim imprecision. An ancient cupboard of sorts contained a primitive shower bath; but there were no other facilities. Going out two or three times a day for a meal, or a cup of coffee, or an extravagant purchase at a delicatessen, afforded me a small *distraction*. In the next block I found a cinema that specialized in old horse operas and a tiny brothel with four whores ranging in age from eighteen to thirty-eight, the youngest being also the plainest.

I was to spend many years in Paris, tied to that dismal city by the threads of a Russian writer's livelihood. Nothing then, and nothing now, in backcast, had or has for me any of the spell that enthralled my compatriots. I am not thinking of the blood spot on the darkest stone of its darkest street; that is *hors-concours* in the way of horror; I just mean that I regarded Paris, with its gray-toned days and charcoal nights, merely as the chance setting for the most authentic and faithful joys of my life: the colored phrase in my mind under the drizzle, the white page under the desk lamp awaiting me in my humble home.

2

Since 1925 I had written and published four novels; by the beginning of 1934 I was on the point of completing my fifth, *Krasnyy Tsilindr* (*The Red Top Hat*), the story of a beheading. None of those books exceeded ninety thousand words but my method of choosing and blending them could hardly be called a timesaving expedient.

A first draft, made in pencil, filled several blue *cahiers* of the kind used in schools, and upon reaching the saturation point of revision presented a chaos of smudges and scriggles. To this corresponded the disorder of the text which followed a regular sequence only for a few pages, being then interrupted by some chunky passage that belonged to a later, or earlier, part of the story. After sorting out and repaginating all this, I applied myself to the next stage: the fair copy. It was tidily written with a fountain pen in a fat and sturdy exercise book or ledger. Then an orgy of new corrections would blot out by degrees all the pleasure of specious perfection. A third phase started where legibility stopped. Poking with slow and rigid fingers at the keys of my trusty old *mashinka* ('machine'), Count Starov's wedding present, I would be able to type some three hundred words in one hour instead of the round thousand with which some popular novelist of the previous century could cram it in longhand.

In the case of *The Red Top Hat*, however, the neuralgic aches which had been spreading through my frame like an inner person of pain, all angles and claws, for the last three years, had now attained my extremities, and made the task of typing a fortunate impossibility. By economizing on my favorite nutriments, such as *foie gras* and Scotch whisky, and postponing the making of a new suit, I calculated that my modest income allowed me to hire an expert typist, to whom I would dictate my corrected manuscript during, say, thirty carefully planned afternoons. I therefore inserted a prominent wanter, with name and telephone, in the *Novosti*.

Among the three or four typists who offered their services, I chose Lyubov Serafimovna Savich, the granddaughter of a country priest and the daughter of a famous SR (Social Revolutionist) who had recently died in Meudon upon completing his biography of Alexander the First (a tedious work in two volumes entitled *The Monarch and the Mystic*, now available to American students in an indifferent translation, Harvard, 1970).

Lyuba Savich started working for me on February 1, 1934. She came as often as necessary and was willing to stay any number of hours (the record she set on an especially memorable occasion was from one to eight). Had there been a Miss Russia and had the age of prize misses been prolonged to just under thirty, beautiful Lyuba would have won the title. She was a tall woman with slim ankles, big breasts, broad shoulders, and a pair of gay blue eyes in a round rosy face. Her auburn hair must have always felt as being in a state of imminent disarray for she constantly stroked its side wave, in a graceful elbow-raised gesture, when talking to me. *Zdraste*, and once more *zdraste*, Lyubov Serafimovna – and, oh, what a delightful amalgam that was, with *lyubov* meaning 'love,' and Serafim ('seraph') being the Christian name of a reformed terrorist!

As a typist L.S. was magnificent. Hardly had I finished dictating one sentence, as I paced back and forth, than it had reached her furrow like a handful of grain, and with one eyebrow raised she was already looking at me, waiting for the next strewing. If a sudden alteration for the better occurred to me in mid session, I preferred not to spoil the wonderful give-and-take rhythm of our joint work by introducing painful pauses of word weighing – especially enervating and sterile when a self-conscious author is aware that the bright lady at the waiting typewriter is longing to come up with a helpful suggestion; I contented myself therefore with marking the passage in my manuscript so as later to desecrate with my scrawl her immaculate creation; but she was only glad, of course, to retype the page at her leisure.

We usually had a ten-minute break around four – or four-thirty if

I could not rein in snorting Pegasus on the dot. She would retire for a minute, closing one door after another with a really unearthly gentleness, to the humble *toilettes* across the corridor, and would reappear, just as silently, with a repowdered nose and a repainted smile, and I would have ready for her a glass of *vin ordinaire* and a pink gaufrette. It was during those innocent intervals that there began a certain thematic movement on the part of fate.

Would I like to know something? (Dilatory sip and lip lick.) Well, at all my five public readings since the first on September 3, 1928, in the Salle Planiol, she had been present, she had applauded till her palms (showing palms) ached, and had made up her mind that next time she'd be smart and plucky enough to push her way through the crowd (yes, crowd – no need to smile ironically) with the firm intention of clasping my hand and pouring out her soul in a single word, which, however, she could never find – and that's why, inexorably, she would always be left standing and beaming like a fool in the middle of the vacated hall. Would I despise her for having an album with reviews of my books pasted in – Morozov's and Yablokov's lovely essays as well as the trash of such hacks as Boris Nyet, and Boyarski? Did I know it was *she* who had left that mysterious bunch of irises on the spot where the urn with my wife's ashes had been interred four years ago? Could I imagine that she could recite by heart every poem I had published in the *émigré* press of half-a-dozen countries? Or that she remembered thousands of enchanting minutiae scattered through all my novels such as the mallard's quack-quack (in *Tamara*) 'which to the end of one's life would taste of Russian black bread because one had shared it with ducks in one's childhood,' or the chess set (in *Pawn Takes Queen*) with a missing Knight 'replaced by some sort of counter, a little orphan from another, unknown, game?'

All this was spread over several sessions and distilled very cunningly, and already by the end of February when a copy of *The Red Top Hat*, an impeccable typescript, lapped in an opulent envelope, had been delivered by hand (hers again) to the offices of *Patria* (the foremost Russian magazine in Paris), I felt enmeshed in a bothersome web.

Not only had I never experienced the faintest twinge of desire in regard to beautiful Lyuba, but the indifference of my senses was turning to positive repulsion. The softer her glances fluttered, the more ungentlemanly my reaction became. Her very refinement had a dainty edge of vulgarity that infested with the sweetness of decay her entire personality. I began to notice with growing irritation such pathetic things as her odor, a quite respectable perfume (*Adoration*, I think) precariously overlaying the natural smell of a Russian maiden's seldom bathed body: for an hour or so *Adoration* still held, but after that the underground would start to conduct more and more frequent forays, and when she raised her arms to put on her hat – but never mind, she was a well-meaning creature, and I hope she is a happy grandmother today.

I would be a cad to describe our last meeting (March 1 of the same year). Suffice it to say that in the middle of typing a rhymed Russian translation that I had made of Keats' *To Autumn* ('Season of mists and mellow fruitfulness') she broke down, and tormented me till at least eight P.M. with her confessions and tears. When at last she left, I lost another hour composing a detailed letter asking her never to come back. Incidentally, it was the first time that an unfinished leaf was left by her in my typewriter. I removed it and rediscovered it several weeks later among my papers, and then deliberately preserved it because it was Annette who completed the job, with a couple of typos and an x-ed erasure in the last lines – and something about the juxtaposition appealed to my combinational slant.

3

In this memoir my wives and my books are interlaced monogram-
matically like some sort of watermark or *ex libris* design; and in
writing this oblique autobiography – oblique, because dealing mainly
not with pedestrian history but with the mirages of romantic and
literary matters – I consistently try to dwell as lightly as inhumanly
possible on the evolution of my mental illness. Yet Dementia is one
of the characters in my story.

By the mid-Thirties little had changed in my health since the first
half of 1922 and its awful torments. My battle with factual, respectable
life still consisted of sudden delusions, sudden reshufflings – kaleido-
scopic, stained-glass reshufflings! – of fragmented space. I still felt
Gravity, that infernal and humiliating contribution to our perceptual
world, grow into me like a monstrous toenail in stabs and wedges of
intolerable pain (incomprehensible to the happy simpleton who finds
nothing fantastic and agonizing in the escape of a pencil or penny
under something – under the desk on which one will live, under the
bed on which one will die). I still could not cope with the abstraction
of direction in space, so that any given stretch of the world was either
permanently 'right-hand' or permanently 'left-hand,' or at best the
one could be changed to the other only by a spine-dislocating effort
of the will. Oh, how things and people tortured me, my dear heart,
I could not tell you! In point of fact you were not yet even born.

Sometime in the mid-Thirties, in black accursed Paris, I remember
visiting a distant relative of mine (a niece of the LATH lady!). She
was a sweet old stranger. She sat all day in a straight-back armchair
exposed to the continuous attacks of three, four, more than four,
deranged children, whom she was paid (by the Destitute Russian

Noblewomen's Aid Association) to watch, while their parents were working in places not so dreadful and dreary in themselves as dreary and difficult to reach by public conveyance. I sat on an old hassock at her feet. Her talk flowed on and on, smooth, untroubled, reflecting the image of radiant days, serenity, wealth, goodness. Yet all the time this or that poor little monster with a slavering mouth and a squint would move upon her from behind a screen or a table and rock her chair or clutch at her skirt. When the squealing became too loud she would only wince a little which hardly affected her reminiscent smile. She kept a kind of fly whisk within easy reach and this she occasionally brandished to chase away the bolder aggressors; but all the time, all the time, she continued her purling soliloquy and I understood that I, too, should ignore the rude turmoil and din around her.

I submit that my life, my plight, the voice of words that was my sole joy and the secret struggle with the wrong shape of things, bore some resemblance to that poor lady's predicament. And mind you, those were my best days, with only a pack of grimacing goblins to hold at bay.

The zest, the strength, the clarity of my art remained unimpaired – at least to a certain extent. I enjoyed, I persuaded myself to enjoy, the solitude of work and that other, even more subtle solitude, the solitude of an author facing, from behind the bright shield of his manuscript, an amorphous audience, barely visible in its dark pit.

The jumble of spatial obstacles separating my bedside lamp from the illumined islet of a public lectern was abolished by the magic of thoughtful friends who helped me to get to this or that remote hall without my having to tussle with horribly small and thin, sticky, bus-ticket slips or to venture into the thunderous maze of the *Métro*. As soon as I was safely platformed with my typed or handwritten sheets at breastbone level on the desk before me, I forgot all about the presence of three hundred eavesdroppers. A decanter of watered vodka, my only lectorial whim, was also my only link with the material universe. Similar to a painter's spotlight on the brown brow of some ecstatical ecclesiastic at the moment of divine revelation, the radiance enclosing me brought out with oracular accuracy every imperfection in my text. A memoirist has noted that not only did I slow down now and then while unclipping a pencil and replacing a comma by a semicolon, but that I had been known to stop and frown over a sentence and reread it, and cross it out, and insert a correction and 're-mouth the whole passage with a kind of defiant complacency.'

My handwriting was good in fair copies, but I felt more comfortable with a typescript before me, and I was again without an expert typist. To insert the same wanter in the same paper would have been foolhardy: what if it were to bring back Lyuba, flushed with renewed hope, and rewind that damned cycle all over again?

I rang up Stepanov, thinking he might help; he guessed he could, and after a muffled confabulation with his fussy wife, just on the brim of the membrane (all I made out was 'mad people are unpredictable'), she took over. They knew a very decent girl who had worked at the Russian nursery school 'Passy na Rousi' to which Dolly had gone four or five years ago. The girl's name was Anna Ivanovna Blagovo. Did I know Oksman, the owner of the Russian bookshop on rue Cuvier?

'Yes, slightly. But I want to ask you –'

'Well,' she went on, interrupting me, 'Annette *sekretarstvovala* for him while his regular typist was hospitalized, but she is now quite well again, and you might –'

'That's fine,' I said, 'but I want to ask you, Berta Abramovna, why did you accuse me of being an "unpredictable madman"? I can assure you that I am not in the habit of raping young women –'

'*Gospod' s vami, golubchik!* (What an idea, my dear!)' exclaimed Mrs. Stepanov and proceeded to explain that she had been scolding her absentminded husband for sitting down on her new handbag when attending to the telephone.

Although I did not believe one word of her version (too quick! too glib!), I pretended to accept it and promised to look up her bookseller. A few minutes later as I was about to open the window and strip in front of it (at moments of raw widowerhood a soft black night in the spring is the most soothing *voyeuse* imaginable), Berta Stepanov telephoned to say that the oxman (what a shiver my Iris derived from Dr. Moreau's island zoo – especially from such bits as the 'screaming shape,' still half-bandaged, escaping out of the lab!) would be up till dawn in his shop, among nightmare-inherited ledgers. She knew, hey-hey (Russian chuckle), that I was a noctambule, so perhaps I might like to stroll over to the Boyan Bookshop *sans tarder*, without retardment, vile term. I might, indeed.

After that jarring call, I saw little to choose between the tossings of insomnia and a walk to rue Cuvier which leads to the Seine, where according to police statistics an average of forty foreigners and God knows how many unfortunate natives drown yearly between wars. I have never experienced the least urge to commit suicide, that silly waste of selfhood (a gem in any light). But I must admit that on that particular night on the fourth or fifth or fiftieth anniversary of my darling's death, I must have looked pretty suspect, in my black suit and dramatic muffler, to an average policeman of the riparian department. And it is a particularly bad sign when a hatless person sobs as he walks, being moved not by lines he might have composed himself but by something he hideously mistakes for his own and presently flinches, yet is too much of a coward to make amends:

> *Zvezdoobraznost' nebesnyh zvyozd*
> *Vidish' tol'ko skvoz' slyozy . . .*
> (Heavenly stars are seen as stellate only through tears.)

I am much bolder now, of course, much bolder and prouder than the ambiguous hoodlum caught progressing that night between a seemingly endless fence with its tattered posters and a row of spaced streetlamps whose light would delicately select for its heart-piercing game overhead a young emerald-bright linden leaf. I now confess that I was bothered that night, and the next and some time before, by a dream feeling that my life was the non-identical twin, a parody, an inferior variant of another man's life, somewhere on this or another earth. A demon, I felt, was forcing me to impersonate that other man, that other writer who was and would always be incomparably greater, healthier, and crueler than your obedient servant.

4

The 'Boyan' publishing firm (Morozov's and mine was the 'Bronze Horseman,' its main rival), with a bookshop (selling not only *émigré* editions but also tractor novels from Moscow) and a lending library, occupied a smart three-story house of the *hôtel particulier* type. In my day it stood between a garage and a cinema: forty years before (in the vista of reverse metamorphosis) the former had been a fountain and the latter a group of stone nymphs. The house had belonged to the Merlin de Malaune family and had been acquired at the turn of the century by a Russian cosmopolitan, Dmitri de Midoff who with his friend S. I. Stepanov established there the headquarters of an anti-despotic conspiracy. The latter liked to recall the sign language of old-fashioned rebellion: the half-drawn curtain and alabaster vase revealed in the drawing-room window so as to indicate to the expected guest from Russia that the way was clear. An aesthetic touch graced revolutionary intrigues in those years. Midoff died soon after World War One, and by that time the Terrorist party, to which those cozy people belonged, had lost its 'stylistic appeal' as Stepanov himself put it. I do not know who later acquired the house or how it happened that Oks (Osip Lvovich Oksman, 1885?–1943?) rented it for his business.

The house was dark except for three windows: two adjacent rectangles of light in the middle of the upper-floor row, d8 and e8, Continental notation (where the letter denotes the file and the number the rank of a chess square) and another light just below at e7. Good God, had I forgotten at home the note I had scribbled for the unknown Miss Blagovo? No, it was still there in my breast pocket under the old, treasured, horribly hot and long Trinity College muffler. I hesitated between a side door on my right – marked *Magazin* – and the main entrance, with a chess coronet above the bell. Finally I chose the coronet. We were playing a *Blitz* game: my opponent moved at once, lighting the vestibule fan at d6. One could not help wondering if under the house there might not exist the five lower floors which would complete the chessboard and that somewhere, in subterranean mystery, new men might not be working out the doom of a fouler tyranny.

Oks, a tall, bony, elderly man with a Shakespearean pate, started to tell me how honored he was at getting a chance to welcome the author of *Camera* – here I thrust the note I carried into his extended palm and prepared to leave. He had dealt with hysterical artists before. None could resist his bland bookside manner.

'Yes, I know all about it,' he said, retaining and patting my hand. 'She'll call you; though, to tell the truth, I do not envy anybody having to use the services of that capricious, absentminded young lady. We'll go up to my study, unless you prefer – no, I don't think so,' he continued, opening a double door on the left and dubiously switching on the light for a moment to reveal a chilly reading room in which a long baize-covered table, dingy chairs, and the cheap busts of Russian classics contradicted a lovely painted ceiling swarming with naked children among purple, pink, and amber clusters of grapes. On the right (another tentative light snapped) a short passage led to the shop proper where I recalled having once had a row with a pert old female who objected to my not wishing to pay for a few copies of my own novel. So we walked up the once noble stairs, which now had something seldom seen even in Viennese dream comics, namely disparate balustrades, the sinistral one an ugly new ramp-and-railing affair and the other, the original ornate set of battered, doomed, but still charming carved wood with supports in the form of magnified chess pieces.

'I am honored –' began Oks all over again, as we reached his so-called *Kabinet* (study), at e7, a room cluttered with ledgers, packed books, half-unpacked books, towers of books, heaps of newspapers, pamphlets, galleys, and slim white paperback collections of poems – tragic offals, with the cool, restrained titles then in fashion – *Prokhlada* ('coolness'), *Sderzhannost'* ('restraint').

He was one of those persons who for some reason or other are often interrupted, but whom no force in our blessed galaxy will prevent from completing their sentence, despite new interruptions, of an elemental or poetical nature, the death of his interlocutor ('I was just saying to him, doctor –'), or the entrance of a dragon. In fact it would seem that those interruptions actually help to polish the phrase and give it its final form. In the meantime the agonizing itch of its being unfinished poisons the mind. It is worse than the pimple which cannot be sprung before one gets home, and is almost as bad as a lifer's recollection of that last little rape nipped in the sweet bud by the intrusion of an accursed policeman.

'I am deeply honored,' finished at last Oks, 'to welcome to this historic house the author of *Camera Obscura*, your finest book in my modest opinion!'

'It ought to be modest,' I said, controlling myself (opal ice in Nepal before the avalanche), 'because, you idiot, the title of *my* novel is *Camera Lucida*.'

'There, there,' said Oks (really a very dear man and a gentleman), after a terrible pause during which all the remainders opened like fairy-tale flowers in a fancy film, 'A slip of the tongue does not deserve such a harsh rebuke. *Lucida, Lucida,* by all means! *A propos* – concerning Anna Blagovo (another piece of unfinished business – or, who knows, a touching attempt to divert and pacify me with an interesting anecdote), I am not sure you know that I am Berta's first cousin. Thirty-five years ago in St. Petersburg she and I worked in the same student organization. We were preparing the assassination of the Premier. How far all that is! His daily route had to be closely established; I was one of the observers. Standing at a certain corner every day in the disguise of a vanilla-ice-cream vendor! Can you imagine that? Nothing came of our plans. They were thwarted by Azef, the great double agent.'

I saw no point in prolonging my visit, but he produced a bottle of cognac, and I accepted a drink, for I was beginning to tremble again.

'Your *Camera*,' he said, consulting a ledger, 'has been selling not badly in my shop, not badly at all: twenty-three – sorry, twenty-five – copies in the first half of last year, and fourteen in the second. Of course, genuine fame, not mere commercial success, depends on the behavior of a book in the Lending Department, and there all your titles are hits. Not to leave this unsubstantiated, let us go up to the stacks.'

I followed my energetic host to the upper floor. The lending library spread like a gigantic spider, bulged like a monstrous tumor, oppressed the brain like the expanding world of delirium. In a bright oasis amidst the dim shelves I noticed a group of people sitting around an oval table. The colors were vivid and sharp but at the same time remote-looking as in a magic-lantern scene. A good deal of red wine and golden brandy accompanied the animated discussion. I recognized the critic Basilevski, his sycophants Hristov and Boyarski, my friend Morozov, the novelists Shipogradov and Sokolovski, the honest nonentity Suknovalov, author of the popular social satire *Geroy nashey ery* ('Hero of Our Era') and two young poets, Lazarev (collection *Serenity*) and Fartuk (collection *Silence*). Some of the heads turned toward us, and the benevolent bear Morozov even struggled to his feet, grinning – but my host said they were having a business meeting and should be left alone.

'You have glimpsed,' he added, 'the parturition of a new literary review, *Prime Numbers*; at least they *think* they are parturiating: actually, they are boozing and gossiping. Now let me show you something.'

He led me to a distant corner and triumphantly trained his flash-light on the gaps in *my* shelf of books.

'Look,' he cried, 'how many copies are out. All of *Princess Mary* is out, I mean *Mary* – damn it, I mean *Tamara*. I love *Tamara*, I mean your *Tamara*, not Lermontov's or Rubinstein's. Forgive me. One gets so confused among so many damned masterpieces.'

I said I was not feeling well and would like to go home. He offered to accompany me. Or would I like a taxi? I did not. He kept furtively directing at me the electric torch through his incarnadined fingers to see if I was not about to faint. With soothing sounds he led me down a side staircase. The spring night, at least, felt real.

After a moment of rumination and an upward glance at the lighted windows, Oks beckoned to the night watchman who was stroking the sad little dog of a dog-walking neighbor. I saw my thoughtful companion shake hands with the gray-cloaked old fellow, then point to the light of the revelers, then look at his watch, then tip the man, and shake hands with him in parting, as if the ten-minute walk to my lodgings were a perilous pilgrimage.

'*Bon,*' he said upon rejoining me. 'If you don't want a taxi, let us set out on foot. He will take care of my imprisoned visitors. There are heaps of things I want you to tell me about your work and your life. Your *confrères* say you are "arrogant and unsocial" as Onegin describes himself to Tatiana but we can't all be Lenskis, can we? Let me take advantage of this pleasant stroll to describe my two meetings with your celebrated father. The first was at the opera in the days of the First Duma. I knew, of course, the portraits of its most prominent members. From high up in the gods I, a poor student, saw him appear in a rosy loge with his wife and two little boys, one of which must have been you. The other time was at a public discussion of current politics in the auroral period of the Revolution; he spoke immediately after Kerenski, and the contrast between our fiery friend and your father, with his English *sangfroid* and absence of gesticulation –'

'My father,' I said, 'died six months before I was born.'

'Well, I seem to have goofed again (*opyat' oskandalisya*),' observed Oks, after taking quite a minute to find his handkerchief, blow his nose with the grandiose deliberation of Varlamov in the role of Gogol's Town Mayor, wrap up the result, and pocket the swaddle. 'Yes, I'm not lucky with you. Yet that image remains in my mind. The contrast was truly remarkable.'

I was to run into Oks again, three or four times at least, in the course of the dwindling years before World War Two. He used to welcome me with a knowing twinkle as if we shared some very private and rather naughty secret. His superb library was eventually grabbed by the Germans who then lost it to the Russians, even better grabbers in that time-honored game. Osip Lvovich himself was to die when attempting an intrepid escape – when almost having escaped – barefoot, in bloodstained underwear, from the 'experimental hospital' of a Nazi concentration camp.

5

My father was a gambler and a rake. His society nickname was Demon. Vrubel has portrayed him with his vampire-pale cheeks, his diamond eyes, his black hair. What remained on the palette has been used by me, Vadim, son of Vadim, for touching up the father of the passionate siblings in the best of my English romaunts, *Ardis* (1970).

The scion of a princely family devoted to a gallery of a dozen Tsars, my father resided on the idyllic outskirts of history. His politics were of the casual, reactionary sort. He had a dazzling and complicated sensual life, but his culture was patchy and commonplace. He was born in 1865, married in 1896, and died in a pistol duel with a young Frenchman on October 22, 1898, after a card-table fracas at Deauville, some resort in gray Normandy.

There might be nothing particularly upsetting about a well-meaning, essentially absurd and muddled old duffer mistaking me for some other writer. I myself have been known, in the lecture hall, to say Shelley when I meant Schiller. But that a fool's slip of the tongue or error of memory should establish a sudden connection with another world, so soon after my imagining with especial dread that I might be permanently impersonating somebody living as a real being beyond the constellation of my tears and asterisks – *that* was unendurable, *that* dared not happen!

As soon as the last sound of poor Oksman's farewells and excuses had subsided, I tore off the striped woollen snake strangling me and wrote down in cipher every detail of my meeting with him. Then I drew a thick line underneath and a caravan of question marks.

Should I ignore the coincidence and its implications? Should I, on the contrary, repattern my entire life? Should I abandon my art, choose another line of achievement, take up chess seriously, or become, say, a lepidopterist, or spend a dozen years as an obscure scholar making a Russian translation of *Paradise Lost* that would cause hacks to shy and asses to kick? But only the writing of fiction, the endless re-creation of my fluid self could keep me more or less sane. All I did finally was drop my pen name, the rather cloying and somehow misleading 'V. Irisin' (of which my Iris herself used to say that it sounded as if I were a villa), and revert to my own family name.

It was with this name that I decided to sign the first installment of my new novel *The Dare* for which the *émigré* magazine *Patria* was waiting. I had finished rewriting in reptile-green ink (a placebo to enliven my task) a second or third fair copy of the opening chapter, when Annette Blagovo came to discuss hours and terms.

She came on May 2, 1934, half-an-hour late, and as persons do who have no sense of duration, laid the blame for her lateness on her innocent watch, an object for measuring motion, not time. She was a graceful blonde of twenty-six years or so, with very attractive though not exceptionally pretty features. She wore a gray tailor-made jacket over a white silk blouse that looked frilly and festive because of a kind of bow between the lapels, to one of which was pinned a bunchlet of violets. Her short smartly cut gray skirt had a nice dash about it, and all in all she was far more chic and *soignée* than an average Russian young lady.

I explained to her (in what struck her – so she told me much later – as the unpleasantly bantering tone of a cynic sizing up a possible conquest) that I proposed to dictate to her every afternoon 'right into the typewriter' (*pryamo v mashinku*) heavily corrected drafts or else chunks and sausages of fair copy that I would probably revise 'in the lonely hours of night,' to quote A. K. Tolstoy, and have her retype next day. She did not remove her close-fitting hat, but peeled off her gloves and, pursing her bright pink freshly painted mouth, put on large tortoiseshell-rimmed glasses, and the effect somehow enhanced her looks: she desired to see my machine (her icy demureness would have turned a saint into a salacious jester), had to hurry to another appointment but just wanted to check if she could use it. She took off her green cabochon ring (which I was to find after her departure) and seemed about to tap out a quick sample but a second glance satisfied her that my typewriter was of the same make as her own.

Our first session proved pretty awful. I had learned my part with the care of a nervous actor, but did not reckon with the kind of fellow performer who misses or fluffs every other cue. She asked me not to go so fast. She put me off by fatuous remarks: 'There is no such expression in Russian,' or 'Nobody knows that word (*vzvoden*', a welter) – why don't you just say '"big wave"' if that's what you mean?' When anger affected my rhythm and it took me some time to unravel the end of a sentence in its no longer familiar labyrinth of cancellations and carets, she would sit back and wait like a provocative martyr and stifle a yawn or study her fingernails. After three hours of work, I examined the result of her dainty and impudent rattle. It teemed with misspellings, typos, and ugly erasures. Very meekly I said that she seemed unaccustomed to deal with literary (i.e. non-humdrum) stuff. She answered I was mistaken, she loved literature. In fact, she said, in just the past five months she had read Galsworthy (in Russian), Dostoyevski (in French), General Pudov-Usurovski's huge historical novel *Tsar Bronshteyn* (in the original), and *L'Atlantide* (which I had not heard of but which a dictionary ascribes to Pierre Benoît, *romancier français né à Albi*, a hiatus in the Tarn). Did she know Morozov's poetry? No, she did not much care for poetry in any form; it was inconsistent with the tempo of modern life. I chided her for not having read any of my stories or novels, and she looked annoyed and perhaps a little frightened (fearing, the little goose, I might dismiss her), and presently was giving me a curiously erotic satisfaction by promising me that now she would look up *all* my books and would certainly know by heart *The Dare*.

The reader must have noticed that I speak only in a very general way about my Russian fictions of the Nineteen-Twenties and Thirties, for I assume that he is familiar with them or can easily obtain them in their English versions. At this point, however, I must say a few words about *The Dare* (*Podarok Otchizne* was its original title, which can be translated as 'a gift to the fatherland'). When in 1934 I started to dictate its beginning to Annette, I knew it would be my longest novel. I did not foresee however that it would be almost as long as

General Pudov's vile and fatuous 'historical' romance about the way
the Zion Wisers usurped St. Rus. It took me about four years in all
to write its four hundred pages, many of which Annette typed at least
twice. Most of it had been serialized in *émigré* magazines by May, 1939,
when she and I, still childless, left for America; but in book form, the
Russian original appeared only in 1950 (Turgenev Publishing House,
New York), followed another decade later by an English translation,
whose title neatly refers not only to the well-known device used to
bewilder noddies but also to the daredevil nature of Victor, the hero
and part-time narrator.

The novel begins with a nostalgic account of a Russian childhood
(much happier, though not less opulent than mine). After that comes
adolescence in England (not unlike my own Cambridge years); then
life in *émigré* Paris, the writing of a first novel (*Memoirs of a Parrot
Fancier*) and the tying of amusing knots in various literary intrigues.
Inset in the middle part is a complete version of the book my Victor
wrote 'on a dare': this is a concise biography and critical appraisal of
Fyodor Dostoyevski, whose politics my author finds hateful and
whose novels he condemns as absurd with their black-bearded killers
presented as mere negatives of Jesus Christ's conventional image, and
weepy whores borrowed from maudlin romances of an earlier age.
The next chapter deals with the rage and bewilderment of *émigré*
reviewers, all of them priests of the Dostoyevskian persuasion;
and in the last pages my young hero accepts a flirt's challenge and
accomplishes a final gratuitous feat by walking through a perilous
forest into Soviet territory and as casually strolling back.

I am giving this summary to exemplify what even the poorest
reader of my *Dare* must surely retain, unless electrolysis destroys
some essential cells soon after he closes the book. Now part of
Annette's frail charm lay in her forgetfulness which veiled everything
toward the evening of everything, like the kind of pastel haze that
obliterates mountains, clouds, and even its own self as the summer
day swoons. I know I have seen her many times, a copy of *Patria* in
her languid lap, follow the printed lines with the pendulum swing of
eyes suggestive of reading, and actually reach the 'To be continued'
at the end of the current installment of *The Dare*. I also know that

she had typed every word of it and most of its commas. Yet the fact remains that she retained nothing – perhaps in result of her having decided once for all that my prose was not merely 'difficult' but hermetic ('nastily hermetic,' to repeat the compliment Basilevski paid me the moment he realized – a moment which came in due time – that his manner and mind were being ridiculed in Chapter Three by my gloriously happy Victor). I must say I forgave her readily her attitude to my work. At public readings, I admired her public smile, the 'archaic' smile of Greek statues. When her rather dreadful parents asked to see my books (as a suspicious physician might ask for a sample of semen), she gave them to read by mistake another man's novel because of a silly similarity of titles. The only real shock I experienced was when I overheard her informing some idiot woman friend that my *Dare* included biographies of 'Chernolyubov and Dobroshevski'! She actually started to argue when I retorted that only a lunatic would have chosen a pair of third-rate publicists to write about – spoonerizing their names in addition!

6

I have noticed, or seem to have noticed, in the course of my long life, that when about to fall in love or even when still unaware of having fallen in love, a dream would come, introducing me to a latent inamorata at morning twilight in a somewhat infantile setting, marked by exquisite aching stirrings that I knew as a boy, as a youth, as a madman, as an old dying voluptuary. The sense of recurrence ('seem to have noticed') is very possibly a built-in feeling: for instance I may have had that dream only once or twice ('in the course of my long life') and its familiarity is only the dropper that comes with the drops. The place in the dream, per contra, is not a familiar room but one remindful of the kind we children awake in after a Christmas masquerade or midsummer name day, in a great house, belonging to strangers or distant cousins. The impression is that the beds, two small beds in the present case, have been put in and placed against the opposite walls of a room that is not a bedroom at heart, a room with no furniture except those two separate beds: property masters are lazy, or economical, in one's dreams as well as in early novellas.

In one of the beds I find myself just awoken from some secondary dream of only formulary importance; and in the far bed against the right-hand wall (direction also supplied), a girl, a younger, slighter, and gayer Annette in this particular variant (summer of 1934 by daytime reckoning), is playfully, quietly talking to herself but actually, as I understand with a delicious quickening of the nether pulses, is feigning to talk, is talking for my benefit, so as to be noticed by me.

My next thought – and it intensifies the throbbings – concerns the strangeness of boy and girl being assigned to sleep in the same makeshift room: by error, no doubt, or perhaps the house was full and the distance between the two beds, across an empty floor, might have been deemed wide enough for perfect decorum in the case of children (my average age has been thirteen all my life). The cup of pleasure is brimming by now and before it spills I hasten to tiptoe across the bare parquet from my bed to hers. Her fair hair gets in the way of my kisses, but presently my lips find her cheek and neck, and her nightgown has buttons, and she says the maid has come into the room, but it is too late, I cannot restrain myself, and the maid, a beauty in her own right, looks on, laughing.

That dream I had a month or so after I met Annette, and her image in it, that early version of her voice, soft hair, tender skin, obsessed me and amazed me with delight – the delight of discovering I loved little Miss Blagovo. At the time of the dream she and I were still on formal terms, super-formal in fact, so I could not tell it to her with the necessary evocations and associations (as set down in these notes); and merely saying 'I dreamt of you' would have amounted to the thud of a platitude. I did something much more courageous and honorable. Before revealing to her what she called (speaking of another couple) 'serious intentions' – and before even solving the riddle of *why* really I loved her – I decided to tell her of my incurable illness.

She was elegant, she was languid, she was rather angelic in one sense, and dismally stupid in many others. I was lonely, and frightened, and reckless with lust – not sufficiently reckless, however, not to warn her by means of a vivid instance – half paradigm and half object lesson – of what she laid herself open to by consenting to marry me.

Milostivaya Gosudarynya

   Anna Ivanovna!

[Anglice *Dear Miss Blagovo*]

   Before entertaining you viva-voce of a subject of the utmost importance, I beg you to join me in the conduct of an experiment that will describe better than a learned article would one of the typical facets of my displaced mental crystal. So here goes.

   With your permission it is night now and I am in bed (decently clad, of course, and with every organ in decent repose), lying supine, and imagining an ordinary moment in an ordinary place. To further protect the purity of the experiment, let the visualized spot be an invented one. I imagine myself coming out of a bookshop and pausing on the curb before crossing the street to the little sidewalk café directly opposite. No cars are in sight. I cross. I imagine myself reaching the little café. The afternoon sun occupies one of its chairs and the half of a table, but otherwise its open-air section is empty and very inviting: nothing but brightness remains of the recent shower. And here I stop short as I recollect that I had an umbrella.

   I do not intend to bore you, glubokouvazhaemaya (dear) Anna Ivanovna, and still less do I wish to crumple this third or fourth poor sheet with the crashing sound only punished paper can make; but the scene is not sufficiently abstract and schematic, so let me retake it.

   I, your friend and employer Vadim Vadimovich, lying in bed on my back in ideal darkness (I got up a minute ago to recurtain the moon that peeped between the folds of two paragraphs), I imagine diurnal Vadim Vadimovich crossing a street from a bookshop to a sidewalk café. I am encased in my vertical self: not looking down but ahead, thus only indirectly aware of the blurry front of my corpulent figure, of the alternate points of my shoes, and of the rectangular form of the parcel under my arm. I imagine myself walking the twenty paces needed to reach the opposite sidewalk, then stopping with an unprintable curse and deciding to go back for the umbrella I left in the shop.

There is an affliction still lacking a name; there is, Anna (you must permit me to call you that, I am ten years your senior and very ill), something dreadfully wrong with my sense of direction, or rather my power over conceived space, because at this juncture I am unable to execute mentally, in the dark of my bed, the simple about-face (an act I perform without thinking in physical reality!) which would allow me to picture instantly in my mind the once already traversed asphalt as now being before me, and the vitrine of the bookshop being now within sight and not some-where behind.

Let me dwell briefly on the procedure involved; on my inability to follow it consciously in my mind – my unwieldy and disobedient mind! In order to make myself imagine the pivotal process I have to force an opposite revolution of the decor: I must try, dear friend and assistant, to swing the entire length of the street, with the massive façades of its houses before and behind me, from one direction to another in the slow wrench of a half circle, which is like trying to turn the colossal tiller of a rusty recalcitrant rudder so as to transform oneself by conscious degrees from, say, an east-facing Vadim Vadimovich into a west-sun-blinded one. The mere thought of that action leads the bedded recliner to such a muddle and dizziness that one prefers scrapping the about-face altogether, wiping, so to speak, the slate of one's vision, and beginning the return journey in one's imagination as if it were an initial one, without any previous crossing of the street, and therefore without any of the intermediate horror – the horror of struggling with the steerage of space and crushing one's chest in the process!

Voilà. Sounds rather tame, doesn't it, en fait de démence, and, indeed, if I stop brooding over the thing, I decrease it to an insignificant flaw – the missing pinkie of a freak born with nine fingers. Considering it closer, however, I cannot help suspecting it to be a warning symptom, a foreglimpse of the mental malady that is known to affect eventually the entire brain. Even that malady may not be as imminent and grave as the storm signals suggest; I only want you to be aware of the situation before proposing to you, Annette. Do not write, do not phone, do not mention this letter, if and when you come Friday afternoon; but, please, if you do, wear, in propitious sign, the Florentine hat that looks like a cluster of wild flowers. I want you to celebrate your resemblance to the fifth girl from left to right, the flower-decked blonde with the straight nose and serious gray eyes, in Botticelli's Primavera, an allegory of Spring, my love, my allegory.

On Friday afternoon, for the first time in two months she came 'on the dot' as my American friends would say. A wedge of pain replaced my heart, and little black monsters started to play musical chairs all over my room, as I noticed that she wore her usual recent hat, of no interest or meaning. She took it off before the mirror and suddenly invoked Our Lord with rare emphasis.

'*Ya idiotka*,' she said, 'I'm an idiot. I was looking for my pretty wreath, when papa started to read to me something about an ancestor of yours who quarreled with Peter the Terrible.'

'Ivan,' I said.

'I didn't catch the name, but I saw I was late and pulled on (*natsepila*) this *shapochka* instead of the wreath, your wreath, the wreath you ordered.'

I was helping her out of her jacket. Her words filled me with dream-free wantonness. I embraced her. My mouth sought the hot hollow between neck and clavicle. It was a brief but thorough embrace, and I boiled over, discreetly, deliciously, merely by pressing myself against her, one hand cupping her firm little behind and the other feeling the harp strings of her ribs. She was trembling all over. An ardent but silly virgin, she did not understand why my grip had relaxed with the suddenness of sleep or windlorn sails.

Had she read only the beginning and end of my letter? Well, yes, she had skipped the poetical part. In other words, she had not the slightest idea what I was driving at? She promised, she said, to reread it. She had grasped, however, that I loved her? She had, but how could she be sure that I *really* loved her? I was so strange, so, so – she couldn't express it – yes, STRANGE in every respect. She never had met anyone like me. Whom then did she meet, I inquired: trepanners? trombonists? astronomists? Well, mostly military men, if I wished to know, officers of Wrangel's army, gentlemen, interesting people, who spoke of danger and duty, of bivouacs in the steppe. Oh, but look here, I too can speak of 'deserts idle, rough quarries, rocks' – No, she said, they did not *invent*. They talked of spies they had hanged, they talked of international politics, of a new film or book that explained the meaning of life. And never one unchaste joke, not one horrid risqué comparison. . . . As in my books? Examples, examples! No, she would not give examples. She would not be pinned down to whirl on the pin like a wingless fly.

Or butterfly.

We were walking, one lovely morning, on the outskirts of Bellefontaine. Something flicked and lit.

'Look at that harlequin,' I murmured, pointing cautiously with my elbow.

Sunning itself against the white wall of a suburban garden was a flat, symmetrically outspread butterfly, which the artist had placed at a slight angle to the horizon of his picture. The creature was painted a smiling red with yellow intervals between black blotches; a row of blue crescents ran along the inside of the toothed wing margins. The only feature to rate a shiver of squeamishness was the glistening sweep of bronzy silks coming down on both sides of the beastie's body.

'As a former kindergarten teacher I can tell you,' said helpful Annette, 'that it's a most ordinary nettlefly *(krapivnitsa)*. How many little hands have plucked off its wings and brought them to me for approval!'

It flicked and was gone.

8

In view of the amount of typing to be done, and of her doing it so slowly and badly, she made me promise not to bother her with what Russians call 'calf cuddlings' during work. At other times all she allowed me were controlled kisses and flexible holds: our first embrace had been 'brutal' she said (having caught on very soon after that in the matter of certain male secrets). She did her best to conceal the melting, the helplessness that overwhelmed her in the natural course of caresses when she would begin to palpitate in my arms before pushing me away with a puritanical frown. Once the back of her hand chanced to brush against the taut front of my trousers; she uttered a chilly *'pardon'* (Fr.), and then went into a sulk upon my saying I hoped she had not hurt herself.

I complained of the ridiculous obsolete turn our relationship was taking. She thought it over and promised that as soon as we were 'officially engaged,' we would enter a more modern era. I assured her I was ready to proclaim its advent any day, any moment.

She took me to see her parents with whom she shared a two-room apartment in Passy. He had been an army surgeon before the Revolution and, with his close-cropped gray head, clipped mustache, and neat imperial, bore a striking resemblance (abetted no doubt by the eager spirit that patches up worn parts of the past with new impressions of the same order) to the kindly but cold-fingered (and cold-earlobed) doctor who treated the 'inflammation of the lungs' I had in the winter of 1907.

As with so many Russians *émigrés* of declining strength and lost professions, it was hard to say what exactly were Dr. Blagovo's personal resources. He seemed to spend life's overcast evening either reading his way through sets of thick magazines (1830 to 1900 or 1850 to 1910), which Annette brought him from Oksman's Lending Library, or sitting at a table and filling by means of a regularly clicking tobacco injector the semitransparent ends of carton-tubed cigarettes of which he never consumed more than thirty per day to avoid intercadence at night. He had practically no conversation and could not retell correctly any of the countless historical anecdotes he found in the battered tomes of *Russkaya Starina* ('Russian ancientry') – which explains where Annette got her inability to remember the poems, the essays, the stories, the novels she had typed for me (my grumble is repetitious, I know, but the matter rankles – a word which comes from *dracunculus*, a 'baby dragon'). He was also one of the last gentlemen I ever met who still wore a dickey and elastic-sided boots.

He asked me – and that remained his only memorable question – why I did not use in print the title which went with my thousand-year-old name. I replied that I was the kind of snob who assumes that bad readers are by nature aware of an author's origins but who hopes that good readers will be more interested in his books than in his stemma. Dr. Blagovo was a stupid old bloke, and his detachable cuffs could have been cleaner; but today, in sorrowful retrospect, I treasure his memory: he was not only the father of my poor Annette, but also the grandfather of my adored and perhaps still more unfortunate daughter.

Dr. Blagovo (1867–1940) had married at the age of forty a provincial belle in the Volgan town of Kineshma, a few miles south from one of my most romantic country estates, famous for its wild ravines, now gravel pits or places of massacre, but *then* magnificent evocations of sunken gardens. She wore elaborate make-up and spoke in simpering accents, reducing nouns and adjectives to over-affectionate forms which even the Russian language, a recognized giant of diminutives, would only condone on the wet lips of an infant or tender nurse ('Here,' said Mrs. Blagovo, 'is your *chaishko s molochishkom* [teeny tea with weeny milk]'). She struck me as an extraordinarily garrulous, affable, and banal lady, with a good taste in clothes (she worked in a *salon de couture*). A certain tenseness could be sensed in the atmosphere of the household. Annette was obviously a difficult daughter. In the

brief course of my visit I could not help noticing that the voice of
the parent addressing her developed little notes of obsequious panic
(*notki podobostrastnoy paniki*). Annette would occasionally curb with
an opaque, almost ophidian, look, her mother's volubility. As I was
leaving, the old girl paid me what she thought was a compliment:
'You speak Russian with a Parisian *grasseyement* and your manners
are those of an Englishman.' Annette, behind her, uttered a low
warning growl.

That same evening I wrote to her father informing him that she
and I had decided to marry; and on the following afternoon, when
she arrived for work, I met her in morocco slippers and silk dressing
gown. It was a holiday – the Festival of Flora – I said, indicating, with
a not wholly normal smile, the carnations, camomiles, anemones,
asphodels, and blue cockles in blond corn, which decorated my room
in our honor. Her gaze swept over the flowers, champagne, and caviar
canapés; she snorted and turned to flee; I plucked her back into the
room, locked the door and pocketed its key.

I do not mind recalling that our first tryst was a flop. It took me
so long to persuade her that this was the day, and she made such a
fuss about which ultimate inch of clothing could be removed and
which parts of her body Venus, the Virgin, and the *maire* of our
arrondissement allowed to be touched, that by the time I had her in a
passably convenient position of surrender, I was an impotent wreck.
We were lying naked, in a loose clinch. Presently her mouth opened
against mine in her first free kiss. I regained my vigor. I hastened
to possess her. She exclaimed I was disgustingly hurting her and
with a vigorous wriggle expulsed the blooded and thrashing fish.
When I tried to close her fingers around it in humble substitution,
she snatched her hand away, calling me a dirty *débauché* (*gryaznyy
razvratnik*). I had to demonstrate myself the messy act while she
looked on in amazement and sorrow.

We did better next day, and finished the flattish champagne; I never
could quite tame her, though. I remember most promising nights in
Italian lakeside hotels when everything was suddenly botched by her
misplaced primness. But on the other hand I am happy now that I
was never so vile and inept as to ignore the exquisite contrast between

her irritating prudery and those rare moments of sweet passion when her features acquired an expression of childish concentration, of solemn delight, and her little moans just reached the threshold of my undeserving consciousness.

9

By the end of the summer, and of the next chapter of *The Dare*, it became clear that Dr. Blagovo and his wife were looking forward to a regular Greek-Orthodox wedding – a taper-lit gold-and-gauze ceremony, with high priest and low priest and a double choir. I do not know if Annette was astonished when I said I intended to cut out the mummery and prosaically register our union before a municipal officer in Paris, London, Calais, or on one of the Channel Islands; but she certainly did not mind astonishing her parents. Dr. Blagovo requested an interview in a stiffly worded letter ('Prince! Anna has informed us that you would prefer –'); we settled for a telephone conversation: two minutes of Dr. Blagovo (including pauses caused by his deciphering a hand that must have been the despair of apothecaries) and five of his wife, who after rambling about irrelevant matters entreated me to reconsider my decision. I refused, and was set upon by a go-between, good old Stepanov, who rather unexpectedly, given his liberal views, urged me in a telephone call from somewhere in England (where the Borgs now lived) to keep up a beautiful Christian tradition. I changed the subject and begged him to arrange a beautiful literary *soirée* for me upon his return to Paris.

In the meantime some of the gayer gods came with gifts. Three windfalls scatter-thudded around me in a simultaneous act of celebration: *The Red Topper* was bought for publication in English with a two-hundred-guinea advance; James Lodge of New York offered for *Camera Lucida* an even handsomer sum (one's sense of beauty was easily satisfied in those days); and a contract for the cinema rights to a short story was being prepared by Ivor Black's half-brother in Los Angeles. I had now to find adequate surroundings for completing *The*

Dare in greater comfort than that in which I wrote its first part; and immediately after that, or concurrently with its last chapter, I would have to examine, and, no doubt, revise heavily, the English translation now being made of my *Krasnyy Tsilindr* by an unknown lady in London (who rather inauspiciously had started to suggest, before a roar of rage stopped her, that 'certain passages, not quite proper or too richly or obscurely phrased, would have to be toned down, or omitted altogether, for the benefit of the sober-minded English reader'). I also expected to have to face a business trip to the United States.

For some odd psychological reason, Annette's parents, who kept track of those developments, were now urging her to go through no matter what form of marriage, civil or pagan (*grazhdanskiy ili basurmanskiy*), without delay. Once that little tricolor farce over, Annette and I paid our tribute to Russian tradition by traveling from hotel to hotel during two months, going as far as Venice and Ravenna, where I thought of Byron and translated Musset. Back in Paris, we rented a three-room apartment on the charming rue Guevara (named after an Andalusian playwright of long ago) a two-minute walk from the Bois. We usually lunched at the nearby Le Petit Diable Boiteux, a modest but excellent restaurant, and had cold cuts for dinner in our kitchenette. I had somehow expected Annette to be a versatile cook, and she did improve later, in rugged America. On rue Guevara her best achievement remained the Soft-Boiled Egg: I do not know how she did it, but she managed to prevent the fatal crack that produced an ectoplasmic swell in the dancing water when I took over.

She loved long walks in the park among the sedate beeches and the prospective-looking babes; she loved cafés, fashion shows, tennis matches, circular bike races at the Vélodrome, and especially the cinema. I soon realized that a little recreation put her in a lovemaking mood – and I was frightfully amorous and strong in our four last years in Paris, and quite unable to stand capricious denials. I drew the line, however, at an overdose of athletic sports – a metronomic tennis ball twanging to and fro or the ghastly hairy legs of hunchbacks on wheels.

The second part of the Thirties in Paris happened to be marked by a marvelous surge of the exiled arts, and it would be pretentious and foolish of me not to admit that whatever some of the more dishonest critics wrote about me, I stood at the peak of that period. In the halls where readings took place, in the back rooms of famous cafés, at private literary parties, I enjoyed pointing out to my quiet and stylish companion the various ghouls of the inferno, the crooks and the creeps, the benevolent nonentities, the groupists, the guru nuts, the pious pederasts, the lovely hysterical Lesbians, the gray-locked old realists, the talented, illiterate, intuitive new critics (Adam Atropovich was their unforgettable leader).

I noted with a sort of scholarly pleasure (like that of tracking down parallel readings) how attentive, how eager to honor her were the three or four, always black-suited, grandmasters of Russian letters (people I admired with grateful fervor, not only because their high-principled art had enchanted my prime, but also because the banishment of their books by the Bolshevists represented the greatest indictment, absolute and immortal, of Lenin's and Stalin's regime). No less *empressés* around her (perhaps in subliminal zeal to earn some of the rare praise I deigned to bestow on the pure voice of the impure) were certain younger writers whom their God had created two-faced: despicably corrupt or inane on one side of their being and shining with poignant genius on the other. In a word, her appearance in the *beau monde* of *émigré* literature echoed amusingly Chapter Eight of *Eugene Onegin* with Princess N.'s moving coolly through the fawning ballroom throng.

I might have been displeased by the tolerance she showed Basil-evski (knowing none of his works and only vaguely aware of his preposterous reputation) had it not occurred to me that the theme of her sympathy was repeating, as it were, the friendly phase of my own initial relations with that *faux bonhomme.* From behind a more or less Doric column I overheard him asking my naïve gentle Annette had she any idea why I hated so fiercely Gorki (for whom he cultivated total veneration). Was it because I resented the world fame of a proletarian? Had I really read any of that wonderful writer's books? Annette had looked puzzled but all at once a charming childish smile illumined her whole face and she recalled *The Mother*, a corny Soviet film that I had criticized, she said, 'because the tears rolling down the faces were too big and too slow.'

'Aha! That explains a lot,' proclaimed Basilevski with gloomy satisfaction.

10

I received the typed translations of *The Red Topper* (sic) and *Camera Lucida* virtually at the same time, in the autumn of 1937. They proved to be even more ignoble than I expected. Miss Haworth, an Englishwoman, had spent three happy years in Moscow where her father had been Ambassador; Mr. Kulich was an elderly Russian-born New Yorker who signed his letters Ben. Both made identical mistakes, choosing the wrong term in their identical dictionaries, and with identical recklessness never bothering to check the treacherous homonym of a familiar-looking word. They were blind to contextual shades of color and deaf to nuances of noise. Their classification of natural objects seldom descended from the class to the family; still more seldom to the genus in the strict sense. They confused the specimen with the species; Hop, Leap, and Jump wore in their minds the drab uniform of regimented synonymity; and not one page passed without a boner. What struck me as especially fascinating, in a dreadful diabolical way, was their taking for granted that a respectable author could have written this or that descriptive passage, which their ignorance and carelessness had reduced to the cries and grunts of a cretin. In all their habits of expression Ben Kulich and Miss Haworth were so close that I now think they might have been secretly married to one another and had corresponded regularly when trying to settle a tricky paragraph; or else, maybe, they used to meet midway for lexical picnics on the grassy lip of some crater in the Azores.

It took me several months to revise those atrocities and dictate my revisions to Annette. She derived her English from the four years she had spent at an American boarding school in Constantinople (1920–1924), the Blagovos' first stage of westward expatriation. I was amazed to see how fast her vocabulary grew and improved in the performance of her new functions and was amused by the innocent pride she took in correctly taking down the blasts and sarcasms I directed in letters to Allan & Overton, London, and James Lodge, New York. In fact, her *doigté* in English (and French) was better than in the typing of Russian texts. Minor stumbles were, of course, bound to occur in any language. One day, in referring to the carbon copy of a spate of corrections already posted to my patient Allan, I discovered a trivial slip she had made, a mere typo ('here' instead of 'hero,' or perhaps 'that' instead of 'hat,' I don't even remember – but there was an 'h' somewhere, I think) which, however, gave the sentence a dismally flat, but, alas, not implausible sense (verisimilitude has been the undoing of many a conscientious proofreader). A telegram could eliminate the fault incontinently, but an overworked edgy author finds such events jarring – and I voiced my annoyance with unwarranted vehemence. Annette started looking for a telegram form in the (wrong) drawer and said, without raising her head:

'She would have helped you so much better than I, though I really am doing my best (*strashno starayus'*, trying terribly).'

We never referred to Iris – that was a tacit condition in the code of our marriage – but I instantly understood that Annette meant *her* and not the inept English girl whom an agency had sent me several weeks before and got back with wrappage and string. For some occult reason (overwork again) I felt the tears welling and before I could get up and leave the room, I found myself shamelessly sobbing and hitting a fat anonymous book with my fist. She glided into my arms, also weeping, and that same evening we went to see René Clair's new film, followed by supper at the Grand Velour.

During those months of correcting and partly rewriting *The Red Topper* and the other thing, I began to experience the pangs of a strange transformation. I did not wake up one Central European morning as a great scarab with more legs than any beetle can have, but certain excruciating tearings of secret tissues did take place in me. The Russian typewriter was closed like a coffin. The end of *The Dare* had been delivered to *Patria*. Annette and I planned to go in the spring to England (a plan never executed) and in the summer of 1939 to America (where she was to die fourteen years later). By the middle of 1938 I felt I could sit back and quietly enjoy both the private praise bestowed upon me by Andoverton and Lodge in their letters and the public accusations of aristocratic obscurity which facetious criticules in the Sunday papers directed at the style of such passages in the English versions of my two novels as had been authored by me alone. It was, however, quite a different matter 'to work without net' (as Russian acrobats say), when attempting to compose a novel straight in English, for now there was no Russian safety net spread below, between me and the lighted circlet of the arena.

As was also to happen in regard to my next English books (including the present sketch), the title of my first one came to me at the moment of impregnation, long before actual birth and growth. Holding that name to the light, I distinguished the entire contents of the semitransparent capsule. The title was to be without any choice or change: *See under Real*. A preview of its eventual tribulations in the catalogues of public libraries could not have deterred me.

The idea may have been an oblique effect of the insult dealt by the two bunglers to my careful art. An English novelist, a brilliant and unique performer, was supposed to have recently died. The story of his life was being knocked together by the uninformed, coarse-minded, malevolent Hamlet Godman, an Oxonian Dane, who found in this grotesque task a Kovalevskian 'outlet' for the literary flops that his proper mediocrity fully deserved. The biography was being edited, rather unfortunately for its reckless concocter, by the indignant brother of the dead novelist. As the opening chapter unfolded its first reptilian coil (with insinuations of 'masturbation guilt' and the castration of toy soldiers) there commenced what was to me the delight and the magic of my book: fraternal footnotes, half-a-dozen lines per page, then more, then much more, which started to question, then refute, then demolish by ridicule the would-be biographer's doctored anecdotes and vulgar inventions. A multiplication of such notes at the bottom of the page led to an ominous increase (no doubt disturbing to clubby or convalescent readers) of astronomical symbols bespeckling the text. By the end of the biographee's college years the height of the critical apparatus had reached one third of each page.

Editorial warnings of a national disaster – flooded fields and so on – accompanied a further rise of the water line. By page 200 the footnote material had crowded out three-quarters of the text and the type of the note had changed, psychologically at least (I loathe typographical frolics in books) from brevier to long primer. In the course of the last chapters the commentary not only replaced the entire text but finally swelled to boldface. 'We witness here the admirable phenomenon of a bogus *biographie romancée* being gradually supplanted by the true story of a great man's life.' For good measure I appended a three-page account of the great annotator's academic career: 'He now teaches Modern Literature, including his brother's works, at Paragon University, Oregon.'

This is the description of a novel written almost forty-five years ago and probably forgotten by the general public. I have never reread it because I reread (*je relis, perechityvayu* – I'm teasing an adorable mistress!) only the page proofs of my paperbacks; and for reasons which, I am sure, J. Lodge finds judicious, the thing is still in its hard-cover instar. But in rosy retrospect I feel it as a pleasurable event, and have completely dissociated it in my mind from the terrors and torments that attended the writing of that rather lightweight little satire.

Actually, its composition, despite the pleasure (maybe also noxious) that the iridescent bubbles in my alembics gave me after a night of inspiration, trial, and triumph (look at the harlequins, everybody look – Iris, Annette, Bel, Louise, and you, you, my ultimate and immortal one!), almost led to the dementia paralytica that I feared since youth.

In the world of athletic games there has never been, I think, a World Champion of Lawn Tennis *and* Ski; yet in two Literatures, as dissimilar as grass and snow, I have been the first to achieve that kind of feat. I do not know (being a complete non-athlete, whom the sports pages of a newspaper bore almost as much as does its kitchen section) what physical stress may be involved in serving one day a sequence of thirty-six aces at sea level and on the next soaring from a ski jump 136 meters through bright mountain air. Colossal, no doubt, and, perhaps, inconceivable. But I have managed to transcend the rack and the wrench of literary metamorphosis.

We think in images, not in words; all right; when, however, we compose, recall, or refashion at midnight in our brain something we wish to say in tomorrow's sermon, or have said to Dolly in a recent dream, or wish we had said to that impertinent proctor twenty years ago, the images we think in are, of course, verbal – and even audible if we happen to be lonely and old. We do not usually think in words, since most of life is mimodrama, but we certainly do imagine words when we need them, just as we imagine everything else capable of being perceived in this, or even in a still more unlikely, world. The book in my mind appeared at first, under my right cheek (I sleep on my non-cardial side), as a varicolored procession with a head and a tail, winding in a general western direction through an attentive town. The children among you and all my old selves on their thresholds were being promised a stunning show. I then saw the show in full detail with every scene in its place, every trapeze in the stars. Yet it was not a masque, not a circus, but a bound book, a short novel in a tongue as far removed as Thracian or Pahlavi from the fata-morganic prose that I had willed into being in the desert of exile. An upsurge of nausea overcame me at the thought of imagining a hundred-thousand adequate words and I switched on the light and called to Annette in the adjacent bedroom to give me one of my strictly rationed tablets.

The evolution of my English, like that of birds, had had its ups and downs. A beloved Cockney nurse had looked after me from 1900 (when I was one year old) to 1903. She was followed by a succession of three English governesses (1903–1906, 1907–1909, and November, 1909, to Christmas of the same year) whom I see over the shoulder of time as representing, mythologically, Didactic Prose, Dramatic Poetry, and the Erotic Idyll. My grand-aunt, a dear person with uncommonly liberal views, gave in, however, to domestic considerations, and discharged Cherry Neaple, my last shepherdess. After an interlude of Russian and French pedagogy, two English tutors more or less succeeded each other between 1912 and 1916, rather comically overlapping in the spring of 1914 when they competed for the favors of a young village beauty who had been my girl in the first place. English fairy tales had been replaced around 1910 by the B.O.P., immediately followed by all the Tauchnitz volumes that had accumulated in the family libraries. Throughout adolescence I read, in pairs, and both with the same rich thrill, *Othello* and *Onegin*, Tyutchev and Tennyson, Browning and Blok. During my three Cambridge years (1919–1922) and thereafter, till April 23, 1930, my domestic tongue remained English, while the body of my own Russian works started to grow and was soon to disorb my household gods.

So far so good. But the phrase itself is a glib cliché; and the question confronting me in Paris, in the late Thirties, was precisely could I fight off the formula and rip up the ready-made, and switch from my glorious self-developed Russian, not to the dead leaden English of the high seas with dummies in sailor suits, but an English I alone would be responsible for, in all its new ripples and changing light?

I daresay the description of my literary troubles will be skipped by the common reader; yet for my sake, rather than his, I wish to dwell mercilessly on a situation that was bad enough before I left Europe but almost killed me during the crossing.

Russian and English had existed for years in my mind as two worlds detached from one another. (It is only today that some interspatial contact has been established: 'A knowledge of Russian,' writes George Oakwood in his astute essay on my *Ardis*, 1970, 'will help you to relish much of the wordplay in the most English of the author's English novels; consider for instance this: "The champ and the chimp came all the way from Omsk to Neochomsk." What a delightful link between a real round place and "ni-o-chyom," the About-Nothing land of modern philosophic linguistics!') I was acutely aware of the syntactic gulf separating their sentence structures. I feared (un-reasonably, as was to transpire eventually) that my allegiance to Russian grammar might interfere with an apostatical courtship. Take tenses: how different their elaborate and strict minuet in English from the free and fluid interplay between the present and the past in their Russian counterpart (which Ian Bunyan has so amusingly compared in last Sunday's NYT to 'a dance of the veil performed by a plump graceful lady in a circle of cheering drunks'). The fantastic number of natural-looking nouns that the British and the Americans apply in lovely technical senses to very specific objects also distressed me.

What is the exact term for the little cup in which you place the diamond you want to cut? (We call it 'dop,' the pupal case of a butterfly, replied my informer, an old Boston jeweler who sold me the ring for my third bride). Is there not a nice special word for a pigling? ('I am toying with "snork"; said Professor Noteboke, the best translator of Gogol's immortal *The Carrick*'). I want the right word for the break in a boy's voice at puberty, I said to an amiable opera basso in the adjacent deck chair during my first transatlantic voyage. ('I think,' he said, 'it's called "ponticello," a small bridge, *un petit pont, mostik*. . . . Oh, you're Russian too?')

The traversal of my particular bridge ended, weeks after landing, in a charming New York apartment (it was leant to Annette and me by a generous relative of mine and faced the sunset flaming beyond Central Park). The neuralgia in my right forearm was a gray adumbration compared to the solid black headache that no pill could pierce. Annette rang up James Lodge, and he, out of the misdirected kindness of his heart, had an old little physician of Russian extraction examine me. The poor fellow drove me even crazier than I was by not only insisting on discussing my symptoms in an execrable version of the language I was trying to shed, but on translating into it various irrelevant terms used by the Viennese Quack and his apostles (*simbolizirovanie, mortidnik*). Yet his visit, I must confess, strikes me in retrospect as a most artistic coda.

PART THREE

I

Neither *Slaughter in the Sun* (as the English translation of *Camera Lucida* got retitled while I lay helplessly hospitalized in New York) nor *The Red Topper* sold well. My ambitious, beautiful, strange *See under Real* shone for a breathless instant on the lowest rung of the bestseller list in a West Coast paper, and vanished for good. In those circumstances I could not refuse the lectureship offered me in 1940 by Quirn University on the strength of my European reputation. I was to develop a plump tenure there and expand into a Full Professor by 1950 or 1955: I can't find the exact date in my old notes.

Although I was adequately remunerated for my two weekly lectures on European Masterpieces and one Thursday seminar on Joyce's *Ulysses* (from a yearly 5000 dollars in the beginning to 15,000 in the Fifties) and had furthermore several splendidly paid stories accepted by *The Beau and the Butterfly*, the kindest magazine in the world, I was not really comfortable until my *Kingdom by the Sea* (1962) atoned for a fraction of the loss of my Russian fortune (1917) and bundled away all financial worries till the end of worrisome time. I do not usually preserve cuttings of adverse criticism and envious abuse; but I do treasure the following definition: 'This is the only known case in history when a European pauper ever became his own American uncle [*amerikanskiy dyadyushka, oncle d'Amérique*],' so phrased by my faithful Zoilus, Demian Basilevski; he was one of the very few larger saurians in the *émigré* marshes who followed me in 1939 to the hospitable and altogether admirable U.S.A., where with egg-laying promptness he founded a Russian-language quarterly which he is still directing today, thirty-five years later, in his heroic dotage.

The furnished apartment we finally rented on the upper floor of a handsome house (10 Buffalo St.) was much to my liking because of an exceptionally comfortable study with a great bookcase full of works on American lore including an encyclopedia in twenty volumes. Annette would have preferred one of the *dacha-like* structures which the Administration also showed us; but she gave in when I pointed out to her that what looked snug and quaint in summer was bound to be chilly and weird the rest of the year.

Annette's emotional health caused me anxiety: her graceful neck seemed even longer and thinner. An expression of mild melancholy lent a new, unwelcome, beauty to her Botticellian face: its hollowed outline below the zygoma was accentuated by her increasing habit of sucking in her cheeks when hesitative or pensive. All her cold petals remained closed in our infrequent lovemaking. Her abstraction grew perilous: stray cats at night knew that the same erratic deity that had not shut the kitchen window would leave ajar the door of the fridge; her bath regularly overflowed while she telephoned, knitting her innocent brows (what on earth did she care for *my* pains, *my* welling insanity!), to find out how the first-floor person's migraine or meno-pause was faring; and that vagueness of hers in relation to me was also responsible for her omitting a precaution she was supposed to take, so that by the autumn, which followed our moving into the accursed Langley house, she informed me that the doctor she had just consulted looked the very image of Oksman and that she was two-months pregnant.

An angel is now waiting under my restless heels. Doomful despair would invade my poor Annette when she tried to cope with the intricacies of an American household. Our landlady, who occupied the first floor, resolved her perplexities in a jiffy. Two ravishing wiggly-bottomed Bermudian coeds, wearing their national costume, flannel shorts and open shirts, and practically twins in appearance, who took the celebrated 'Hotel' course at Quirn, came to cook and char for her, and she offered to share with us their services.

'She's a veritable angel,' confided Annette to me in her touchingly phony English.

I recognized in the woman the Assistant Professor of Russian whom I had met in a brick building on the campus when the head of her remarkably dreary department, meek myopic old Noteboke, invited me to attend an Advanced Group Class (*My govorim po-russki. Vy govorite? Pogovorimte togda* – that kind of awful stuff). Happily I had no connection whatever with Russian grammar at Quirn – except that my wife was eventually saved from utter boredom by being engaged to help beginners under Mrs. Langley's direction.

Ninel Ilinishna Langley, a displaced person in more senses than one, had recently left her husband, the 'great' Langley, author of *A Marxist History of America*, the bible (now out of print) of a whole generation of morons. I do not know the reason of their separation (after one year of American Sex, as the woman told Annette, who relayed the information to me in a tone of idiotic condolence); but I did have the occasion of seeing and disliking Professor Langley at an official dinner on the eve of his departure for Oxford. I disliked him for his daring to question my teaching *Ulysses* my way – in a purely textual light, without organic allegories and quasi-Greek myths and that sort of tripe; his 'Marxism,' on the other hand, was a pleasantly comic and very mild affair (too mild, perhaps, for his wife's taste) compared to the general attitude of ignorant admiration which American intellectuals had toward Soviet Russia. I remember the sudden hush, and furtive exchange of incredulous grimaces, when at a party, given for me by the most eminent member of our English department, I described the Bolshevist state as Philistine in repose and bestial in action; internationally vying in rapacious deceit with the praying mantis; doctoring the mediocrity of its literature by first sparing a few talents left over from a previous period and then blotting them out with their own blood. One professor, a left-wing moralist and dedicated muralist (he was experimenting that year with automobile paint), stalked out of the house. He wrote me next day, however, a really magnificent, larger-than-nature letter of apology saying that he could not be really cross with the author of *Esmeralda and Her Parandrus* (1941), which despite its 'motley style and baroque imagery' was a masterpiece 'pinching strings of personal poignancy which he, a committed artist, never knew could vibrate in him.' Reviewers of my books took the same line, chiding me formally for underestimating the 'greatness' of Lenin, yet paying me compliments of a kind that could not fail to touch, in the long run, even me, a scornful and austere author, whose homework in Paris had never received its due. Even the President of Quirn, who timorously sympathized with the fashionable Sovietizers, was really on my side: he told me when he called on us (while Ninel crept up to grow an ear on our landing) that he was proud, etc., and had found my 'last (?) book very interesting' though he could not help regretting that I took every opportunity of criticizing 'our Great Ally' in my classes. I answered, laughing, that this criticism was a child's caress when set alongside the public lecture on 'The Tractor in Soviet Literature' that I planned to deliver at the end of the term. He laughed, too, and asked Annette what it was like to live with a genius (she only shrugged her pretty shoulders). All this was *très américain* and thawed a whole auricle in my icy heart.

But to return to good Ninel.

She had been christened Nonna at birth (1902) and renamed twenty years later Ninel (or Ninella), as petitioned by her father, a Hero of Toil and a toady. She wrote it Ninella in English but her friends called her Ninette or Nelly just as my wife's Christian name Anna (as Nonna liked to observe) turned into Annette and Netty.

Ninella Langley was a stocky, heavily built creature with a ruddy and rosy face (the two tints unevenly distributed), short hair dyed a mother-in-law ginger, brown eyes even madder than mine, very thin lips, a fat Russian nose, and three or four hairs on her chin. Before the young reader heads for Lesbos, I wish to say that as far as I could discover (and I am a peerless spy) there was nothing sexual in her ludicrous and unlimited affection for my wife. I had not yet acquired the white Desert Lynx that Annette did not live to see, so it was Ninella who took her shopping in a dilapidated jalopy while the resourceful lodger, sparing the copies of his own novels, would autograph for the grateful twins old mystery paperbacks and unreadable pamphlets from the Langley collection in the attic whose dormer looked out obligingly on the road to, and from, the Shopping Center. It was Ninella who kept her adored 'Netty' well supplied with white knitting wool. It was Ninella who twice daily invited her for a cup of coffee or tea in her rooms; but the woman made a point of avoiding our flat, at least when we were at home, under the pretext that it still reeked of her husband's tobacco: I rejoined that it was my own pipe – and later, on the same day, Annette told me I really ought not to smoke so much, especially indoors; and she also upheld another absurd complaint coming from downstairs, namely, that I walked back and forth too late and too long, right over Ninella's forehead. Yes – and a third grievance: why didn't I put back the encyclopedia volumes in alphabetic order as her husband had always been careful to do, for (he said) 'a misplaced book is a lost book' – quite an aphorism.

Dear Mrs. Langley was not particularly happy about her job. She owned a lakeside bungalow ('Rustic Roses') thirty miles north of Quirn, not very far from Honeywell College, where she taught summer school and with which she intended to be even more closely associated, if a 'reactionary' atmosphere persisted at Quirn. Actually, her only grudge was against decrepit Mme. de Korchakov, who had accused her, in public, of having a *sdobnyy* ('mellow') Soviet accent and a provincial vocabulary – all of which could not be denied, although Annette maintained I was a heartless bourgeois to say so.

2

The infant Isabel's first four years of life are so firmly separated in my consciousness by a blank of seven years from Bel's girlhood that I seem to have had two different children, one a cheerful red-cheeked little thing, and the other her pale and morose elder sister.

I had laid in a stock of ear plugs; they proved superfluous: no crying came from the nursery to interfere with my work – *Dr. Olga Repnin*, the story of an invented Russian professor in America, which was to be published (after a bothersome spell of serialization entailing endless proofreading) by Lodge in 1946, the year Annette left me, and acclaimed as 'a blend of humor and humanism' by alliteration-prone reviewers, comfortably unaware of what I was to prepare some fifteen years later for their horrified delectation.

I enjoyed watching Annette as she took color snapshots of the baby and me in the garden. I loved perambulating a fascinated Isabel through the groves of larches and beeches along Quirn Cascade River, with every loop of light, every eyespot of shade escorted, or so it seemed, by the baby's gay approbation. I even agreed to spend most of the summer of 1945 at Rustic Roses. There, one day, as I was returning with Mrs. Langley from the nearest liquor store or newspaper stand, something she said, some intonation or gesture, released in me the passing shudder, the awful surmise, that it was not with my wife but with me that the wretched creature had been in love from the very start.

The torturous tenderness I had always felt for Annette gained new poignancy from my feelings for our little child (I 'trembled' over her as Ninella put it in her coarse Russian, complaining it might be bad for the baby, even if one 'subtracted the overacting'). That was the human side of our marriage. The sexual side disintegrated altogether.

For quite a time after her return from the maternity ward, echoes of her pangs in the darkest corridors of my brain and a frightening stained window at every turn – the afterimage of a wounded orifice – pursued me and deprived me of all my vigor. When everything in me healed, and my lust for her pale enchantments rekindled, its volume and violence put an end to the brave but essentially inept efforts she had been making to reestablish some sort of amorous harmony between us without departing one jot from the puritanical norm. She now had the gall – the pitiful girlish gall – to insist I see a psychiatrist (recommended by Mrs. Langley) who would help me to think 'softening' thoughts at moments of excessive engorgement. I said her friend was a monster and she a goose, and we had our worst marital quarrel in years.

The creamy-thighed twins had long since returned with their bicycles to the island of their birth. Plainer young ladies came to help with the housekeeping. By the end of 1945 I had virtually ceased visiting my wife in her cold bedroom.

Sometime in mid-May, 1946, I traveled to New York – a five-hour train trip – to lunch with a publisher who was offering me better terms for a collection of stories (*Exile from Mayda*) than good Lodge. After a pleasant meal, in the sunny haze of that banal day, I walked over to the Public Library, and by a banal miracle of synchronization she came dancing down those very steps, Dolly von Borg, now twenty-four, as I trudged up toward her, a fat famous writer in his powerful forties. Except for a gleam of gray in the abundant fair mane that I had cultivated for my readings in Paris, more than a decade ago, I do not believe I could have changed sufficiently to warrant her saying, as she began doing, that she would never have recognized me had she not been so fond of the picture of meditation on the back of *See under*. I recognized her because I had never lost track of her image, readjusting it once in a while: the last time I had notched the score was when her grandmother, in response to my wife's Christmas greetings, in 1939, sent us from London a postcard-size photo of a bare-shouldered flapper with a fluffy fan and false eyelashes in some high-school play, terribly chi-chi. In the two minutes we had on those steps – she pressing with both hands a book to her breast, I at a lower level, standing with my right foot placed on the next step, her step, and slapping my knee with a glove (many a tenor's only known gesture) – in those two minutes we managed to exchange quite a lot of plain information.

She was now studying the History of the Theater at Columbia University. Parents and grandparents were tucked away in London. I had a child, right? Those shoes I wore were lovely. Students called my lectures fabulous. Was I happy?

I shook my head. When and where could I see her?

She had always had a crush on me, oh yes, ever since I used to mesmerize her in my lap, playing sweet Uncle Gasper, muffing every other line, and now all had come back and she certainly wished to do something about it.

She had a remarkable vocabulary. Summarize her. Mirages of motels in the eye of the penholder. Did she have a car?

Well, that was rather sudden (laughing). She could borrow, perhaps, his old sedan though he might not like the notion (pointing to a nondescript youth who was waiting for her on the sidewalk). He had just bought a heavenly Hummer to go places with her.

Would she mind telling me *when* we could meet, please.

She had read all my novels, at least all the English ones. Her Russian was rusty!

The hell with my novels! When?

I had to let her think. She might visit me at the end of the term. Terry Todd (now measuring the stairs with his eyes, preparing to mount) had briefly been a student of mine; he got a D minus for his first paper and quit Quirn.

I said I consigned all the D people to everlasting oblivion. Her 'end of the term' might bend away into Minus Eternity. I required more precision.

She would let me know. She would call me next week. No, she would not part with her own telephone number. She told me to look at that clown (he was now coming up the steps). Paradise was a Persian word. It was simply Persian to meet again like that. She might drop in at my office for a few moments, just to chat about old times. She knew how busy –

'Oh, Terry: this is *the* writer, the man who wrote *Emerald and the Pander.*'

I do not recall what I had planned to look up in the library. Whatever it was, it was not that unknown book. Aimlessly I walked up and down several halls; abjectly visited the W.C.; but simply could not, short of castrating myself, get rid of her new image in its own portable sunlight – the straight pale hair, the freckles, the banal pout, the Lilithan long eyes – though I knew she was only what one used to call a 'little tramp' and, perhaps, *because* she was just that.

I gave my penultimate 'Masterpieces' lecture of the spring term. I gave my ultimate one. An assistant distributed the blue books for the final examination in that course (which I had curtailed for reasons of health) and collected them while three or four hopeless hopefuls still kept scribbling madly in separate spots of the hall. I held my last Joyce seminar of the year. Little Baroness Borg had forgotten the end of the dream.

In the last days of the spring term a particularly stupid baby-sitter told me that some girl whose name she had not quite caught – Tallbird or Dalberg – had phoned that she was on her way to Quirn. It so happened that a Lily Talbot in my Masterpieces class had missed the examination. On the following day I walked over to my office for the ordeal of reading the damned heap on my desk. Quirn University Official Examination Book. All academic work is conducted on the assumption of general horror. Write on the consecutive right- and left-hand pages. What does 'consecutive' really mean, Sir? Do you want us to describe *all* the birds in the story or only one? As a rule, one-tenth of the three hundred minds preferred the spelling 'Stern' to 'Sterne' and 'Austin' to 'Austen.'

The telephone on my spacious desk (it 'slept two' as my ribald neighbor Professor King, an authority on Dante, used to say) rang, and this Lily Talbot started to explain, volubly, unconvincingly, in a kind of lovely, veiled, and confidential voice, why she had not taken the examination. I could not remember her face or her figure, but the subdued melody tickling my ear contained such intimations of young charm and surrender that I could not help chiding myself for overlooking her in my class. She was about to come to the point when an eager childish rap at the door diverted my attention. Dolly walked in, smiling. Smiling, she indicated with a tilt of her chin that the receiver should be cradled. Smiling, she swept the examination books off the desk and perched upon it with her bare shins in my face. What might have promised the most refined ardors turned out to be the tritest scene in this memoir. I hastened to quench a thirst that had been burning a hole in the mixed metaphor of my life ever since I had fondled a quite different Dolly thirteen years earlier. The ultimate convulsion rocked the desk lamp, and from the class just across the corridor came a burst of applause at the end of Professor King's last lecture of the season.

When I came home, I found my wife alone on the porch swinging gently if not quite straight in her favorite glider and reading the *Krasnaya Niva* ('Red Corn'), a Bolshevist magazine. Her purveyor of *literatura* was away giving some future mistranslators a final examination. Isabel had been out of doors and was now taking a nap in her room just above the porch.

In the days when the *bermudki* (as Ninella indecently called them) used to minister to my humble needs, I experienced no guilt after the operation and confronted my wife with my usual, fondly ironical smile; but on *this* occasion I felt my flesh coated with stinging slime, and my heart missed a thump, when she said, glancing up and stopping the line with her finger: 'Did that girl get in touch with you at your office?'

I answered as a fictional character might 'in the affirmative': 'Her people,' I added, 'wrote you, it appears, about her coming to study in New York, but you never showed me that letter. *Tant mieux*, she's a frightful bore.'

Annette looked utterly confused: 'I'm speaking,' she said, 'or trying to speak, about a student called Lily Talbot who telephoned an hour ago to explain why she missed the exam. Who is *your* girl?'

We proceeded to disentangle the two. After some moral hesitation ('You know, we both owe a lot to her grandparents') Annette conceded we really need not entertain little strays. She seemed to recall the letter because it contained a reference to her widowed mother (now moved to a comfortable home for the old into which I had recently turned my villa at Carnavaux – despite my lawyer's well-meaning objections). Yes, yes, she had mislaid it – and would find it some day in some library book that had never been returned to an unattainable library. A strange appeasement was now flowing through my poor veins. The romance of her absentmindedness always made me laugh heartily. I laughed heartily. I kissed her on her infinitely tender-skinned temple.

'How does Dolly Borg look now?' asked Annette. 'She used to be a very homely and very brash little brat. Quite repulsive, in fact.'

'That's what she still is,' I practically shouted, and we heard little Isabel crow: *'Ya prosnulas',',* through the yawn of the window: 'I am awake.' How lightly the spring cloudlets scudded! How glibly that red-breasted thrush on the lawn pulled out its unbroken worm! Ah – and there was Ninella, home at last, getting out of her car, with the string-bound corpses of *cahiers* under her sturdy arm. 'Gosh,' said I to myself, in my ignoble euphoria, 'there's something quite nice and cozy about old Ninel after all!' Yet only a few hours later the light of Hell had gone out, and I writhed, I wrung my four limbs, yes, in an agony of insomnia, trying to find some combination between pillow and back, sheet and shoulder, linen and leg, to help me, help me, oh, help me to reach the Eden of a rainy dawn.

3

The increasing disarray of my nerves was such that the bother of getting a driver's license could not be contemplated: hence I had to rely on Dolly's use of Todd's dirty old sedan in order to seek the conventional darkness of country lanes that were difficult to find and disappointing when found. We had three such rendezvous, near New Swivington or thereabouts, in the complicated vicinity of Casanovia of all places, and despite my muddled condition I could not help noticing that Dolly welcomed the restless wanderings, the wrong turns, the torrents of rain which attended our sordid little affair. 'Just think,' she said one especially boggy June night in unknown surroundings, 'how much simpler things would be if somebody explained the situation to your wife, just think!'

On realizing she had gone too far with that proposed thought, Dolly changed tactics and rang me up at my office to tell me with a great show of jubilant excitement that Bridget Dolan, a medical student and a cousin of Todd's, was offering us for a small remuneration her flat in New York on Monday and Thursday afternoons when she worked as a nurse at the Holy Something Hospital. Inertia rather than Eros caused me to give it a try; I kept up the pretext of having to complete the literary research I was supposed to be conducting in the Public Library, and traveled in a crowded Pullman from one nightmare to another.

She met me in front of the house, strutting in triumph, brandishing a little key that caught a glint of sun in the hothouse mizzle. I was so very weak from the journey that I had trouble getting out of the taxi, and she helped me to the front door, chattering the while like a bright child. Fortunately the mysterious flat was on the ground floor – I could not have faced a lift's closure and spasm. A surly janitrix (reminding me in mnemonic reverse of the Cerberean bitches in the hotels of Soviet Siberia which I was to stop at a couple of decades later) insisted on my writing down my name and address in a ledger ('That's the rule,' sang out Dolly, who had already picked up some intones of local delivery). I had the presence of mind to put down the dumbest address I could produce at the moment, Dumbert Dumbert, Dumberton. Dolly, humming, added unhurriedly my raincoat to those hanging in a communal hallway. If she had ever experienced the pangs of neuralgic delirium, she would not have fumbled with that key when she knew quite well that the door of what should have been an exquisitely private apartment was not even properly closed. We entered a preposterous, evidently ultra-modern living room with painted hard furniture and one lone little white rocker supporting a plush biped rat instead of a sulky child. Doors were still with me, were always with me. The one on the left, being slightly ajar, let in voices from an adjacent suite or asylum. 'There's a party going on there!' I expostulated, and Dolly deftly and softly drew that door almost shut. 'They're a nice friendly group,' she said, 'and it's really too warm in these rooms to choke every chink. Second on the right. Here we are.'

Here we were. Nurse Dolan for the sake of atmosphere and professional empathy had rigged up her bedroom in hospital style: a snow-pure cot with a system of levers that would have rendered even Big Peter (in the *Red Topper*) impotent; whitewashed commodes and glazed cabinets; a bedhead chart dear to humorists; and a set of rules tacked to the bathroom door.

'Now off with that jacket,' cried Dolly gaily, 'while I unlace those lovely shoes' (crouching nimbly, and nimbly recrouching, at my retreating feet).

I said: 'You have lost your mind, my dear, if you think I could contemplate making love in this appalling place.'

'What do you want then'? she asked, angrily brushing away a strand of hair from her flushed face and uncoiling back to her natural length: 'Where would you find another such dandy, hygienic, utterly –'

A visitor interrupted her: a brown, gray-cheeked old dackel

carrying horizontally a rubber bone in its mouth. It entered from the parlor, placed the obscene red thing on the linoleum, and stood looking at me, at Dolly, at me again, with melancholy expectation on its raised dogface. A pretty bare-armed girl in black slipped in, grabbed the animal, kicked its toy back into the parlor, and said: 'Hullo, Dolly! If you and your friend want some drinks afterwards, please join us. Bridget phoned she'd be home early. It's J.B.'s birthday.'

'Righto, Carmen,' replied Dolly, and turning to me continued in Russian: 'I think you need that drink right away. Oh, come along! And for God's sake leave that jacket and waistcoat here. You are drenched with sweat.'

She forced me out of the room; I went rumbling and groaning; she gave a perfunctory pat to the creaseless cot and followed the man of snow, the man of tallow, the dying lopsided man.

Most of the party had now invaded the parlor from the next room. I cringed and tried to hide my face as I recognized Terry Todd. He raised his glass in delicate congratulation. What that slut had done to ensure a thwarted beau's complicity, I shall never know; but I should never have put her in my *Krasnyy Tsilindr*; that's the way you breed live monsters – from little ballerinas in books. Another person I had once seen already – in a car that kept passing us somewhere in the country – a young actor with handsome Irish features, pressed upon me what he called a Honolulu Cooler, but at the eoan stage of an attack I am beyond alcohol, so could only taste the pineapple part of the mixture. Amidst a circle of sycophants a bull-size old fellow in a short-sleeved shirt monogrammed 'J.B.' posed, one hairy arm around Dolly, for a naughty shot that his wife snapped. Carmen removed my sticky glass on her neat little tray with a pillbox and a thermometer in the corner. Not finding a seat, I had to lean against the wall, and the back of my head caused a cheap abstract in a plastic frame to start swinging above me: it was stopped by Todd who had sidled up to me and now said, lowering his voice: 'Everything is settled, Prof, to everybody's satisfaction. I've kept in touch with Mrs. Langley, sure I have, she and the missus are writing you. I believe they've already left, the kid thinks you're in Heaven – now, now, what's the matter?'

I am not a fighter. I only hurt my hand against a tall lamp and lost both shoes in the scuffle. Terry Todd vanished – forever. The telephone was being used in one room and ringing in the other. Dolly, retransformed by the alchemy of her blazing anger – and now untellable from the little girl who had hurled a three-letter French word at me when I told her I found it wiser to stop taking advantage of her grandfather's hospitality – virtually tore my necktie in two, yelling she could easily get me jailed for rape but preferred to see me crawling back to my consort and harem of baby-sitters (her new vocabulary, though, remained richly theatrical, even when she shrieked).

I felt trapped like a silver pea teased into the center of a toy maze. A threatening crowd, held back by J.B., the head doctor, separated me from the exit; so I retreated to Bridget's private wardette and saw, with a sense of relief (also 'eoan' alas) that beyond a previously unnoticed, half-opened French window there extended to a fabulous distance an inner court, or only one comforting part of an inner court, with lightly robed patients circulating in a geometry of lawns and garden walks, or quietly sitting on benches. I staggered out, and as my white-socked feet touched the cool turf I noticed that the vagabond wench had undone the ankle strings of the long linen underpants I was wearing. Somehow, somewhere, I had shed and lost all the rest of my clothes. As I stood there, my head brimming with a blackness of pain seldom known before, I became aware of a flurry of motion beyond the court. Far, far away, nurse Dolan or Nolan (at that distance such nice distinctions no longer mattered) emerged from a wing of the hospital and came running to my assistance. Two males followed her with a stretcher. A helpful patient gathered up the blanket they had dropped.

'You know, you know . . . you should have never done that,' she cried panting. 'Don't move, they'll help you to get up (I had collapsed on the turf). If you'd escaped after surgery you might have died right where you are. On such a lovely day, too!'

And so I was carried by two sturdy palanquiners who stank all the way (the hind bearer solidly, the front man in rhythmic wafts) not to Bridget's bed but to a real hospital cot in a ward for three between two old men, both dying of cerebritis.

4

The step I have taken, Vadim, is not subject to discussion (ne podlezhit obsuzhdeniyu). *You must accept my departure as a* fait accompli.[1] *Had I really loved you I would not have left you; but I never loved you really, and maybe your escapade – which no doubt is not your first since our arrival in this sinister* (zloveshchuyu) *'free' country[2] – is for me a mere pretext for leaving you.*

We have never been very happy together, you and I, during our twelve[3] years of marriage. You regarded me from the start as a cute, dutiful, but definitely disappointing little circus animal[4] which you tried to teach immoral disgusting tricks – condemned as such *according to the faithful companion without whom I might not have survived in ghastly 'Kvirn'[5] by the latest scientific stars of our fatherland. I, on the other hand, was so painfully nonplussed by your* trenne (sic)[6] de vie, *your habits, your black-locked[7] friends, your decadent novels, and – why not admit it? – your pathological revolt against Art and Progress in the Soviet Land, including the restoration of lovely old churches,[8] that I would have divorced you, had I dared upset[9] poor papa and mama who were so eager in their dignity and naïveté to have their daughter addressed – by whom, good Lord? – as 'Your Serenity'* (Siyatel'stvo).

Now comes a serious demand, an absolute injunction. Never, never – at least while I am still alive – never, I repeat, shall you try to communicate with the child. I do not know – Nelly is better versed in this – what the legal situation is, but I know that in certain respects you are a gentleman and it is to the gentleman that I say and shout: Please, please, keep away! If some dreadful American illness strikes me, then remember I wish her to be brought up as a Russian Christian.[10]

I was sorry to learn about your hospitalization. This is your second, and I hope last, attack of neurasthenia[11] since the time we made the mistake of leaving

Europe instead of waiting quietly for the Soviet Army to liberate it from the fascists. Good-bye.

P.S. Nelly wishes to add a few lines.

Thank you, Netty. I shall indeed be brief. The information imparted to us by your girlfriend's fiancé and his mother,[12] a saintly woman of infinite compassion and common sense, lacked, fortunately, the element of dreadful surprise. A roommate of Berenice Mudie (the one that stole the cut-crystal decanter Netty gave me) had already been spreading certain odd rumors a couple of years ago; I tried to protect your sweet wife by not allowing that gossip to reach her or at least by drawing her attention to it in a very oblique, half-humorous way long after those prostitutes had gone. But now let us talk turkey.[13]

There can be no problem, I am sure, in separating your things from hers. She says: 'Let him take the countless copies of his novels and all the tattered dictionaries'; but she must be allowed to keep her household treasures such as my little birthday gifts to her – the silver-plated caviar bowl as well as the six pale-green handblown wine glasses, etc.

I can especially sympathize with Netty in this domestic catastrophe because my own marriage resembled hers in many, many ways. It began so auspiciously! I was stranded and lost in a territory suddenly occupied by Estonian fascists, a poor little war-tossed Moscow girl,[14] when I first met Professor Langley in quite romantic circumstances: I was interpreting for him (the study of foreign languages stands at a remarkable level in the Soviet Land); but when I was shipped with other DP's to the U.S. and we met again and married, all went wrong – he ignored me in the daytime, and our nights were full of incompatibility.[15] One good consequence is that I inherited, so to speak, a lawyer, Mr. Horace Peppermill, who has consented to grant you a consultation and help you to settle all business details. It will be wise on your part to follow Professor Langley's example and give your wife a monthly allowance while placing a sizable 'guarantee sum' in the bank which can be available to her in extreme cases and, naturally, after your demise or during an overprotracted terminal illness. We do not have to remind you that Mrs. Blagovo should continue to receive regularly her usual check until further notice.

The Quirn house will be offered for sale immediately – it is overflowing with odious memories. Consequently, as soon as they let you out, which I hope will happen without retardment (bez zamedleniya, sans tarder), move out of the house, please.[16] I am not on speaking terms with Miss Myrna Soloway – or, in reality, simply

Soloveychik – of my department, but I understand she is very good at ferreting out places for rent.

We have fine weather here after all that rain. The lake is beautiful at this time of the year! We are going to refurnish our dear little dacha. Its only drawback in one sense (an asset in all others!) is that it stands a wee bit apart from civilization or at least from Honeywell College. The police are always on the lookout for bathers in the nude, prowlers, etc. We are seriously thinking of acquiring a big Alsatian![17]

COMMENTARY

1. *En français dans le texte.*

2. The first two or three lines are no doubt authentic, but then come various details which convince me that not Netty but Nelly masterminded the entire communication. Only a Soviet woman would speak like that of America.

3. At first typed 'fourteen' but expertly erased and replaced by the correct 'twelve,' as seen clearly in the carbon copy that I found pinned, 'just in case,' to the blotter in my study. Netty would have been totally incapable of producing such a clean typescript – especially with the New Orthography machine used by her friend.

4. The term in the text is *durovskiy zveryok*, meaning a small animal trained by the famous Russian clown Durov, a reference less familiar to my wife than to a person of the older generation to which her friend belonged.

5. Contemptuous transliteration of 'Quirn.'

6. Symptomatic misspelling of *train*. Annette's French was excellent. Ninette's French (as well as her English) was a joke.

7. My wife coming as she did from an obscurant Russian milieu was no paragon of racial tolerance; but she would never have used the vulgar anti-Semitic phraseology typical of her friend's character and upbringing.

8. The interpolation of those 'lovely old churches' is a stock platitude of Soviet patriotism.

9. Actually my wife rather liked to upset her people on every possible occasion.

10. I might have done something about it had I known for sure *whose* wish it was. To spite her parents – a strange but constant policy on her part – Annette never went to church, not even at Easter. As to Mrs. Langley, devotional decorum was the motto; the woman made the sign of the cross every time American Jupiter split the black clouds.

11. 'Neurasthenia' indeed!

12. A totally new character – this mother. Myth? Impersonation act? I turned to Bridget for some explanation; she said there was no such person around (the real Mrs. Todd died long ago) and advised me 'to drop the subject' with the irritating curtness of one dismissing a topic as the product of another's delirium. I am ready to agree that my recollection of the scene at her apartment is tainted by the state I was in, but that 'saintly mother' must remain an enigma.

13. *En Anglais dans le texte.*

14. The little Muscovite must have been around forty at the time.

15. *En Anglais dans le texte.*

16. This I did not dream of doing before my lease expired, which it did on August 1, 1946.

17. Let us refrain from a final comment.

Good-bye, Netty and Nelly. Good-bye, Annette and Ninette. Good-bye, Nonna Anna.

PART FOUR

I

Learning to drive that 'Caracal' (as I fondly called my new white coupé) had its comic as well as dramatic side, but after two flunks and a few little repairs, I found myself legally and physically fit at last to spin off West on a protracted tour. There was, true, a moment of acute distress, as the first distant mountains disowned suddenly any likeness to lilac clouds, when I recalled the trips Iris and I used to make to the Riviera in our old Icarus. If she did occasionally allow me to take the wheel, it was only in a spirit of fun, for she was such a sportive girl. With what sobs I now remembered the time when I managed to hit the postman's bicycle which had been left leaning against a pink wall at the entrance of Carnavaux, and how my Iris doubled up in beautiful mirth as the thing slithered off in front of us!

I spent what remained of the summer exploring the incredibly lyrical Rocky Mountain states, getting drunk on whiffs of Oriental Russia in the sagebrush zone and on the North Russian fragrances so faithfully reproduced above timberline by certain small bogs along trickles of sky between the snowbank and the orchid. And yet – was that all? What form of mysterious pursuit caused me to get my feet wet like a child, to pant up a talus, to stare every dandelion in the face, to start at every colored mote passing just beyond my field of vision? What was the dream sensation of having come empty-handed – without what? A gun? A wand? This I dared not probe lest I wound the raw fell under my thin identity.

Skipping the academic year, in a kind of premature 'sabbatical leave' that left the Trustees of Quirn University speechless, I wintered in Arizona where I tried to write *The Invisible Lath*, a book rather similar to that in the reader's hands. No doubt I was not ready for it and perhaps toiled too much over inexpressible shades of emotion; anyway I smothered it under too many layers of sense as a Russian peasant woman, in her stuffy log house, might overlay (*zaspat'*) her baby in heavy oblivion after making hay or being thrashed by her drunken husband.

I pushed on to Los Angeles – and was sorry to learn that the cinema company I had counted upon was about to fold after Ivor Black's death. On my way back, in early spring, I rediscovered the dear phantasmata of my childhood in the tender green of aspen groves at high altitudes here and there, on conifer-clothed ridges. For almost six months I roamed again from motel to motel, several times having my car scratched and cracked by cretinous rival drivers and finally trading it in for a sedate Bellargus sedan of a celestial blue that Bel was to compare with that of a Morpho.

Another odd thing: with prophetic care I took down in my diary all my stops, all my motels (*Mes Moteaux* as Verlaine might have said!), the Lakeviews, the Valley Views, the Mountain Views, the Plumed Serpent Court in New Mexico, the Lolita Lodge in Texas, Lone Poplars, that if recruited might have patrolled a whole river, and enough sunsets to keep all the bats of the world – and one dying genius – happy. LATH, LATH, Look At The Harlequins! Look at that strange fever rash of viatic tabulation in which I persevered as if I knew that those motor courts prefigured the stages of my future travels with my darling daughter.

In late August, 1947, suntanned, and more edgy than ever, I returned to Quirn and transferred my belongings from storage to the new dwelling (1 Larchdell Road) found for me by efficient and cute Miss Soloway. This was a charming two-storied gray-stone house, with a picture window and a white grand in the long drawing-room, three virginal bedrooms upstairs and a library in the basement. It had belonged to the late Alden Landover, the greatest American belle-lettrist of the half-century. With the help of the beaming Trustees – and rather taking advantage of their joy at welcoming me back to Quirn – I resolved to buy that house. I loved its scholarly odor, a treat seldom granted to my exquisitely sensitive Brunn's membrane, and I also loved its picturesque isolation amidst a tremendous unkempt garden above a larched and golden-rodded steep slope.

To keep Quirn grateful, I also decided to reorganize completely my contribution to its fame. I scrapped my Joyce seminar which in 1945 had attracted (if that is the word) only six students – five grim graduates and one not quite normal sophomore. In compensation I added a third lecture in Masterpieces (now including *Ulysses*) to my weekly quota. The chief innovation, however, lay in my bold presentation of knowledge. During my first years at Quirn I had accumulated two thousand pages of literary comments typed out by my assistant (I notice I have not introduced him yet: Waldemar Exkul, a brilliant young Balt, incomparably more learned than I; *dixi*, Ex!). These I had the Photostat people multiply to accommodate at least three hundred students. At the end of every week each received a batch of the forty pages that I had recited to them, with certain addenda, in the lecture hall. The 'certain addenda' were a concession to the Trustees who reasonably remarked that without this catch nobody would need to attend my classes. The three hundred copies of the two thousand typed pages were to be signed by the readers and returned to me before the final examination. There were flaws at first in the system (for example, only 153 incomplete sets, many unsigned, were returned in 1948) but on the whole it worked, or should have worked.

Another decision I took was to make myself more available to faculty members than I had been before. The red needle of my dial scale now quiver-stopped at a very conservative figure, when, stark naked, arms hanging like those of a clumsy troglodyte, I stood on the fatal platform and with the help of my new housemaid, an enchanting black girl with an Egyptian profile, managed to make out what lay midway in the blur between my reading glasses and my long-distance ones: a great triumph, which I marked by acquiring several new 'costumes,' as my Dr. Olga Repnin says in the novel of that name – 'I don't know (all "o's" as in "don" and "anon") why your horseband wears such not modern costumes.' I visited quite frequently the Pub, a college tavern, where I tried to mix with white-shoed young males, but somehow ended up by getting involved with professional barmaids. And I entered in my pocket diary the addresses of some twenty fellow professors.

Most treasured among my new friends was a frail-looking, sad-looking, somewhat monkey-faced man with a shock of black hair, gray-streaked at fifty-five, the enchantingly talented poet Audace whose paternal ancestor was the eloquent and ill-fated Girondist of that name (*'Bourreau, fais ton devoir envers la Liberté!'*) but who did not know a word of French and spoke American with a flat Midwestern accent. Another interesting glimpse of descent was provided by Louise Adamson, the young wife of our Chairman of English: her grandmother, Sybil Lanier, had won the Women's National Golf Championship in 1896 at Philadelphia!

Gerard Adamson's literary reputation was immensely superior to that of the immensely more important, bitter, and modest Audace. Gerry was a big flabby hulk of a man who must have been nearing sixty when after a life of aesthetic asceticism he surprised his special coterie by marrying that porcelain-pretty and very fast girl. His famous essays – on Donne, on Villon, on Eliot – his philosophic poetry, his recent *Laic Litanies* and so forth meant nothing to me, but he was an appealing old drunk, whose humor and erudition could break the resistance of the most unsociable outsider. I caught myself enjoying the frequent parties at which good old Noteboke and his sister Phoneme, the delightful Kings, the Adamsons, my favorite poet, and a dozen other people did all they could to entertain and comfort me.

Louise, who had an inquisitive aunt at Honeywell, kept me informed, at tactful intervals, of Bel's well-being. One spring day in 1949 or 1950 I happened to stop at the Plaza Liquor Store in Rosedale after a business meeting with Horace Peppermill and was about to back out of the parking lot when I saw Annette bending over a baby carriage in front of a grocery store at the other end of the shopping area. Something about her inclined neck, her melancholy concentration, the ghost of a smile directed at the child in the stroller, sent such a pang of pity through my nervous system that I could not resist accosting her. She turned toward me and even before I uttered some wild words – of regret, of despair, of tenderness – there she was shaking her head, forbidding me to come near. *'Nikogda,'* she murmured, 'never,' and I could not bear to decipher the expression on her pale drawn face. A woman came out of the shop and thanked her for tending the little stranger – a pale and thin infant, looking almost as ill as Annette. I hurried back to the parking lot, scolding myself for not realizing at once that Bel must be a girl of seven or eight by this time. Her mother's moist starry stare kept pursuing me for several nights; I even felt too ill to attend an Easter party at one of the friendly Quirn houses.

During this or some other period of despondency, I heard one day the hall bell tinkle, and my Negro maid, little Nefertitty as I had dubbed her, hasten to open the front door. Slipping out of bed I pressed my bare flesh to the cool window ledge but was not in time to glimpse the entrant or entrants, no matter how far I leant out into a noisy spring downpour. A freshness of flowers, clusters and clouds of flowers, reminded me of some other time, some other casement. I made out part of the Adamsons' glossy black car beyond the garden gate. Both? She alone? *Solus rex?* Both, alas – to judge by the voices reaching me from the hallway through my transparent house. Old Gerry, who disliked unnecessary stairs and had a morbid fear of contagion, remained in the living room. Now his wife's steps and voice were coming up. We had kissed for the first time a few days before, in the Notebokes' kitchen – rummaging for ice, finding fire. I had good reason to hope that the intermission before the obligatory scene would be brief.

She entered, set down two bottles of port for the invalid, and pulled off her wet sweater over her tumbled chestnut-brown, violet-brown curls and naked clavicles. Artistically, strictly artistically, I daresay she was the best-looking of my three major loves. She had upward-directed thin eyebrows, sapphire eyes registering (and that's the right word) constant amazement at earth's paradise (the only one she would ever know, I'm afraid), pink-flushed cheekbones, a rosebud mouth, and a lovely concave abdomen. In less time than it took her husband, a quick reader, to skim down two columns of print, we had 'attired' him. I put on blue slacks and a pink shirt and followed her downstairs.

Her husband sat in a deep armchair, reading a London weekly

bought at the Shopping Center. He had not bothered to take off his horrible black raincoat – a voluminous robe of oilskin that conjured up the image of a stagecoach driver in a lashing storm. He now removed however his formidable spectacles. He cleared his throat with a characteristic rumble. His purple jowls wobbled as he tackled the ordeal of rational speech:

GERRY *Do you ever see this paper, Vadim* (accenting 'Vadim' incorrectly on the first syllable)? *Mister* (naming a particularly lively criticule) *has demolished your Olga* (my novel about the *professorsha*; it had come out only now in the British edition).

VADIM *May I give you a drink? We'll toast him and roast him.*

GERRY *Yet he's right, you know. It is your worst book.* Chute complète, *says the man. Knows French, too.*

LOUISE *No drinks. We've got to rush home. Now heave out of that chair. Try again. Take your glasses and paper. There. Au revoir, Vadim.* I'll bring you those pills *tomorrow morning after I drive* him *to school.*

How different it all was, I mused, from the refined adulteries in the castles of my early youth! Where was the romantic thrill of a glance exchanged with one's new mistress in the presence of a morose colossus – the Jealous Husband? Why did the recollection of the recent embrace not blend any longer as it used to do with the certainty of the next one, forming a sudden rose in an empty flute of crystal, a sudden rainbow on the white wallpaper? What did Emma see a fashionable woman drop into that man's silk hat? Write legibly.

2

The mad scholar in *Esmeralda and Her Parandrus* wreathes Botticelli and Shakespeare together by having Primavera end as Ophelia with all her flowers. The loquacious lady in *Dr. Olga Repnin* remarks that tornadoes and floods are really sensational only in North America. On May 17, 1953, several papers printed a photograph of a family, complete with birdcage, phonograph, and other valuable possessions, riding it out on the roof of their shack in the middle of Rosedale Lake. Other papers carried the picture of a small Ford caught in the upper branches of an intrepid tree with a man, a Mr. Byrd, whom Horace Peppermill said he knew, still in the driver's seat, stunned, bruised, but alive. A prominent personality in the Weather Bureau was accused of criminally delayed forecasts. A group of fifteen schoolchildren who had been taken to see a collection of stuffed animals donated by Mrs. Rosenthal, the benefactor's widow, to the Rosedale Museum, were safe in the sudden darkness of that sturdy building when the twister struck. But the prettiest lakeside cottage got swept away, and the drowned bodies of its two occupants were never retrieved.

Mr. Peppermill, whose natural faculties were no match for his legal acumen, warned me that if I desired to relinquish the child to her grandmother in France, certain formalities would have to be complied with. I observed quietly that Mrs. Blagovo was a half-witted cripple and that my daughter, whom her schoolteacher harbored, should be brought by that person to my house AT ONCE. He said he would fetch her himself early next week.

After weighing and reweighing every paragraph of the house, every parenthesis of its furniture, I decided to lodge her in the former bedroom of the late Landover's companion whom he called his nurse or his fiancée depending on his mood of the moment. This was a lovely chamber, east of mine, with lilac butterflies enlivening its wallpaper and a large, low, flouncy bed. I peopled its white bookshelf with Keats, Yeats, Coleridge, Blake, and four Russian poets (in the New Orthography). Although I told myself with a sigh that she would, no doubt, prefer 'comics' to my dear bespangled mimes and their wands of painted lath, I felt compelled in my choice by what is termed the 'ornamental instinct' among ornithologists. Moreover, knowing well how essential a pure strong light is to reading in bed, I asked Mrs. O'Leary, my new charwoman and cook (borrowed from Louise Adamson who had left with her husband for a long sojourn in England) to screw a couple of hundred-watt bulbs into a tall bedside lamp. Two dictionaries, a writing pad, a little alarm clock, and a Junior Manicure Set (suggested by Mrs. Noteboke, who had a twelve-year-old daughter) were attractively placed on a spacious and stable bedtable. All this was but a rough, naturally. The fair copy would come in due time.

Landover's nurse or fiancée could rush to his assistance either along a short passage or through the bathroom between the two bedrooms: Landover had been a large man and his long deep tub was a soaker's delight. Another, narrower bathroom followed Bel's bedroom easterly – and here I really missed my dainty Louise when racking my brain for the correct epithet between well-scrubbed and perfumed. Mrs. Noteboke could not help me: her daughter, who used the messy parental facilities, had no time for silly deodorants and loathed 'foam.' Wise old Mrs. O'Leary, on the other hand, held before her mind's eye Mrs. Adamson's creams and crystals in a Flemish artist's detail and made me long for her employer's speedy return by conjuring up that picture, which she then proceeded to simplify, but not vulgarize, while retaining such major items as the huge sponge, the jumbo cake of lavender soap, and a delicious toothpaste.

Walking still farther sunriseward, we reach the corner guest room (above the round dining room at the east end of the first floor); this I transformed with the help of a handyman, Mrs. O'Leary's cousin, into an efficiently furnished studio. It contained, when I finished with it, a couch with boxy pillows, an oak desk with a revolving chair, a steel cabinet, a bookcase, *Klingsor's Illustrated Encyclopedia* in twenty volumes, crayons, writing tablets, state maps, and (to cite the *School Buyer's Guide* for 1952–1953) 'a globe ball that lifts out of a cradle so that every child can hold the world in his or her lap.'

Was that all? No. I found for the bedroom a framed photograph of her mother, Paris, 1934, and for the studio a reproduction in color of Levitan's *Clouds above a Blue River* (the Volga, not far from my Marevo), painted around 1890.

Peppermill was to bring her on May 21, around four P.M. I had to fill somehow the abyss of the afternoon. Angelic Ex had already read and marked the entire batch of exams, but he thought I might want to see some of the works he had reluctantly failed. He had dropped in some time on the eve and had left them downstairs on the round table in the round room next to the hallway at the west end of the house. My poor hands ached and trembled so dreadfully that I could hardly leaf through those poor *cahiers*. The round window gave on the driveway. It was a warm gray day. Sir! I need a passing mark desperately. *Ulysses* was written in Zurich and Greece and therefore consists of too many foreign words. One of the characters in Tolstoy's *Death of Ivan* is the notorious actress Sarah Bernard. Stern's style is very sentimental and illiterative. A car door banged. Mr. Peppermill came with a duffel bag in the wake of a tall fair-haired girl in blue jeans carrying, and slowing down, to change from hand to hand, an unwieldy valise.

Annette's moody mouth and eyes. Graceful but plain.

Fortified by a serenacin tablet, I received my daughter and lawyer with the neutral dignity for which effusive Russians in Paris used to detest me so heartily. Peppermill accepted a drop of brandy. Bel had a glass of peach juice and a brown biscuit. I indicated to Bel – who was displaying her palms in a polite Russian allusion – the dining-room toilet, an old-fashioned touch on the architect's part. Horace Peppermill handed me a letter from Bel's teacher Miss Emily Ward. Fabulous Intelligence Quotient of 180. Menses already established. Strange, marvelous child. One does not quite know whether to curb or encourage such precocious brilliance. I accompanied Horace halfway back to his car, fighting off, successfully, the disgraceful urge to tell him how staggered I was by the bill his office had recently sent me.

'Let me now show you your *apartámenty*. You speak Russian, don't you?'

'I certainly do, but I can't write it. I also know a little French.'

She and her mother (whom she mentioned as casually as if Annette were in the next room copying something for me on a sound-less typewriter) had spent most of last summer at Carnavaux with *babushka*. I would like to have learned what room exactly Bel had occupied in the villa, but an oddly obtrusive, though irrelevant-looking, recollection somehow prevented me from asking: shortly before her death Iris had dreamed one night that she had given birth to a fat boy with dusky red cheeks and almond eyes and the blue shadow of mutton chops: 'A horrible Omarus K.'

Oh yes, said Bel, she had loved it. Especially the path down, down to the sea and the aroma of rosemary (*chudnyy zapakh rozmarina*). I was tortured and charmed by her 'shadowless' *émigré* Russian, untainted, God bless Annette, by the Langley woman's fruity Sovietisms.

Did Bel recognize me? She looked me over with serious gray eyes.

'I recognize your hands and your hair.'

'*On se tutoie* in Russian henceforward. All right. Let's go upstairs.'

She approved of the studio: 'A schoolroom in a picture book.' She opened the medicine chest in her bathroom. 'Empty – but I know what I'll put there.' The bedroom 'enchanted' her. *Ocharovatel'no!* (Annette's favorite praise word.) She criticized, though, the bedside bookshelf: 'What, no Byron? No Browning? Ah, Coleridge! The little golden sea snakes. Miss Ward gave me an anthology for Russian Easter: I can recite your last duchess – I mean "My Last Duchess." '

I caught my breath with a moan. I kissed her. I wept. I sat, shak-ing, on a fragile chair that creaked in response to my hunched-up paroxysm. Bel stood looking away, looking up at a prismatic reflection on the ceiling, looking down at her luggage, which Mrs. O'Leary, a dumpy but doughty woman, had already brought up.

I apologized for my tears. Bel inquired in a socially perfect let's-change-the-subject manner if there was a television set in the house. I said we'd get one tomorrow. I would leave her now to her own devices. Dinner in half-an-hour. She had noticed, she said, that a picture she'd like to see was being shown in town. After dinner we drove to The Strand Theater.

Says a scribble in my diary: Does not much care for boiled chicken. *The Black Widow*. With Gene, Ginger, and George. Have passed the 'illiterative' sentimentalist and all the rest.

3

If Bel is alive today, she is thirty-two – exactly your age at the moment of writing (February 15, 1974). The last time I saw her, in 1959, she was not quite seventeen; and between eleven and a half and seventeen and a half she has changed very slightly in the medium of memory, where blood does not course through immobile time as fast as it does in the perceptual present. Especially unaffected by linear growth is my vision of her pertaining to 1953–1955, the three years in which she was totally and uniquely mine: I see it today as a composite portrait of rapture, in which a mountain in Colorado, my translating *Tamara* into English, Bel's high school accomplishments, and an Oregon forest intergrade in patterns of transposed time and twisted space that defy chronography and charting.

One change, one gradational trend I must note, however. This was my growing awareness of her beauty. Scarcely a month after her arrival I was already at a loss to understand how she could have struck me as 'plain.' Another month elapsed and the elfin line of her nose and upper lip in profile came as an 'expected revelation' – to use a formula I have applied to certain prosodic miracles in Blake and Blok. Because of the contrast between her pale-gray iris and very black lashes, her eyes seemed rimmed with kohl. Her hollowed cheek and long neck were pure Annette, but her fair hair, which she wore rather short, gave off a richer sheen as if the tawny strands were mixed with gold-olive ones in thick straight stripes of alternate shades. All this is easily described and this also goes for the regular striation of bright bloom along the outside of forearm and leg, which, in fact, smacks of self-plagiarism, for I had given it both to Tamara and Esmeralda, not counting several incidental lassies in my short stories (see for

example page 537 of the *Exile from Mayda* collection, Goodminton,
New York, 1947). The general type and bone structure of her pubescent
radiance cannot be treated, however, with a crack player's brio and
chalk-biting serve. I am reduced – a sad confession! – to something I
have also used before, and even in this book – the well-known method
of degrading one species of art by appealing to another. I am thinking
of Serov's *Five-petaled Lilac*, oil, which depicts a tawny-haired girl of
twelve or so sitting at a sun-flecked table and manipulating a raceme
of lilac in search of that lucky token. The girl is no other than Ada
Bredow, a first cousin of mine whom I flirted with disgracefully that
very summer, the sun of which ocellates the garden table and her
bare arms. What hack reviewers of fiction call 'human interest' will
now overwhelm my reader, the gentle tourist, when he visits the
Hermitage Museum in Leningrad, where I have seen with my own
rheumy eyes, on a visit to Sovietland a few years ago, that picture
which belonged to Ada's grandmother before being handed over to
the People by a dedicated purloiner. I believe that this enchanting
little girl was the model of my partner in a recurrent dream of mine
with a stretch of parquetry between two beds in a makeshift demonic
guest room. Bel's resemblance to her – same cheekbones, same chin,
same knobby wrists, same tender flower – can be only alluded to, not
actually listed. But enough of this. I have been trying to do something
very difficult and I will tear it up if you say I have succeeded too well,
because I do not want, and never wanted, to succeed, in this dismal
business of Isabel Lee – though at the same time I was intolerably
happy.

When asked – at last! – had she loved her mother (for I could not
get over Bel's apparent indifference to Annette's terrible death) she
thought for such a long time that I decided she had forgotten my
question, but finally (like a chessplayer resigning after an abyss of
meditation), she shook her head. What about Nelly Langley? This
she answered at once: Langley was mean and cruel and hated her,
and only last year whipped her; she had welts all over (uncovering for
display her right thigh, which now, at least, was impeccably white and
smooth).

The education she got in Quirn's best private school for Young

Ladies (you, her coeval, were there for a few weeks, in the same class, but you and she somehow missed making friends with each other) was supplemented by the two summers we spent roaming all over the Western states. What memories, what lovely smells, what mirages, near-mirages, substantiated mirages, accumulated along Highway 138 – Sterling, Fort Morgan (El. 4325), Greeley, well-named Loveland – as we approached the paradise part of Colorado!

From Lupine Lodge, Estes Park, where we spent a whole month, a path margined with blue flowers led through aspen groves to what Bel drolly called The Foot of the Face. There was also the Thumb of the Face, at its southern corner. I have a large glossy photograph taken by William Garrell who was the first, I think, to reach The Thumb, in 1940 or thereabouts, showing the East Face of Longs Peak with the checkered lines of ascent superimposed in a loopy design upon it. On the back of this picture – and as immortal in its own little right as the picture's subject – a poem by Bel, neatly copied in violet ink, is dedicated to Addie Alexander, 'First woman on Peak, eighty years ago.' It commemorates our own modest hikes:

> *Longs' Peacock Lake:*
> *the Hut and its Old Marmot;*
> *Boulderfield and its Black Butterfly;*
> *And the intelligent trail.*

She had composed it while we were sharing a picnic lunch, somewhere between those great rocks and the beginning of The Cable, and after testing the result mentally a number of times, in frowning silence, she finally scribbled it on a paper napkin which she handed to me with my pencil.

I told her how wonderful and artistic it was – particularly the last line. She asked: what's 'artistic'? I said: 'Your poem, you, your way with words.'

In the course of that ramble, or perhaps on a latter occasion, but certainly in the same region, a sudden storm swept upon the glory of the July day. Our shirts, shorts, and loafers seemed to dwindle to nothing in the icy mist. A first hailstone hit a tin can, another my bald spot. We sought refuge in a cavity under a jutting rock. Thunderstorms to me are agony. Their evil pressure destroys me; their lightning forks through my brain and breast. Bel knew this; huddling against me (for my comfort rather than hers!), she kept giving me a quick little kiss on the temple at every bang of thunder, as if to say: That one's over, you're still safe. I now felt myself longing for those crashes never to cease; but presently they turned to half-hearted rumbles, and the sun found emeralds in a patch of wet turf. She could not stop shivering, though, and I had to thrust my hands under her skirt and rub her thin body, till it glowed, so as to ward off 'pneumonia' which she said, laughing jerkily, was a 'new,' was a 'moon,' was a 'new moon' and a 'moan,' a 'new moan,' thank you.

There is a hollow of dimness again in the sequence, but it must have been soon after that, in the same motor court, or in the next, on the way home, that she slipped into my room at dawn, and sat down on my bed – move your legs – in her pyjama top to read me another poem:

> *In the dark basement, I stroked*
> *the silky head of a wolf.*
> *When the light returned*
> *and all cried: 'Ah!,'*
> *it turned out to be only*
> *Médor, a dead dog.*

I again praised her talent, and kissed her more warmly, perhaps, than the poem deserved; for, actually, I found it rather obscure, but did not say so, and presently she yawned and fell asleep on my bed, a practice I usually did not tolerate. Today, however, on rereading those strange lines, I see through their starry crystal the tremendous commentary I could write about them, with galaxies of reference marks and footnotes like the reflections of brightly lit bridges spanning black water. But my daughter's soul is hers, and my soul is mine, and may Hamlet Godman rot in peace.

4

As late as the start of the 1954–1955 school year, with Bel nearing her thirteenth birthday, I was still deliriously happy, still seeing nothing wrong or dangerous, or absurd or downright cretinous, in the relationship between my daughter and me. Save for a few insignificant lapses – a few hot drops of overflowing tenderness, a gasp masked by a cough and that sort of stuff – my relations with her remained essentially innocent. But whatever qualities I might have possessed as a Professor of Literature, nothing but incompetence and a reckless laxity of discipline can I see today in the rearview reflection of that sweet wild past.

Others forestalled me in perspicacity. My first critic happened to be Mrs. Noteboke, a stout dark lady in suffragettish tweeds, who instead of keeping her Marion, a depraved and vulgar nymphet, from snooping on a schoolmate's home life, lectured me on the upbringing of Bel and strongly advised my hiring an experienced, preferably German, governess to look after her day and night. My second critic – a much more tactful and understanding one – was my secretary, Myrna Soloway, who complained that she could not keep track of the literary magazines and clippings in my mail – because of their being intercepted by an unscrupulous and avid little reader – and who gently added that Quirn High School, the last refuge of common sense in my incredible plight, was astounded by Bel's lack of manners almost as much as by her intelligence and familiarity with 'Proust and Prévost.' I spoke to Miss Lowe, the rather pretty petite headmistress, and she mentioned 'boarding facilities,' which sounded like some kind of wooden jail, and the even more dismal ('with all those rippling birdcalls and wickering trills in the woods, Miss Lowe – in the woods'!) 'summer instruction' to replace the 'eccentricities of an artist's ("A great artist's, Professor") household.' She pointed out to the giggling and apprehensive artist that a young daughter should be treated as a potential component of our society and not as a fancy pet. Throughout that talk I could not shake off the feeling of its all being a nightmare that I had had or would have in some other existence, some other bound sequence of numbered dreams.

An atmosphere of vague distress was gathering (to speak in verbal clichés about a cliché situation) around my metaphorical head, when there occurred to me a simple and brilliant solution of all my problems and troubles.

The tall looking glass before which many of Landover's houris had onduled in their brief brown glory now served me to behold the image of a lion-hued fifty-five-year-old would-be athlete performing waist-slimming and chest-expanding exercises by means of an 'Elmago' ('Combines the mechanical know-how of the West with the magic of Mithra'). It was a good image. An old telegram (found unopened in an issue of *Artisan*, a literary review, filched by Bel from the hallway table), was addressed to me by a Sunday paper in London, asking me to comment on the rumors – which I had already heard – to the effect that I was the main candidate in the abstract scramble for what our American kid brothers called 'the most prestigious prize in the world.' This, too, might impress the rather success-minded person I had in view. Finally, I knew that in the vacational months of 1955 a series of strokes had killed off in London poor old Gerry Adamson, a great guy, and that Louise was free. Too free in fact. An urgent letter I now wrote her, summoning her back to Quirn at once, for a serious Discussion of a matter concerning both her and me, reached her only after describing a comic circle via four fashionable spots on the Continent. I never saw the wire she said she sent me from New York on October 1.

On October 2, an abnormally warm day, the first of a week-long series, Mrs. King telephoned in the afternoon to invite me with rather enigmatic little laughs to an 'impromptu *soirée*, in a few hours, say at nine P.M. after you have tucked in your adorable daughter.' I agreed to come because Mrs. King was an especially nice soul, the kindest on the campus.

I had a black headache and decided that a two-mile walk in the cool clear night would do me good. My dealings with space and spatial transitions are so diabolically complicated that I do not recall whether I really walked, or drove, or limited myself to pacing up and down the open gallery running along the front side of our second floor, or what.

The first person to whom my hostess introduced me – with a subdued fanfare of social elation – was the 'English' cousin with whom Louise had been staying in Devonshire, Lady Morgain, 'daughter of our former Ambassador and widow of the Oxford medievalist' – shadowy figures on a briefly lit screen. She was a rather deaf and decidedly dotty witch in her middle fifties, comically coiffured and dowdily dressed, and she and her belly advanced upon me with such energetic eagerness that I scarcely had time to sidestep the well-meant attack before getting wedged 'between the books and the bottles' as poor Gerry used to say in reference to academic cocktails. I passed into a different, far more stylish world as I bent to kiss Louise's expertly swanned cool little hand. My dear old Audace welcomed me with the kind of Latin accolade that he had especially developed to mark the highest degree of spiritual kinship and mutual esteem. John King, whom I had seen on the eve in a college corridor, greeted me with raised arms as if the fifty hours elapsed since our last chat had been magically blown-up into half a century. We were only six people in a spacious parlor, not counting two painted girl-children in Tyrolean dress, whose presence, identity, and very existence have remained to this day a familiar mystery – familiar, because such zigzag cracks in the plaster are typical of the prisons or palaces into which recrudescent derangement merrily leads me whenever I have prepared to make, as I was to do now, a difficult, climactic announcement that demanded absolute clarity of concentration. So, as I just said, we were only six animal people in that room (and two little phantoms), but through the translucid unpleasant walls I could make out – without looking! – rows and tiers of dim spectators, with the sense of a sign in my brain meaning 'standing room only' in the language of madness.

We were now sitting at a round clockfaced table (practically undistinguishable from the one in the Opal Room of my house, west of the albino Stein), Louise at twelve o'clock, Professor King at two, Mrs. Morgain at four, Mrs. King in green silk at eight, Audace at ten, and I at six, presumably, or a minute past, because Louise was not quite opposite, or maybe she had pushed her chair a sixty-second space closer to Audace although she had sworn to me on the *Social Register* as well as on a *Who's Who* that he had never made that pass at her somehow suggested by his magnificent little poem in the *Artisan*.

> *Speaking of, ah, yesternights,*
> *I had you, dear, within earshot*
> *of that party downstairs,*
> *on the broad bed of my host*
> *piled with the coats of your guests,*
> *old macks, mock minks,*
> *one striped scarf (mine),*
> *a former flame's furs*
> *(more rabbit than flipperling),*
> *yea, a mountain of winters,*
> *like that upon which flunkeys sprawl*
> *in the vestibule of the Opera,*
> *Canto One of* Onegin,
> *where under the chandeliers*
> *of a full house, you, dear,*
> *should have been the dancer*
> *flying, like fluff, in a decor*
> *of poplars and fountains.*

I started to speak in the high, clear, insolent voice (taught me by Ivor on the beach of Cannice) by which I instilled the fear of Phoebus when inaugurating a recalcitrant seminar in my first years of teaching at Quirn: 'What I plan to discuss is the curious case of a close friend of mine whom I shall call –'

Mrs. Morgain set down her glass of whisky and leaned toward me confidentially: 'You know I met little Iris Black in London, around

1919, I guess. Her father was a business friend of my father, the Ambassador. I was a starry-eyed American gal. She was a fantastic beauty and *most* sophisticated. I remember how thrilled I was later to learn that she had gone and married a Russian Prince!'

'Fay,' cried Louise from twelve to four: 'Fay! His Highness is making his throne speech.'

Everyone laughed, and the two bare-thighed Tyrolean children chasing each other around the table bounced across my knees and were gone again.

'I shall call this close friend of mine, whose case we are about to examine, Mr. Twidower, a name with certain connotations, as those of you who remember the title story in my *Exile from Mayda* will note.'

(Three people, the Kings and Audace, raised three hands, looking at one another in shared smugness.)

'This person, who is in the mighty middle of life, thinks of marry-ing a third time. He is deeply in love with a young woman. Before proposing to her, however, honesty demands that he confess he is suffering from a certain ailment. I wish they would stop jolting my chair every time they run by. "Ailment" is perhaps too strong a term. Let's put it this way: there are certain flaws, he says, in the mechanism of his mind. The one he told me about is harmless in itself but very distressing and unusual, and may be a symptom of some imminent, more serious disorder. So here goes. When this person is lying in bed and imagining a familiar stretch of street, say, the right-hand sidewalk from the Library to, say –'

'The Liquor Store,' put in King, a relentless wag.

'All right, Recht's Liquor Store. It is about three hundred yards away –'

I was again interrupted, this time by Louise (whom, in fact, I was solely addressing). She turned to Audace and informed him that she could never visualize any distance in yards unless she could divide it by the length of a bed or a balcony.

'Romantic,' said Mrs. King. 'Go on, Vadim.'

'Three hundred paces away along the same side as the College Library. Now comes my friend's problem. He can walk in his mind there and back but he can't perform in his mind the actual about-face that transforms "there" into "back." '

'Must call Rome,' muttered Louise to Mrs. King, and was about to leave her seat, but I implored her to hear me out. She resigned herself, warning me however that she could not understand a word of my peroration.

'Repeat that bit about twisting around in your mind,' said King. 'Nobody understood.'

'I did,' said Audace: 'We suppose the Liquor Store happens to be closed, and Mr. Twidower, who is a friend of mine too, turns on his heel to go back to the Library. In the reality of life he performs this action without a hitch or hiatus, as simply and unconsciously as we all do, even if the artist's critical eye does see – *A toi*, Vadim.'

'Does see,' I said, accepting the relay-race baton, 'that, depending on the speed of one's revolution, palings and awnings pass counter-wise around you either with the heavy lurch of a merry-go-round or (saluting Audace) in a single brisk flip like that of the end of a striped scarf (Audace smiled, acknowledging the Audacianism) that one flings over one's shoulder. But when one lies immobile in bed and rehearses or rather replays in one's mind the process of turning, in the manner described, it is not so much the pivotal swing which is hard to perceive mentally – it is its result, the reversion of vista, the transformation of direction, *that's* what one vainly strives to imagine. Instead of the liquor-store direction smoothly turning into the opposite one, as it does in the simplicity of waking life, poor Twidower is baffled –'

I had seen it coming but had hoped that I would be allowed to complete my sentence. Not at all. With the infinitely slow and silent movement of a gray tomcat, which he resembled with his bristly whiskers and arched back, King left his seat. He started to tiptoe, with a glass in each hand, toward the golden glow of a densely populated sideboard. With a dramatic slap of both hands against the edge of the table I caused Mrs. Morgain to jump (she had either dozed off or aged tremendously in the last few minutes) and stopped old King in his tracks; he silently turned like an automaton (illustrating my story) and as silently stole back to his seat with the empty Arabesque glasses.

'The mind, my friend's mind, is baffled, as I was saying, by something dreadfully strainful and irksome in the machinery of the change from one position to another, from east to west or west to east, from one damned nymphet to another – I mean I'm losing the thread of my tale, the zipper of thought has stuck, this is absurd –'

Absurd and very embarrassing. The two cold-thighed, cheesy-necked girleens were now engaged in a quarrelsome game as to who should sit on my left knee, that side of my lap where the honey was, trying to straddle Left Knee, warbling in Tyrolese and pushing each other off, and cousin Fay kept bending toward me and saying with a macabre accent: *'Elles vous aiment tant!'* Finally I pinched and twisted the nearest buttock, and with a squeal they resumed their running around, like that eternal little pleasure-park train, brushing the brambles.

I still could not disentangle my thoughts, but Audace came to my rescue.

'To conclude,' he said (and an audible ouf! was emitted by cruel Louise), 'our patient's trouble concerns not a certain physical act but the imagining of its performance. All he can do in his mind is omit the swiveling part altogether and shift from one visual plane to another with the neutral flash of a slide change in a magic lantern, whereupon he finds himself facing in a direction which has lost, or rather never contained, the idea of "oppositeness." Does anybody wish to comment?'

After the usual pause that follows such offers, John King said: 'My advice to your Mr. Twitter is to dismiss that nonsense once for all. It's charming nonsense, it's colorful nonsense, but it's also harmful nonsense. Yes, Jane?'

'My father,' said Mrs. King, 'a professor of botany, had a rather endearing quirk: he could memorize historical dates and telephone numbers – for example our number 9743 – only insofar as they contained primes. In our number he remembered two figures, the second and last, a useless combination; the other two were only black gaps, missing teeth.'

'Oh, that's good,' cried Audace, genuinely delighted.

I remarked it was not at all the same thing. My friend's affliction resulted in nausea, dizziness, *kegelkugel* headache.

'Well yes, I understand, but my father's quirk also had its side effects. It was not so much his inability to memorize, say, his house number in Boston, which was 68 and which he saw every day, but the fact that he could do nothing about it; that nobody, but nobody could explain *why* all he could make out at the far end of his brain was not 68 but a bottomless hole.'

Our host resumed his vanishing act with more deliberation than before. Audace lidded his empty glass with his palm. Though swine-drunk, I longed for mine to be refilled, but was bypassed. The walls of the round room had grown more or less opaque again, God bless them, and the Dolomite Dollies were no longer around.

'In the days when I longed to be a ballerina,' said Louise, 'and was Blanc's little favorite, I always rehearsed exercises in my mind lying in bed, and had no difficulty whatever in imagining swirls and whirls. It is a matter of practice, Vadim. Why don't you just roll over in bed when you want to see yourself walking back to that Library? We must be going now, Fay, it's past midnight.'

Audace glanced at his wristwatch, uttered the exclamation which Time must be sick of hearing, and thanked me for a wonderful evening. Lady Morgain's mouth mimicked the pink aperture of an elephant's trunk as it mutely formed the word 'loo' to which Mrs. King, fussily swishing in green, immediately took her. I remained alone at the round table, then struggled to my feet, drained the rest of Louise's daiquiri, and joined her in the hallway.

She had never melted and shivered so nicely in my embrace as she did now.

'How many quadruped critics,' she asked after a tender pause in the dark garden, 'would accuse you of leg pulling if you published the description of those funny feelings. Three, ten, a herd?'

'Those are not really "feelings" and they are not really "funny." I just wished you to be aware that if I go mad it will be in consequence of my games with the idea of space. "Rolling over" would be cheating and besides would not help.'

'I'll take you to an absolutely divine analyst.'

'That's all you can suggest?'

'Why, yes.'

'Think, Louise.'

'Oh. I'm also going to marry you. Yes, of course, you idiot.'

She was gone before I could reclasp her slender form. The star-dusted sky, usually a scary affair, now vaguely amused me: it belonged, with the autumn *fadeur* of barely visible flowers, to the same issue of *Woman's Own World* as Louise. I made water into a sizzle of asters and looked up at Bel's window, square c2. Lit as brightly as e1, the Opal Room. I went back there and noted with relief that kind hands had cleared and tidied the table, the round table with the opalescent rim, at which I had delivered a most successful introductory lecture. I heard Bel's voice calling me from the upper landing, and taking a palmful of salted almonds ascended the stairs.

5

Rather early next morning, a Sunday, as I stood, shawled in terry cloth, and watched four eggs rolling and bumping in their inferno, somebody entered the living room through a side door that I never bothered to lock.

Louise! Louise dressed up in hummingbird mauve for church. Louise in a sloping beam of mellow October sun. Louise leaning against the grand piano, as if about to sing and looking around with a lyrical smile.

I was the first to break our embrace.

VADIM No, darling, no. My daughter may come down any minute. Sit down.

LOUISE (*examining an armchair and then settling in it*) Pity. You know, I've been here many times before! In fact I was laid on that grand at eighteen. Aldy Landover was ugly, unwashed, brutal – and absolutely irresistible.

VADIM Listen, Louise. I have always found your free, frivolous style very fetching. But you will be moving into this house very soon now, and we want a little more dignity, don't we?

LOUISE We'll have to change that blue carpet. It makes the Stein look like an iceberg. And there should be a riot of flowers. So many big vases and not one Strelitzia! There was a whole shrub of lilac down there in my time.

VADIM It's October, you know. Look, I hate to bring this up, but isn't your cousin waiting in the car? It would be very irregular.

LOUISE Irregular, my foot. She won't be up before lunch. Ah, Scene Two.

(*Bel wearing only slippers and a cheap necklace of iridescent glass – a Riviera souvenir – comes down at the other end of the living room beyond the piano.*

She has already turned kitchenward showing the beaupage back of her head and delicate shoulder blades when she becomes aware of our presence and retraces her steps.)

BEL (*addressing me and casually squinting at my amazed visitor*) Ya bezumno golodnaya (*I'm madly hungry*).

VADIM Louise dear, this is my daughter Bel. She's walking in her sleep, really, hence the, uh, non-attire.

LOUISE Hullo, Annabel. The non-attire is very becoming.

BEL (*correcting Louise*) Isa.

VADIM Isabel, this is Louise Adamson, an old friend of mine, back from Rome. I hope we'll be seeing a lot of her.

BEL How do you do (*question-markless*).

VADIM Well, run along, Bel, and put on something. Breakfast is ready. (*To Louise*) Would you like to have breakfast too? Hard-boiled eggs? A Coke with a straw? (*Pale violin climbing stairs*)

LOUISE Non, merci. I'm flabbergasted.

VADIM Yes, things have been getting a little out of hand, but you'll see, she's a special child, there's no other child like her. All we need is your presence, your touch. She has inherited the habit of circulating in a state of nature from me. An Edenic gene. Curious.

LOUISE Is this a two-people nudist colony or has Mrs. O'Leary also joined?

VADIM (*laughing*) No, no, she's not here on Sundays. Everything is fine, I assure you. Bel is a docile angel. She –

LOUISE (*rising to leave*) There she comes to be fed (*Bel descends the stairs in a skimpy pink robe*). Drop in around tea time. Fay is being taken by Jane King to a lacrosse game in Rosedale. (*Exits*)

BEL Who's she? Former student of yours? Drama? Elocution?

VADIM (*moving fast*) Bozhe moy! (*good Lord!*). The eggs! They must be as hard as jade. Come along. I'll acquaint you with the situation, as your schoolmistress says.

6

The grand was the first to go – it was carried out by a gang of staggering iceberg movers and donated by me to Bel's school, which I had reasons to pamper: I am not an easily frightened man but when I am frightened I am very much frightened, and at a second interview that I had had with the schoolmistress, my impersonation of an indignant Charles Dodgson was only saved from failure by the sensational news of my being about to marry an irreproachable socialite, the widow of our most pious philosopher. Louise, per contra, regarded the throwing out of a symbol of luxury as a personal affront and a crime: a concert piano of that kind costs, she said, as least as much as her old Hecate convertible, and she was not quite as wealthy as, no doubt, I thought she was, a statement representing that knot in Logic: the double-hitch lie which does not make one truth. I appeased her by gradually overcrowding the Music Room (if a time series be transformed into sudden space) with the modish gadgets she loved, singing furniture, miniature TV sets, stereorphics, portable orchestras, better and better video sets, remote-control instruments for turning those things on or off, and an automatic telephone dialer. For Bel's birthday she gave her a Rain Sound machine to promote sleep; and to celebrate *my* birthday she murdered a neurotic's night by getting me a thousand-dollar bedside Pantomime clock with twelve yellow radii on its black face instead of figures, which made it look blind to me or feigning blindness like some repulsive beggar in a hideous tropical town; in compensation that terrible object possessed a secret beam that projected Arabic numerals (2:00, 2:05, 2:10, 2:15, and so forth) on the ceiling of my new sleeping quarters, thus demolishing the sacred, complete, agonizingly achieved occlusion of its oval window. I said I'd buy a gun and shoot it in the mug, if she did not send it back to the fiend who sold it to her. She replaced it by 'something especially made for people who like originality,' namely a silver-plated umbrella stand in the shape of a giant jackboot – there was 'something about rain strangely attractive to her' as her 'analyst' wrote me in one of the silliest letters that man ever wrote to man. She was also fond of small expensive animals, but here I stood firm, and she never got the long-coated Chihuahua she coldly craved.

I did not expect much of Louise the Intellectual. The only time I saw her shed big tears, with interesting little howls of real grief, was when on the first Sunday of our marriage all the newspapers carried photographs of the two Albanian authors (a bald-domed old epicist and a long-haired woman compiler of children's books) who shared out between them the Prestigious Prize that she had told everybody I was sure to win that year. On the other hand she had only flipped through my novels (she was to read more attentively, though, *A Kingdom by the Sea*, which I began slowly to pull out of myself in 1957 like a long brain worm, hoping it would not break), while consuming all the 'serious' bestsellers discussed by sister consumers belonging to the Literary Group in which she liked to assert herself as a writer's wife.

I also discovered that she considered herself a connoisseur of Modern Art. She blazed with anger at me when I said I doubted that the appreciation of a green stripe across a blue background had *any* connection with its definition in a glossy catalogue as 'producing a virtually Oriental atmosphere of spaceless time and timeless space.' She accused me of trying to wreck her entire view of the world by maintaining – in a facetious vein, she hoped – that only a Philistine misled by the solemn imbeciles paid to write about exhibitions could tolerate rags, rinds, and fouled paper rescued from a garbage can and discussed in terms 'of warm splashes of color' and 'good-natured irony.' But perhaps most touching and terrible of all was her honestly believing that painters painted 'what they felt'; that a rather rough and rumpled landscape dashed off in the Provence might be gratefully and proudly interpreted by art students if a psychiatrist explained to them that the advancing thundercloud represented the artist's clash with his father, and the rolling grainfield the early death of his mother in a shipwreck.

I could not prevent her from purchasing specimens of the pictorial art in vogue but I judiciously steered some of the more repulsive objects (such as a collection of daubs produced by 'naïve' convicts) into the round dining room where they swam blurrily in the candlelight when we had guests for supper. Our routine meals generally took place in the snackbar niche between the kitchen and the housemaid's quarters. Into that niche Louise introduced her new Cappuccino Espresso Maker, while at the opposite end of the house, in the Opal Room, a heavily built, hedonically appareled bed with a padded headboard was installed for me. The adjacent bathroom had a less comfortable tub than my former one, and certain inconveniences attended my excursions, two or three nights per week, to the connubial chamber – via drawing room, creaky stairs, upper landing, second-floor corridor, and past the inscrutable chink-gleam of Bel's door; but I treasured my privacy more than I resented its drawbacks. I had the 'Turkish *toupet*,' as Louise called it, to forbid her to communicate with me by thumping on her floor. Eventually I had an interior telephone put in my room, to be used only in certain emergencies: I was thinking of such nervous states as the feeling of imminent collapse that I experienced sometimes in my nocturnal bouts with eschatological obsessions; and there was always the half-full box of sleeping pills that only she could have filched.

The decision to let Bel stay in her apartment, with Louise as her only neighbor, instead of refurnishing a spiral of space by allotting those two east-end rooms to Louise – 'perhaps I too need a studio?' – while transferring Bel with bed and books to the Opal Room downstairs and leaving me upstairs in my former bedchamber, was taken by me firmly despite Louise's rather bitchy countersuggestions, such as removing the tools of my trade from the library in the basement and banishing Bel with all her belongings to that warm, dry, nice and quiet lair. Though I knew I would never give in, the very process of shuffling rooms and accessories in my mind made me literally ill. On top of that, I felt, perhaps wrongly, that Louise was enjoying the hideous banality of a stepmother-versus-stepdaughter situation. I did not exactly regret marrying her, I recognized her charm and functional qualities, but my adoration for Bel was the sole splendor, the sole breathtaking mountain in the drab plain of my emotional life. Being in many ways an extraordinarily stupid person, I had simply not reckoned with the tangles and tensions of what was meant to look like a model household. The moment I woke up – or at least the moment I saw that getting up was the only way to fool early-morning insomnia – I started wondering what new project Louise would invent that day with which to harass my girl. When two years later this gray old dolt and his volatile wife, after treating Bel to a tedious Swiss tour, left her in Larive, between Hex and Trex, at a 'finishing' school (finishing childhood, finishing the innocence of young imagination), it was our 1955–1957 period of life *à trois* in the Quirn house, and not my earlier mistakes, that I recalled with curses and sobs.

She and her stepmother stopped speaking to each other altogether; they communicated, if need be, by signs: Louise, for instance, pointing dramatically at the ruthless clock and Bel tapping in the negative on the crystal of her loyal little wristwatch. She lost all affection for me, twisting away gently when I attempted a perfunctory caress. She adopted again the wan absent expression that had dimmed her features at her arrival from Rosedale. Camus replaced Keats. Her marks deteriorated. She no longer wrote poetry. One day as Louise and I were packing for our next trip to Europe (London, Paris, Pisa, Stresa, and – in small print – Larive) I started removing some old maps, Colorado, Oregon, from the silk 'cheek' inside a valise, and the moment my secret prompter uttered that '*shcheka*' I came across a poem of hers written long before Louise's intrusion into her trustful young life. I thought it might do Louise good to read it and handed her the exercise-book page (all ragged along its torn root but still mine) on which the following lines were penciled:

At sixty, if I'll look back,
jungles and hills will hide
the notch, the source, the sand
and a bird's footprints across it.
I'll see nothing at all
with my old eyes,
yet I'll know it was there, the source.

How come, then, that when I look back
at twelve – one fifth of the stretch! –
with visibility presumably better
and no junk in between,

I can't even imagine
that patch of wet sand
and the walking bird
and the gleam of my source?

'Almost Poundian in purity,' remarked Louise – which annoyed me, because I thought Pound a fake.

7

Château Vignedor, Bel's charming boarding school in Switzerland, on a charming hill three hundred meters above charming Larive on the Rhône, had been recommended to Louise in the autumn of 1957 by a Swiss lady in Quirn's French Department. There were two other 'finishing' schools of the same general type that might have done just as well, but Louise set her sights on Vignedor because of a chance remark made not even by her Swiss friend but by a chance girl in a chance travel agency who summed up the qualities of the school in one phrase: 'Many Tunisian princesses.'

It offered five main subjects (French, Psychology, Savoir-vivre, Couture, Cuisine), various sports (under the direction of Christine Dupraz, the once famous skier), and a dozen additional classes on request (which would keep the plainest girl there till she married), including Ballet and Bridge. Another *supplément* – especially suitable for orphans or unneeded children – was a summer trimester, filling up the year's last remaining segment with excursions and nature studies, to be spent by a few lucky girls at the home of the head-mistress, Madame de Turm, an Alpine chalet some twelve hundred meters higher: 'Its solitary light, twinkling in a black fold of the mountains, can be seen,' said the prospectus in four languages, 'from the Château on clear nights.' There was also some kind of camp for differently handicapped local children in different years conducted by our medically inclined sports directress.

1957, 1958, 1959. Sometimes, seldom, hiding from Louise, who objected to Bel's twenty well-spaced monosyllables' costing us fifty dollars, I would call her from Quirn, but after a few such calls I received a curt note from Mme. de Turm, asking me not to upset my daughter by telephoning, and so retreated into my dark shell. Dark shell, dark years of my heart! They coincided oddly with the composition of my most vigorous, most festive, and commercially most successful novel, *A Kingdom by the Sea*. Its demands, the fun and the fancy of it, its intricate imagery, made up in a way for the absence of my beloved Bel. It was also bound to reduce, though I was hardly conscious of that, my correspondence with her (well-meant, chatty, dreadfully artificial letters which she seldom troubled to answer). Even more startling, of course, more incomprehensible to me, in groaning retrospect, is the effect my self-entertainment had on the number and length of our visits between 1957 and 1960 (when she eloped with a progressive blond-bearded young American). You were appalled to learn the other day, when we discussed the present notes, that I had seen 'beloved Bel' only four times in three summers and that only two of our visits lasted as long as a couple of weeks. I must add, however, that she resolutely declined to spend her vacations at home. I ought never, of course, have dumped her in Europe. I should have elected to sweat it out in my hellish household, between a childish woman and a somber child.

The work on my novel also impinged on my marital mores, making of me a less passionate and more indulgent husband: I let Louise go on suspiciously frequent trips to out-of-town unlisted eye specialists and neglected her in the meantime for Rose Brown, our cute housemaid who took three soapshowers daily and thought frilly black panties 'did something to guys.'

But the greatest havoc wrought by my work was its effect on my lectures. To it I sacrificed, like Cain, the flowers of my summers, and, like Abel, the sheep of the campus. Because of it, the process of my academic discarnation reached its ultimate stage. The last vestiges of human interconnection were severed, for I not only vanished physically from the lecture hall but had my entire course taped so as to be funneled through the College Closed Circuit into the rooms of headphoned students. Rumor had it that I was ready to quit; in fact, an anonymous punster wrote in the *Quirn Quarterly*, Spring, 1959: 'His Temerity is said to have asked for a raise before emeriting.'

In the summer of that year my third wife and I saw Bel for the last time. Allan Garden (after whom the genus of the Cape Jasmin should have been named, so great and triumphant was the flower in his buttonhole) had just been united in wedlock to his youthful Virginia, after several years of cloudless concubinage. They were to live to the combined age of 170 in absolute bliss, yet one grim fateful chapter remained to be constructed. I toiled over its first pages at the wrong desk, in the wrong hotel, above the wrong lake, with a view of the wrong *isoletta* at my left elbow. The only right thing was a pregnant-shaped bottle of Gattinara before me. In the middle of a mangled sentence Louise came to join me from Pisa, where I gathered – with amused indifference – that she had recoupled with a former lover. Playing on the strings of her meek uneasiness I took her to Switzer-land, which she detested. An early dinner with Bel was scheduled at the Larive Grand Hotel. She arrived with that Christ-haired youth, both purple trousered. The maître d'hôtel murmured something over the menu to my wife, and she rode up and brought down my oldest necktie for the young lout to put around his Adam's apple and scrawny neck. His grandmother had been related by marriage, so it turned out, to a third cousin of Louise's grandfather, the not quite untarnished Boston banker. This took care of the main course. We had coffee and kirsch in the lounge, and Charlie Everett showed us pictures of the summer Camp for Blind Children (who were spared the sight of its drab locust trees and rings of ashed refuse amidst the riverside bur-docks) which he and Bella (Bella!) were supervising. He was twenty-five years old. He had spent five years studying Russian, and spoke it as fluently, he said, as a trained seal. A sample justified the comparison. He was a dedicated 'revolutionary,' and a hopeless nincompoop, knowing nothing, crazy about jazz, existentialism, Leninism, pacifism, and African Art. He thought snappy pamphlets and catalogues so much more 'meaningful' than fat old books. A sweet, stale, and unhealthy smell emanated from the poor fellow. Throughout the dinner and coffee-drinking ordeal I never once – never once, reader! – looked up at my Bel, but as we were about to part (forever) I did look at her, and she had new twin lines from nostrils to wicks, and she wore granny glasses, and a middle part, and had lost all her pubescent prettiness, remnants of which I had still glimpsed during a visit to Larive a spring and winter ago. They had to be back at half-past-twenty, alas – not really 'alas.'

'Come and see us at Quirn soon, soon, Dolly,' I said, as we all stood on the sidewalk with mountains outlined in solid black against an aquamarine sky, and choughs jacking harshly, flying in flocks to roost, away, away.

I cannot explain the slip, but it angered Bel more than anything had ever angered her at any time.

'What is he saying?' she cried, looking in turn at Louise, at her beau, and again at Louise. 'What does he mean? Why does he call me "Dolly"? Who is she for God's sake? Why, why (turning to me), why did you say that?'

'*Obmolvka, prosti* (lapse of the tongue, sorry),' I replied, dying, trying to turn everything into a dream, a dream about that hideous last moment.

They walked briskly toward their little Klop car, he half-overtaking her, already poking the air with his car key, on her left, on her right. The aquamarine sky was now silent, darkish and empty, save for a star-shaped star about which I wrote a Russian elegy ages ago, in another world.

'What a charming, good-natured, civilized, sexy young fellow,' said Louise as we stamped into the lift. 'Are you in the mood tonight? Right away, Vad?'

PART FIVE

I

This penultimate part of LATH, this spirited episode in my otherwise somewhat passive existence, is horribly hard to set down, reminding me of the pensums, which the cruelest of my French governesses used to inflict upon me – some old saw to be copied *cent fois* (hiss and spittle) – in punishment for my adding my own marginal illustrations to those in her *Petit Larousse* or for exploring under the schoolroom table the legs of Lalage L., a little cousin, who shared lessons with me that unforgettable summer. I have, indeed, repeated the story of my dash to Leningrad in the late nineteen-sixties innumerable times in my mind, to packed audiences of my scribbling or dreaming selves – and yet I keep doubting both the necessity and the success of my dismal task. But you have argued the question, you are tenderly adamant, yes, and your decree is that I should relate my adventure in order to lend a semblance of significance to my daughter's futile fate.

In the summer of 1960, Christine Dupraz, who ran the summer camp for disabled children between cliff and highway, just east of Larive, informed me that Charlie Everett, one of her assistants, had eloped with my Bel after burning – in a grotesque ceremony that she visualized more clearly than I – his passport and a little American flag (bought at a souvenir stall especially for that purpose) 'right in the middle of the Soviet Consul's back garden'; whereupon the new 'Karl Ivanovich Vetrov' and the eighteen-year-old Isabella, a *ci-devant*'s daughter, had gone through some form of mock marriage in Berne and incontinently headed for Russia.

The same mail brought me an invitation to discuss in New York with a famous *compère* my sudden Number One position on the Bestselling Authors list, inquiries from Japanese, Greek, Turkish publishers, and a postcard from Parma with the scrawl: 'Bravo for Kingdom from Louise and Victor.' I never learned who Victor was, by the way.

Brushing all my engagements aside, I surrendered again – after quite a few years of abstinence! – to the thrill of secret investigations. Spying had been my *clystère de Tchékhov* even before I married Iris Black whose later passion for working on an interminable detective tale had been sparked by this or that hint I must have dropped, like a passing bird's lustrous feather, in relation to my experience in the vast and misty field of the Service. In my little way I have been of some help to my betters. The tree, a blue-flowering ash, whose cortical wound I caught the two 'diplomats,' Tornikovski and Kalikakov, using for their correspondence, still stands, hardly scarred, on its hilltop above San Bernardino. But for structural economy I have omitted that entertaining strain from this story of love and prose. Its existence, however, helped me now to ward off – for a while, at least – the madness and anguish of hopeless regret.

It was child's play to find Karl's relatives in the U.S.; namely, two gaunt aunts who disliked the boy even more than they did one another. Aunt Number One assured me he had never left Switzerland – they were still forwarding his Third Class mail to her in Boston. Aunt Number Two, the Philadelphia Fright, said he liked music and was vegetating in Vienna.

I had overestimated my forces. A serious relapse hospitalized me for nearly a whole year. The complete rest ordered by all my doctors was then botched by my having to stand by my publisher in a long legal fight against obscenity charges leveled at my novel by stuffy censors. I was again very ill. I still feel the pressure of the hallucinations that beset me, as my search for Bel got somehow mixed up with the controversy over my novel, and I saw as clearly as one sees mountains or ships, a great building, all windows lit, trying to advance upon me, through this or that wall of the ward, seeking as it were a weak spot to push through and ram my bed.

In the late Sixties I learned that Bel was now definitely married to Vetrov but that he had been sent to some remote place of unspecified work. Then came a letter.

It was forwarded to me by an old respectable businessman (I shall call him A.B.) with a note saying that he was 'in textiles' though by education 'an engineer'; that he represented 'a Soviet firm in the U.S. and vice versa'; that the letter he was enclosing came from a lady working in his Leningrad office (I shall call her Dora) and concerned my daughter 'whom he did not have the honor to know but who, he believed, needed my assistance.' He added that he would be flying back to Leningrad in a month's time and would be glad if I 'contacted him.' The letter from Dora was in Russian.

Much-respected Vadim Vadimovich!

You probably receive many letters from people in our country who manage to obtain your books – not an easy enterprise! The present letter, however, is not from an admirer but simply from a friend of Isabella Vadimovna Vetrov with whom she has been sharing a room for more than a year now.

She is ill, she has no news from her husband, and she is without a kopek.

Please, get in touch with the bearer of this note. He is my employer, and also a distant relative, and has agreed to bring a few lines from you, Vadim Vadimovich, and a little money, if possible, but the main thing, the main thing (glavnoe, glavnoe) is to come in person (lichno). Let him know if you can come and if yes, when and where we could meet to discuss the situation. Everything in life is urgent (speshno, 'pressing,' 'not to be postponed') but some things are dreadfully urgent and this is one of them.

In order to convince you that she is here, with me, telling me to write you and unable to write herself, I am appending a little clue or token that only you and she can decode: '. . . and the intelligent trail (i umnitsa tropka).'

For a minute I sat at the breakfast table – under the compassionate stare of Brown Rose – in the attitude of a cave dweller clasping his hands around his head at the crash of rocks breaking above him (women make the same gesture when something falls in the next room). My decision was, of course, instantly taken. I perfunctorily patted Rose's young buttocks through her light skirt, and strode to the telephone.

A few hours later I was dining with A.B. in New York (and in the course of the next month was to exchange several long-distance calls with him from London). He was a superb little man, perfectly oval in shape, with a bald head and tiny feet expensively shod (the rest of his envelope looked less classy). He spoke friable English with a soft Russian accent, and native Russian with Jewish question marks. He thought that I should begin by seeing Dora. He settled for me the exact spot where she and I might meet. He warned me that in preparing to visit the weird Wonderland of the Soviet Union a traveler's first step was the very Philistine one of being assigned a *nomer* (hotel room) and that only after he had been granted one could the 'visa' be tackled. Over the tawny mountain of 'Bogdan's' brown-speckled, butter-soaked, caviar-accompanied *bliny* (which A.B. forbade me to pay for though I was lousy with *A Kingdom*'s money), he spoke poetically, and at some length, about his recent trip to Tel Aviv.

My next move – a visit to London – would have been altogether delightful, had I not been overwhelmed all the time by anxiety, impatience, anguished forebodings. Through several venturesome gentlemen – a former lover of Allan Andoverton's and two of my late benefactor's mysterious chums – I had retained some innocent ties with the BINT, as Soviet agents acronymize the well-known, too well-known, British intelligence service. Consequently it was possible for me to obtain a false or more-or-less false passport. Since I may want to avail myself again of those facilities, I cannot reveal here my exact alias. Suffice it to say that some teasing similarity with my real family name could make the assumed one pass, if I got caught, for a clerical error on the part of an absentminded consul and for indifference to official papers on that of the deranged bearer. Let us suppose my real name to have been 'Oblonsky' (a Tolstoyan invention); then the false one would be, for example, the mimetic 'O. B. Long,' an oblong blursky, so to speak. This I could expand into, say, Oberon Bernard Long, of Dublin or Dumberton, and live with it for years on five or six continents.

I had escaped from Russia at the age of not quite nineteen, leaving across my path in a perilous forest the felled body of a Red soldier. I had then dedicated half a century to berating, deriding, twisting into funny shapes, wringing out like blood-wet towels, kicking neatly in

Evil's stinkiest spot, and otherwise tormenting the Soviet regime at every suitable turn of my writings. In fact, no more consistent critic of Bolshevist brutality and basic stupidity existed during all that time at the literary level to which my output belonged. I was thus well aware of two facts: that under my own name I would not be given a room at the Evropeyskaya or Astoria or any other Leningrad hotel unless I made some extraordinary amends, some abjectly exuberant recantation; and that if I talked my way to that hotel room as Mr. Long or Blong, and got interrupted, there might be no end of trouble. I decided therefore not to get interrupted.

'Shall I grow a beard to cross the frontier?' muses homesick General Gurko in Chapter Six of *Esmeralda and Her Parandrus*.

'Better than none,' said Harley Q., one of my gayest advisers. 'But,' he added, 'do it before we glue on and stamp O.B.'s picture and don't lose weight afterwards.' So I grew it – during the atrocious heartracking wait for the room I could not mock up and the visa I could not forge. It was an ample Victorian affair, of a nice, rough, tawny shade threaded with silver. It reached up to my apple-red cheekbones and came down to my waistcoat, commingling on the way with my lateral yellow-gray locks. Special contact lenses not only gave another, dumbfounded, expression to my eyes, but somehow changed their very shape from squarish leonine, to round Jovian. Only upon my return did I notice that the old tailor-made trousers, on me and in my bag, displayed my real name on the inside of the waistband.

My good old British passport, which had been handled cursorily by so many courteous officers who had never opened my books (the only real identity papers of its accidental holder), remained, after a procedure, that both decency and incompetence forbid me to describe, physically the same in many respects; but certain of its other features, details of substance and items of information, were, let us say, 'modified' by a new method, an alchemysterious treatment, a technique of genius, 'still not understood elsewhere,' as the chaps in the lab tactfully expressed people's utter unawareness of a discovery that might have saved countless fugitives and secret agents. In other words nobody, no forensic chemist not in the know, could suspect, let alone prove, that my passport was false. I do not know why I dwell on this subject with such tedious persistence. Probably, because I *otlynivayu* – 'shirk' – the task of describing my visit to Leningrad; yet I can't put it off any longer.

2

After almost three months of fretting I was ready to go. I felt lacquered from head to foot, like that naked ephebe, the bright *clou* of a pagan procession, who died of dermal asphyxia in his coat of golden varnish. A few days before my actual departure there occurred what seemed a harmless shift at the time. I was to wing off on a Thursday from Paris. On Monday a melodious female voice reached me at my nostalgically lovely hotel, rue Rivoli, to tell me that something – perhaps a hushed-up crash in a Soviet veil of mist – had clogged the general schedule and that I could board an Aeroflot turboprop to Moscow either this Wednesday or the next. I chose the former, of course, for it did not affect the date of my rendezvous.

My traveling companions were a few English and French tourists and a goodish bunch of gloomy officials from Soviet trade missions. Once inside the aircraft, a certain illusion of cheap unreality enveloped me – to linger about me for the rest of my trip. It was a very warm day in June and the farcical air-conditioning system failed to outvie the whiffs of sweat and the sprayings of *Krasnaya Moskva*, an insidious perfume which imbued even the hard candy (named *Ledenets vzlyotnyy*, 'take-off caramel,' on the wrapper) generously distributed to us before the start of the flight. Another fairy-tale touch was the bright dapple – yellow curlicues and violet eyespots – adorning the blinds. A similarly colored waterproof bag in the seat pocket before me was ominously labeled 'for waste disposal' – such as the disposal of my identity in that fairyland.

My mood and mental condition needed strong liquor rather than another round of *vzlyotnyy* or some nice reading matter; still I accepted a publicity magazine from a stout, unsmiling, bare-armed stewardess in sky blue, and was interested to learn that (in contrast to current triumphs) Russia had not done so well in the Soccer Olympics of 1912 when the 'Tsarist team' (consisting presumably of ten boyars and one bear) lost 12–0 to a German side.

I had taken a tranquilizer and hoped to sleep at least part of the way; but a first, and only, attempt at dozing off was resolutely thwarted by a still fatter stewardess, in a still stronger aura of onion sweat, asking me nastily to draw in the leg that I had stuck out too far into the aisle where she circulated with more and more publicity material. I envied darkly my windowside neighbor, an elderly Frenchman – or, anyway, scarcely a compatriot of mine – with a straggly gray-black beard and a terrible tie, who slept through the entire five-hour flight, disdaining the sardines and even the vodka which I could not resist, though I had a flask of better stuff in my hip pocket. Perhaps historians of photography could help me some day to define how, by precisely what indices, I am enabled to establish that the recollection of an anonymous unplaceable face goes back to 1930–1935, say, and not to 1945–1950. My neighbor was practically the twin of a person I had known in Paris, but who? A fellow writer? A concierge? A cobbler? The difficulty of determination grated less than the riddle of its limits as suggested by the degree of perceived 'shading' and the 'feel' of the image.

I got a closer but still more teasing look at him when, toward the close of our journey, my raincoat fell from the rack and landed upon him, and he grinned amiably enough as he emerged from under the sudden awakener. And I glimpsed again his fleshy profile and thick eyebrow while submitting for inspection the contents of my only valise and fighting the insane urge to question the propriety of the phrasing in the English form of the Customs Declaration: '. . . miniature graphics, slaughtered fowl, live animals and birds.'

I saw him again, but not as clearly, during our transfer by bus from one airport to another through some shabby environs of Moscow – a city which I had never seen in my life and which interested me about as much as, say, Birmingham. On the plane to Leningrad, however, he was again next to me, this time on the inner side. Mixed odors of dour hostess and 'Red Moscow,' with a gradual prevalence of the first ingredient, as our bare-armed angels multiplied their last ministrations, accompanied us from 21:18 to 22:33. In order to draw out my neighbor before he and his riddle vanished, I asked him, in French, if he knew anything about a picturesque group that had boarded our aircraft in Moscow. He replied, with a Parisian *grasseyement*, that they were, he believed, Iranian circus people touring Europe. The men looked like harlequins in mufti, the women like birds of paradise, the children like golden medallions, and there was one dark-haired pale beauty in black bolero and yellow sharovars who reminded me of Iris or a prototype of Iris.

'I hope,' I said, 'we'll see them perform in Leningrad.'

'Pouf!' he rejoined. 'They can't compete with our Soviet circus.'

I noted the automatic 'our.'

Both he and I were billeted in the Astoria, a hideous pile built around World War One, I think. The heavily bugged (I had been taught by Guy Gayley a way of finding that out in one gleeful twinkle) and therefore sheepish-looking room *'de luxe,'* with orange curtains and an orange-draped bed in its old-world alcove, did have a private bath as stipulated, but it took me some time to cope with a convulsive torrent of clay-colored water. 'Red Moscow's' last stand took place on a cake of incarnadine soap. 'Meals,' said a notice, 'may be served in the rooms.' For the heck of it I tried ordering an evening snack; nothing happened, and I spent another hungry hour in the recalcitrant restaurant. The Iron Curtain is really a lampshade: its variety here was gemmed with glass incrustations in a puzzle of petals. The *kotleta po kievski* I ordered took forty-four minutes to come from Kiev – and two seconds to be sent back as a non-cutlet, with a tiny oath (murmured in Russian) that made the waitress start and gape at me and my *Daily Worker*. The Caucasian wine was undrinkable.

A sweet little scene happened to be enacted as I hurried toward the lift, trying to recall where I had put my blessed Burpies. A flushed athletic *liftyorsha* wearing several bead necklaces was in the act of being replaced by a much older woman of the pensioned type, at whom she shouted while stomping out of the lift: *'Ya tebe eto popomnyu, sterva!* (I'll get even with you, dirty bitch)' – and proceeded to barge into me and almost knock me down (I am a large, but fluff-light old fellow). '*Shtoy-ty suyoshsya pod nogi?* (Why do you get underfoot?)' she cried in the same insolent tone of voice which left the night attendant quietly shaking her gray head all the way up to my floor.

Between two nights, two parts of a serial dream, in which I vainly tried to locate Bel's street (whose name, by a superstition current for centuries in conspiratorial circles, I had preferred not to be told), while knowing perfectly well that she lay bleeding and laughing in an alcove diagonally across the room, a few barefooted steps from my bed, I wandered about the city, idly trying to derive some emotional benefit from my being born there almost three-quarters of a century ago. Either because it could never get over the presence of the bog on which a popular bully had built it, or for some other reason (nobody, according to Gogol, knows), St. Petersburg was no place for children. I must have passed there insignificant parts of a few Decembers, and no doubt an April or two; but at least a dozen winters of my nineteen pre-Cambridge ones were spent on Mediterranean or Black Sea coasts. As to summers, to my young summers, all of them had bloomed for me on the great country estates of my family. Thus I realized with silly astonishment that, except for picture postcards (views of conventional public parks with lindens looking like oaks and a pistachio palace instead of the remembered pinkish one, and relentlessly gilded church domes – all of it under an Italianate sky), I had never seen my native city in June or July. Its aspect, therefore, evoked no thrill of recognition; it was an unfamiliar, if not utterly foreign, town, still lingering in some other era: an undefinable era, not exactly remote, but certainly preceding the invention of body deodorants.

Warm weather had come to stay, and everywhere, in travel agencies, in foyers, in waiting rooms, in general stores, in trolleybuses, in elevators, on escalators, in every damned corridor, everywhere, and especially where women worked, or had worked, invisible onion soup was cooking on invisible stoves. I was to remain only a couple of days in Leningrad and had not the time to get used to those infinitely sad emanations.

From travelers I knew that our ancestral mansion no longer existed, that the very lane where it had stood between two streets in the Fontanka area had been lost, like some connective tissue in the process of organic degeneration. What then succeeded in transfixing my memory? That sunset, with a triumph of bronze clouds and flamingo-pink meltings in the far-end archway of the Winter Canalet, might have been first seen in Venice. What else? The shadow of railings on granite? To be quite honest, only the dogs, the pigeons, the horses, and the very old, very meek cloakroom attendants seemed familiar to me. They, and perhaps the facade of a house on Gertsen Street. I may have gone there to some children's fête ages ago. The floral design running above the row of its upper windows caused an eerie shiver to pass through the root of wings that we all grow at such moments of dream-like recollection.

Dora was to meet me Friday morning on the Square of the Arts in front of the Russian Museum near the statue of Pushkin erected some ten years before by a committee of weathermen. An Intourist folder had yielded a tinted photograph of the spot. The meteorological associations of the monument predominated over its cultural ones. Frock-coated Pushkin, the right-side lap of his garment permanently agitated by the Nevan breeze rather than by the violence of lyrical afflatus, stands looking upward and to the left while his right hand is stretched out the other way, sidewise, to test the rain (a very natural attitude at the time lilacs bloom in the Leningrad parks). It had dwindled, when I arrived, to a warm drizzle, a mere murmur in the lindens above the long garden benches. Dora was supposed to be sitting on Pushkin's left, *id est* my right. The bench was empty and looked dampish. Three or four children, of the morose, drab, oddly old-fashioned aspect that Soviet kids have, could be seen on the other side of the pedestal, but otherwise I was loitering all alone, holding the *Humanité* in my hand instead of the *Worker* which I was supposed to signal with discreetly but had not been able to obtain that day. I was in the act of spreading the newspaper on the bench when a lady with the predicted limp came along a garden path toward me. She wore the, also expected, pastel-pink coat, had a clubfoot, and walked with the aid of a sturdy cane. She also carried a diaphanous little umbrella which had not figured in the list of attributes. I dissolved in tears at once (though I was farced with pills). Her gentle beautiful eyes were also wet.

Had I got A.B.'s telegram? Sent two days ago to my Paris address? Hotel Moritz?

'That's garbled,' I said, 'and besides I left earlier. Doesn't matter. Is she much worse?'

'No, no, on the contrary. I knew you would come all the same, but something has happened. Karl turned up on Tuesday while I was in the office and took her away. He also took my new suitcase. He has no sense of ownership. He will be shot some day like a common thief. The first time he got into trouble was when he kept declaring that Lincoln and Lenin were brothers. And last time –'

Nice voluble lady, Dora. What was Bel's illness exactly?

'Splenic anemia. And last time, he told his best student in the language school that the only thing people should do was to love one another and pardon their enemies.'

'An original mind. Where do you suppose –'

'Yes, but the best student was an informer, and Karlusha spent a year in a *tundrovyy* House of Rest. I don't know where he took her now. I even don't know whom to ask.'

'But there must be *some* way. She must be brought back, taken out of this hole, this hell.'

'That's impossible. She adores, she worships Karlusha. *C'est la vie*, as the Germans say. It's a pity A.B. is in Riga till the end of the month. You saw very little of him. Yes, it's a pity, he's a freak and a dear (*chudak i dushka*) with four nephews in Israel, which sounds, he says, as "the dramatic persons in a pseudoclassical play." One of them was my husband. Life gets sometimes very complicated, and the more com-plicated the happier it should be, one would think, but in reality "complicated" always means for some reason *grust' i toska* (sorrow and heartache).'

'But look here, can't *I* do something? Can't I sort of hang around and make inquiries, and perhaps seek advice from the Embassy –'

'She is not English any more and was never American. It's hopeless, I tell you. We were very close, she and I, in my very complicated life, but, imagine, Karl did not allow her to leave at least one little word for me – and for you, of course. She had informed him, unfortunately, that you were coming, and this he could not bear in spite of all the sympathy he works up for all unsympathetic people. You know, I saw your face last year – or was it two years ago? – two years, rather – in a Dutch or Danish magazine, and I would have recognized you at once, anywhere.'

'With the beard?'

'Oh, it does not change you one droplet. It's like wigs or green spectacles in old comedies. As a girl I dreamt of becoming a female clown, "Madam Byron," or "Trek Trek." But tell me, Vadim Vadimovich – I mean Gospodin Long – haven't they found you out? Don't they intend to make much of you? After all, you're the secret pride of Russia. Must you go now?'

I detached myself from the bench – with some scraps of *L'Humanité* attempting to follow me – and said, yes, I had better be going before the pride outstripped the prudence. I kissed her hand whereupon she remarked that she had seen it done only in a movie called *War and Peace*. I also begged her, under the dripping lilacs, to accept a wad of bank notes to be used for any purpose she wished including the price of that suitcase for her trip to Sochi. 'And he also took my whole set of safety pins,' she murmured with her all-beautifying smile.

3

I cannot be sure it was not again my fellow traveler, the black-hatted man, whom I saw hurrying away as I parted with Dora and our National Poet, leaving the latter to worry forever about all that wasted water (compare the Tsarskoselski Statue of a rock-dwelling maiden who mourns her broken but still brimming jar in one of his own poems); but I know I saw Monsieur Pouf at least twice in the restaurant of the Astoria, as well as in the corridor of the sleeping car on the night train that I took in order to catch the earliest Moscow–Paris plane. On that plane he was prevented from sitting next to me by the presence of an elderly American lady, with pink and violet wrinkles and rufous hair: we kept alternately chatting, dozing and drinking Bloody Marshas, *her* joke – not appreciated by our sky-blue hostess. It was delightful to observe the amazement expressed by old Miss Havemeyer (her rather incredible name) when I told her that I had spurned the Intourist's offer of a sightseeing tour of Leningrad; that I had not peeped into Lenin's room in the Smolny; had not visited one cathedral; had not eaten something called 'tabaka chicken'; and that I had left that beautiful, *beautiful* city without seeing a single ballet or variety show. 'I happen to be,' I explained, 'a triple agent and you know how it is –' 'Oh!' she exclaimed, with a pulling-away movement of the torso as if to consider me from a nobler angle. 'Oh! But that's vurry glamorous!'

I had to wait some time for my jet to New York, and being a little tight and rather pleased with my plucky journey (Bel, after all, was not too gravely ill and not too unhappily married; Rosabel sat reading, no doubt, a magazine in the living room, checking in it the Hollywood measurements of her leg, ankle 8½ inches, calf 12½, creamy thigh 19½; and Louise was in Florence or Florida). With a hovering grin, I noticed and picked up a paperback somebody had left on a seat next to mine in the transit lounge of the Orly airport. I was the mouse of fate on that pleasant June afternoon between a shop of wines and a shop of perfumes.

I held in my hands a copy of a Formosan (!) paperback reproduced from the American edition of *A Kingdom by the Sea*. I had not seen it yet – and preferred not to inspect the pox of misprints that, no doubt, disfigured the pirated text. On the cover a publicity picture of the child actress who had played my Virginia in the recent film did better justice to pretty Lola Sloan and her lollypop than to the significance of my novel. Although slovenly worded by a hack with no inkling of the book's art, the blurb on the back of the limp little volume rendered faithfully enough the factual plot of my *Kingdom*.

Bertram, an unbalanced youth, doomed to die shortly in an asylum for the criminal insane, sells for ten dollars his ten-year-old sister Ginny to the middle-aged bachelor Al Garden, a wealthy poet who travels with the beautiful child from resort to resort through America and other countries. A state of affairs that looks at first blush – and 'blush' is the right word – like a case of irresponsible perversion (described in brilliant detail never attempted before) develops by the grees [misprint] *into a genuine dialogue of tender love. Garden's feelings are reciprocated by Ginny, the initial 'victim' who at eighteen, a normal nymph, marries him in a warmly described religious ceremony. All seems to end honky-donky* [sic!] *in foreverlasting bliss of a sort fit to meet the sexual demands of the most rigid, or frigid, humanitarian, had there not been running its chaotic course, in a sheef* [sheaf?] *of parallel lives beyond our happy couple's ken, the tragic tiny* [destiny?] *of Virginia Garden's inconsolable parents, Oliver and* [?], *whom the clever author by every means in his power, prevents from tracking their daughter Dawn* [sic!!]. *A Book-of-the-Decade choice.*

I pocketed it upon noticing that my long-lost fellow-traveler, goat-bearded and black-hatted, as I knew him, had come up from the lavatory or the bar: Would he follow me to New York or was it to be our last meeting? Last, last. He had given himself away: the moment he came near, the moment his mouth opened in the tense-lower-lip shape that discharges, with a cheerless up-and-down shake of the head, the exclamation *'Ekh!,'* I knew not only that he was as Russian as I, but that the ancient acquaintance whom he resembled so strikingly was the father of a young poet, Oleg Orlov, whom I had met in Paris, in the Nineteen-Twenties. Oleg wrote 'poems in prose' (long after Turgenev), absolutely worthless stuff, which his father, a half-demented widower, would try to 'place,' pestering with his son's worthless wares the dozen or so periodicals of the emigration. He could be seen in the waiting room miserably fawning on a harassed and curt secretary, or attempting to waylay an assistant editor between office and toilet, or writing in stoic misery, at a corner of a crowded table, a special letter pleading the cause of some horrible little poem that had been already rejected. He died in the same Home for the Aged where Annette's mother had spent her last years. Oleg, in the meantime, had joined the small number of *littérateurs* who decided to sell the bleak liberty of expatriation for the rosy mess of Soviet pottage. His budtime had kept its promise. The best he had achieved during the last forty or fifty years was a medley of publicity pieces, commercial translations, vicious denunciations, and – in the domain of the arts – a prodigious resemblance to the physical aspect, voice, mannerisms, and obsequious impudence of his father.

'*Ekh!*' he exclaimed, '*Ekh*, Vadim Vadimovich *dorogoy* (dear), aren't you ashamed of deceiving our great warm-hearted country, our benevolent, credulous government, our overworked Intourist staff, in this nasty infantile manner! A Russian writer! Snooping! Incognito! By the way, I am Oleg Igorevich Orlov, we met in Paris when we were young.'

'What do you want, *merzavetz* (you scoundrel)?' I coldly inquired as he plopped into the chair on my left.

He raised both hands in the 'see-I'm-unarmed' gesture: 'Nothing, nothing. Except to ruffle (*potormoshit'*) your conscience. Two courses presented themselves. We had to choose. Fyodor Mihaylovich [?] himself had to choose. Either to welcome you *po amerikanski* (the American way) with reporters, interviews, photographers, girls, garlands, and, naturally, Fyodor Mihaylovich himself [President of the Union of Writers? Head of the "Big House"?]; or else to ignore you – and that's what we did. By the way: forged passports may be fun in detective stories, but our people are just not interested in passports. Aren't you sorry now?'

I made as if to move to another seat, but he made as if to accompany me there. So I stayed where I was, and feverishly grabbed something to read – that book in my coat pocket.

'*Et ce n'est pas tout!*' he went on. 'Instead of writing for us, your compatriots, you, a Russian writer of genius, betray them by concocting, for your paymasters, *this* (pointing with a dramatically quivering index at *A Kingdom by the Sea* in my hands), this obscene novelette about little Lola or Lotte, whom some Austrian Jew or reformed pederast rapes after murdering her mother – no, excuse me – *marrying* mama first before murdering her – we like to legalize everything in the West, don't we, Vadim Vadimovich?'

Still restraining myself, though aware of the uncontrollable cloud of black fury growing within my brain, I said: 'You are mistaken. You are a somber imbecile. The novel I wrote, the novel I'm holding now, is *A Kingdom by the Sea*. You are talking of some other book altogether.'

'*Vraiment?* And maybe you visited Leningrad merely to chat with a lady in pink under the lilacs? Because, you know, you and your friends are phenomenally naïve. The reason Mister (it rhymed with "Easter" in his foul serpent-mouth) Vetrov was permitted to leave a certain labor camp in Vadim – odd coincidence – so he might fetch his wife, is that he has been cured now of his mystical mania – cured by such nutcrackers, such shrinkers as are absolutely unknown in the philosophy of your Western *sharlatany*. Oh yes, precious (*dragotsennyy*) Vadim Vadimovich –'

The swing I dealt old Oleg with the back of my left fist was of quite presentable power, especially if we remember – and I remembered it as I swung – that our combined ages made 140.

There ensued a pause while I struggled back to my feet (unaccustomed momentum had somehow caused me to fall from my seat).

'*Nu, dali v mordu. Nu, tak chtozh?*' he muttered (Well, you've given me one in the mug. Well, what does it matter?). Blood blotched the handkerchief he applied to his fat muzhikian nose.

'*Nu, dali,*' he repeated and presently wandered away.

I looked at my knuckles. They were red but intact. I listened to my wristwatch. It ticked like mad.

PART SIX

I

Speaking of philosophy, I recalled when starting to readjust myself, very temporarily, to the corners and crannies of Quirn, that some- where in my office I kept a bundle of notes (on the Substance of Space), prepared formerly toward an account of my young years and nightmares (the work now known as *Ardis*). I also needed to sort out and remove from my office, or ruthlessly destroy, a mass of miscel- lanea which had accumulated ever since I began teaching.

That afternoon – a sunny and windy September afternoon – I had decided, with the unaccountable suddenness of genuine inspiration, that 1969–1970 would be my last term at Quirn University. I had, in fact, interrupted my siesta that day to request an immediate interview with the Dean. I thought his secretary sounded a little grumpy on the phone; true, I declined to explain anything beforehand, beyond confiding to her, in an informal bantering manner, that the numeral '7' always reminded me of the flag an explorer sticks in the cranium of the North Pole.

After setting out on foot and reaching the seventh poplar I realized that there might be quite a load of papers to bring from my office, so I went back for my car, and then had difficulty in finding a place to park near the library where I intended to return a number of books which were months, if not years, overdue. In result, I was a little late for my appointment with the Dean, a new man and not my best reader. He consulted, rather demonstratively, the clock and muttered he had a 'conference' in a few minutes at some other place, probably invented.

I was amused rather than surprised by the vulgar joy he did not trouble to conceal at the news of my resignation. He hardly heard the reasons which common courtesy impelled me to give (frequent headaches, boredom, the efficiency of modern recording, the comfortable income my recent novel supplied, and so forth). His whole manner changed – to use a cliché he deserves. He paced to and fro, positively beaming. He grasped my hand in a burst of brutal effusion. Certain fastidious blue-blooded animals prefer surrendering a limb to the predator rather than suffer ignoble contact. I left the Dean encumbered with a marble arm that he kept carrying in his prowlings like a trayed trophy, not knowing where to put it down.

So off to my office I stalked, a happy amputee, more than ever eager to clean up drawers and shelves. I began, however, by dashing off a note to the President of the University, another new man, informing him with a touch of French *malice*, rather than English 'malice,' that my entire set of one hundred lectures on European Masterpieces was about to be sold to a generous publisher who offered me an advance of half-a-million bucks (a salubrious exaggeration), thus making transmissions of my course no longer available to students, best regards, sorry not to have met you personally.

In the name of moral hygiene I had got rid long ago of my Bechstein desk. Its considerably smaller substitute contained note paper, scratch paper, office envelopes, photostats of my lectures, a copy of *Dr. Olga Repnin* (hardback) which I had intended for a colleague (but had spoiled by misspelling his name), and a pair of warm gloves belonging to my assistant (and successor) Exkul. Also three boxfuls of paper clips and a half-empty flask of whisky. From the shelves, I swept into the wastebasket, or onto the floor in its vicinity, heaps of circulars, separata, a displaced ecologist's paper on the ravages committed by a bird of some sort, the *Ozimaya Sovka* ('Lesser Winter-Crop Owl'?), and the tidily bound page proofs (mine always come in the guise of long, horribly slippery and unwieldy snakes) of picaresque trash, full of cricks and punts, imposed on me by proud publishers hoping for a rave from the lucky bastard. A mess of business correspondence and my tractatule on Space I stuffed into a large worn folder. Adieu, lair of learning!

Coincidence is a pimp and cardsharper in ordinary fiction but a marvelous artist in the patterns of fact recollected by a non-ordinary memoirist. Only asses and geese think that the re-collector skips this or that bit of his past because it is dull or shoddy (that sort of episode here, for example, the interview with the Dean, and how scrupulously it is recorded!). I was on the way to the parking lot when the bulky folder under my arm – replacing my arm, as it were – burst its string and spilled its contents all over the gravel and grassy border. You were coming from the library along the same campus path, and we crouched side by side collecting the stuff. You were pained you said later (*zhalostno bylo*) to smell the liquor on my breath. On the breath of that great writer.

I say 'you' retroconsciously, although in the logic of life you were not 'you' yet, for we were not actually acquainted and you were to become really 'you' only when you said, catching a slip of yellow paper that was availing itself of a bluster to glide away with false insouciance:

'No, you don't.'

Crouching, smiling, you helped me to cram everything again into the folder and then asked me how my daughter was – she and you had been schoolmates some fifteen years ago, and my wife had given you a lift several times. I then remembered your name and in a photic flash of celestial color saw you and Bel looking like twins, silently hating each other, both in blue coats and white hats, waiting to be driven somewhere by Louise. Bel and you would both be twenty-eight on January 1, 1970.

A yellow butterfly settled briefly on a clover head, then wheeled away in the wind.

'*Metamorphoza*,' you said in your lovely, elegant Russian.

Would I care to have some snapshots (additional snapshots) of Bel? Bel feeding a chipmunk? Bel at the school dance? (Oh, I remember that dance – she had chosen for escort a sad fat Hungarian boy whose father was assistant manager of the Quilton Hotel – I can still hear Louise snorting!)

We met next morning in my carrel at the College Library, and after that I continued to see you every day. I will not suggest, LATH is not meant to suggest, that the petals and plumes of my previous loves are dulled or coarsened when directly contrasted with the purity of your being, the magic, the pride, the reality of your radiance. Yet 'reality' *is* the key word here; and the gradual perception of that reality was nearly fatal to me.

Reality would be only adulterated if I now started to narrate what you know, what I know, what nobody else knows, what shall never, never be ferreted out by a matter-of-fact, father-of-muck, mucking biograffitist. And how did your affair develop, Mr. Blong? Shut up, Ham Godman! And when did you decide to leave together for Europe? Damn you, Ham!

See under Real, my first novel in English, thirty-five years ago!

One little item of subhuman interest I can disclose, however, in this interview with posterity. It is a foolish, embarrassing trifle and I never told you about it, so here goes. It was on the eve of our departure, around March 15, 1970, in a New York hotel. You were out shopping. ('I think' – you said to me just now when I tried to check that detail without telling you why – 'I think I bought a beautiful blue suitcase with a zipper' – miming the word with a little movement of your dear delicate hand – 'which proved to be absolutely useless.') I stood before the closet mirror of my bedroom in the north end of our pretty 'suite,' and proceeded to take a final decision. All right, I could not live without you; but was I worthy of you – I mean, in body and spirit? I was forty-three years older than you. The Frown of Age, two deep lines forming a capital lambda, ascended between my eyebrows. My forehead, with its three horizontal wrinkles that had not really overasserted themselves in the last three decades, remained round, ample and smooth, waiting for the summer tan that would scumble, I knew, the liver spots on my temples. All in all, a brow to be enfolded and fondled. A thorough haircut had done away with the leonine locks; what remained was of a neutral, grayish-dun tint. My large handsome glasses magnified the senile group of wart-like little excrescences under each lower eyelid. The eyes, once an irresistible hazel-green, were now oysterous. The nose, inherited from a succession of Russian boyars, German barons, and, perhaps (if Count Starov who sported some English blood was my real father), at least one Peer of the Realm, had retained its bone hump and tip rime, but had developed on the frontal flesh, within its owner's memory, an aggravating gray hairlet that grew faster and faster between yanks. My dentures did not do justice to my former attractively irregular teeth and (as I told an expensive but obtuse dentist who did not understand what I meant) 'seemed to ignore my smile.' A furrow sloped down from each nosewing, and a jowl pouch on each side of my chin formed in three-quarter-face the banal flexure common to old men of all races, classes, and professions. I doubted that I had been right in shaving off my glorious beard and the trim mustache that had lingered, on try, for a week or so after my return from Leningrad. Still, I passed my face, giving it a C-minus mark.

Since I had never been much of an athlete, the deterioration of my body was neither very marked, nor very interesting. I gave it a C plus, mainly for my routing tank after tank of belly fat in a war with obesity waged between intervals of retreat and rest since the middle Fifties. Apart from incipient lunacy (a problem with which I prefer to deal separately), I had been in excellent health throughout adulthood.

What about the state of my art? What could I offer to you there? You had studied, as I hope you recall, Turgenev in Oxford and Bergson in Geneva, but thanks to family ties with good old Quirn and Russian New York (where a last *émigré* periodical was still deploring, with idiotic innuendoes, my 'apostasy') you had followed pretty closely, as I discovered, the procession of my Russian and English harlequins, followed by a tiger or two, scarlet-tongued, and a libellula girl on an elephant. You had also studied those obsolete photocopies – which proved that my method *avait du bon* after all – *pace* the monstrous accusations leveled at them by a pack of professors in envious colleges.

As I peered, stripped naked and traversed by opaline rays, into another, far deeper mirror, I saw the whole vista of my Russian books and was satisfied and even thrilled by what I saw: *Tamara*, my first novel (1925): a girl at sunrise in the mist of an orchard. A grandmaster betrayed in *Pawn Takes Queen*. *Plenilune*, a moonburst of verse. *Camera Lucida*, the spy's mocking eye among the meek blind. The *Red Top Hat* of decapitation in a country of total injustice. And my best in the series: young poet writes prose on a *Dare*.

That Russian batch of my books was finished and signed and thrust back into the mind that had produced them. All of them had been gradually translated into English either by myself or under my direction, with my revisions. Those final English versions as well as the reprinted originals would be now dedicated to you. That was good. That was settled. Next picture:

My English originals, headed by the fierce *See under Real* (1940), led through the changing light of *Esmeralda and Her Parandrus*, to the fun of *Dr. Olga Repnin* and the dream of *A Kingdom by the Sea*. There was also the collection of short stories *Exile from Mayda*, a distant island; and *Ardis*, the work I had resumed at the time we met – at the time, too, of a deluge of postcards (postcards!) from Louise hinting at last at a move which I wanted her to be the first to make.

If I estimated the second batch at a lower value than the first, it was owing not only to a diffidence some will call coy, others, commendable, and myself, tragic, but also because the contours of my American production looked blurry to me; and they looked that way because I knew I would always keep hoping that my *next* book – not simply the one in progress, like *Ardis* – but something I had never attempted yet, something miraculous and unique, would at last answer fully the craving, the aching thirst that a few disjunct paragraphs in *Esmeralda* and *The Kingdom* were insufficient to quench. I believed I could count on your patience.

2

I had not the slightest desire to reimburse Louise for being forced to shed me; and I hesitated to embarrass her by supplying my lawyer with the list of her betrayals. They were stupid and sordid, and went back to the days when I still was reasonably faithful to her. The 'divorce dialogue,' as Horace Peppermill, Junior, horribly called it, dragged on during the entire spring: You and I spent part of it in London and the rest in Taormina, and I kept putting off talks of *our* marriage (a delay you regarded with royal indifference). What really bothered me was having also to postpone the tedious statement (to be repeated for the fourth time in my life) that would have to precede any such talks. I fumed. It was a shame to leave you in the dark regarding my derangement.

Coincidence, the angel with the eyed wings mentioned before, spared me the humiliating rigmarole that I had found necessary to go through before proposing to each of my former wives. On June 15, at Gandora, in the Tessin, I received a letter from young Horace giving me excellent news: Louise had discovered (*how* does not matter) that at various periods of our marriage I had had her shadowed, in all sorts of fascinating old cities, by a private detective (Dick Cockburn, a staunch friend of mine); that the tapes of love calls and other documents were in my lawyer's hands; and that she was ready to make every possible concession to speed up matters, being anxious to marry again – this time the son of an Earl. And on the same fatidic day, at a quarter past five in the afternoon, I finished transcribing on 733 medium-sized Bristol cards (each holding about 100 words), with a fine-nibbed pen and in my smallest fair-copy hand, *Ardis*, a stylized memoir dealing with the arbored boyhood and ardent youth of a great thinker who by the end of the book tackles the itchiest of all noumenal mysteries. One of the early chapters contained an account (couched in an overtly personal, intolerably tortured tone) of my own tussles with the Specter of Space and the myth of Cardinal Points.

By 5:30 I had consumed, in a fit of private celebration, most of the caviar and all the champagne in the friendly fridge of our bungalow on the green grounds of the Gandora Palace Hotel. I found you on the veranda and told you I would like you to devote the next hour to reading attentively –

'I read everything attentively.'

'– this batch of thirty cards from *Ardis*.' After which I thought you might meet me somewhere on my way back from my late-afternoon stroll: always the same – to the *spartitraffico* fountain (ten minutes) and thence to the edge of a pine plantation (another ten minutes). I left you reclining in a lounge chair with the sun reproducing the amethyst lozenges of the veranda windows on the floor, and barring your bare shins and the insteps of your crossed feet (right toe twitching now and then in some obscure connection with the tempo of assimilation or a twist in the text). In a matter of minutes you would have learned (as only Iris had learned before you – the others were no eaglesses) what I wished you to be aware of when consenting to be my wife.

'Careful, please, when you cross,' you said, without raising your eyes but then looking up and tenderly pursing your lips before going back to *Ardis*.

Ha! Weaving a little! Was that really I, Prince Vadim Blonsky, who in 1815 could have outdrunk Pushkin's mentor, Kaverin? In the golden light of a mere quart of the stuff all the trees in the hotel park looked like araucarias. I congratulated myself on the neatness of my stratagem though not quite knowing whether it concerned my third wife's recorded frolics or the disclosure of my infirmity through a bloke in a book. Little by little the soft spicy air did me good: my soles clung more firmly to gravel and sand, clay and stone. I became aware that I had gone out wearing morocco slippers and a torn, bleached denim trousers-and-top with, paradoxically, my passport in one nipple pocket and a wad of Swiss bank notes in the other. Local people in

Gandino or Gandora, or whatever the town was called, knew the face of the author of *Un regno sul mare* or *Ein Königreich an der See* or *Un Royaume au Bord de la Mer*, so it would have been really fatuous on my part to prepare the cue and the cud for the reader in case a car was really to hit me.

Soon I was feeling so happy and bright that when I passed by the sidewalk café just before reaching the square, it seemed a good idea to stabilize the fizz still ascending in me by means of a jigger of something – and yet I demurred, and passed by, cold-eyed, knowing how sweetly, yet firmly, you disapproved of the most innocent tippling.

One of the streets projecting west beyond the traffic island traversed the Corso Orsini and immediately afterwards, as if having achieved an exhausting feat, degenerated into a soft dusty old road with traces of gramineous growth on both sides, but none of pavement.

I could say what I do not remember having been moved to say in years, namely: My happiness was complete. As I walked, I read those cards with you, at your pace, your diaphanous index at my rough peeling temple, my wrinkled finger at your turquoise temple-vein. I caressed the facets of the Blackwing pencil you kept gently twirling, I felt against my raised knees the fifty-year-old folded chessboard, Nikifor Starov's gift (most of the noblemen were badly chipped in their baize-lined mahogany box!), propped on your skirt with its pattern of irises. My eyes moved with yours, my pencil queried with your own faint little cross in the narrow margin a solecism I could not distinguish through the tears of space. Happy tears, radiant, shamelessly happy tears!

A goggled imbecile on a motorcycle who I thought had seen me and would slow down to let me cross Corso Orsini in peace swerved so clumsily to avoid killing me that he skidded and ended up facing me some way off after an ignominious wobble. I ignored his roar of hate and continued my steady stroll westward in the changed surroundings I have already mentioned. The practically rural old road crept between modest villas, each in its nest of tall flowers and spreading trees. A rectangle of cardboard on one of the west-side wickets said 'Rooms' in German; on the opposite side an old pine supported a sign 'For Sale' in Italian. Again on the left, a more sophisticated houseowner offered 'Lunchings.' Still fairly far was the green vista of the *pineta*.

My thoughts reverted to *Ardis*. I knew that the bizarre mental flaw you were now reading about would pain you; I also knew that its display was a mere formality on my part and could not obstruct the natural flow of our common fate. A gentlemanly gesture. In fact, it might compensate for what you did not yet know, what I would have to tell you too, what I suspected you would call the not quite savory little method (*gnusnovaten'kiy sposob*) of my 'getting even' with Louise. All right – but what about *Ardis*? Apart from my warped mind, did you like it or loathe it?

Composing, as I do, whole books in my mind before releasing the inner word and taking it down in pencil or pen, I find that the final text remains for a while committed to memory, as distinct and perfect as the floating imprint that a light bulb leaves on the retina. I was able therefore to rerun the actual images of those cards you read: they were projected on the screen of my fancy together with the gleam of your topaz ring and the beat of your eyelashes, and I could calculate how far you had read not simply by consulting my watch but by actually following one line after the other to the right-hand brink of each card. The lucidity of the image was correlated with the quality of the writing. You knew my work too well to be ruffled by a too robust erotic detail, or annoyed by a too recondite literary allusion. It was bliss reading *Ardis* with you that way, triumphing that way over the stretch of colored space separating my lane from your lounge chair. Was I an excellent writer? I was an excellent writer. That avenue of statues and lilacs where Ada and I drew our first circles on the dappled sand was visualized and re-created by an artist of lasting worth. The hideous suspicion that even *Ardis*, my most private book, soaked in reality, saturated with sun flecks, might be an unconscious imitation of another's unearthly art, *that* suspicion might come later; at the moment – 6:18 P.M. on June 15, 1970, in the Tessin – nothing could scratch the rich humid gloss of my happiness.

I was now reaching the end of my usual preprandial walk. The *ra-ta-ta, ta-ta, tac* of a typist's finishing a last page came from a window through motionless foliage, reminding me pleasantly that I had long since eschewed the long labor of having my immaculate manuscripts typed when they could be reproduced photographically in one hum. It was now the publisher who bore the brunt of having my hand transformed directly into printed characters; and I know he disliked the procedure as a well-bred entomologist may find revolting an irregular insect's skipping some generally accepted stage of metamorphosis.

Only a few steps – twelve, eleven – remained before I would start to walk back: I felt you were thinking of this in a reversal of distant perception, just as I felt a kind of mental loosening, which told me you had finished reading those thirty cards, placed them in their proper order, tidied the stack by knocking its base slightly against the table, found the elastic lying there in the assumed shape of a heart, banded the batch, carried it to the safety of my desk, and were now preparing to meet me on my way back to Gandora Palace.

A low wall of gray stone, waist-high, paunch-thick, built in the general shape of a transversal parapet, put an end to whatever life the road still had as a town street. A narrow passage for pedestrians and cyclists divided the parapet in the middle, and the width of that gap was preserved beyond it in a path which after a flick or two slithered into a fairly dense young pinewood. You and I had rambled there many times on gray mornings, when lakeside or poolside lost all attraction; but that evening, as usual, I terminated my stroll at the parapet, and stood in perfect repose, facing the low sun, my spread hands enjoying the smoothness of its top edge on both sides of the passage. A tactile something, or the recent *ra-ta-tac*, brought back and completed the image of my 733, twelve centimeters by ten-and-a-half Bristol cards, which you would read chapter by chapter whereupon a great pleasure, a parapet of pleasure, would perfect my task: in my mind there arose, endowed with the clean-cut compactness of some great solid – an altar! a mesa! – the image of the shiny photocopier in one of the offices of our hotel. My trustful hands were still spread, but my soles no longer sensed the soft soil. I wished to go back to you, to life, to the amethyst lozenges, to the pencil lying on the veranda table, and I could not. What used to happen so often in thought, now had happened for keeps: I could not turn. To make that movement would mean rolling the world around on its axis and that was as impossible as traveling back physically from the present moment to the previous one. Maybe I should not have panicked, should have waited quietly for the stone of my limbs to regain some tingle of flesh. Instead, I performed, or imagined performing, a wild wrenching movement – and the globe did not bulge. I must have hung in a spread-eagle position for a little while longer before ending supine on the intangible soil.

PART SEVEN

I

There exists an old rule – so old and trite that I blush to mention it. Let me twist it into a jingle – to stylize the staleness:

> The I of the book
> Cannot die in the book.

I am speaking of serious novels, naturally. In so-called *Planchette-Fiction* the unruffled narrator, after describing his own dissolution, can continue thus: 'I found myself standing on a staircase of onyx before a great gate of gold in a crowd of other bald-headed angels . . .'

Cartoon stuff, folklore rubbish, hilarious atavistic respect for precious minerals!

And yet –

And yet I feel that during three weeks of general paresis (if that is what it was) I have gained some experience; that when my night really comes I shall not be totally unprepared. Problems of identity have been, if not settled, at least set. Artistic insights have been granted. I was allowed to take my palette with me to very remote reaches of dim and dubious being.

Speed! If I could have given my definition of death to the stunned fisherman, to the mower who stopped wiping his scythe with a handful of grass, to the cyclist embracing in terror a willow sapling on one green bank and actually getting up to the top of a taller tree on the opposite side with his machine and girlfriend, to the black horses gaping at me like people with trick dentures all through my strange skimming progress, I would have cried one word: Speed! Not that those rural witnesses ever existed. My impression of prodigious, inexplicable, and to tell the truth rather silly and degrading speed (death is silly, death is degrading) would have been conveyed to a perfect void, without one fisherman tearing by, without one blade of grass bloodied by his catch, without any reference mark altogether. Imagine me, an old gentleman, a distinguished author, gliding rapidly on my back, in the wake of my outstretched dead feet, first through that gap in the granite, then over a pinewood, then along misty water meadows, and then simply between marges of mist, on and on, imagine that sight!

Madness had been lying in wait for me behind this or that alder or boulder since infancy. I got used by degrees to feeling the sepia stare of those watchful eyes as they moved smoothly along the line of my passage. Yet I have known madness not only in the guise of an evil shadow. I have seen it also as a flash of delight so rich and shattering that the very absence of an immediate object on which it might settle was to me a form of escape.

For practical purposes, such as keeping body-mind and mind-body in a state of ordinary balance, so as not to imperil one's life or become a burden to friends or governments, I preferred the latent variety, the awfulness of that watchful thing that meant at best the stab of neuralgia, the distress of insomnia, the battle with inanimate things which have never disguised their hatred of me (the runaway button which *condescends* to be located, the paper clip, a thievish slave, not content to hold a couple of humdrum letters, but managing to catch a precious leaf from another batch), and at worst a sudden spasm of space as when the visit to one's dentist turns into a burlesque party. I preferred the muddle of such attacks to the motley of madness which, after pretending to adorn my existence with special forms of inspiration, mental ecstasy, and so forth, would stop dancing and flitting around me and would pounce upon me, and cripple me, and for all I know destroy me.

2

At the start of the great seizure, I must have been totally incapacitated, from top to toe, while my mind, the images racing through me, the tang of thought, the genius of insomnia, remained as strong and active as ever (except for the blots in between). By the time I had been flown to the Lecouchant Hospital in coastal France, highly recommended by Dr. Genfer, a Swiss relative of its director, I became aware of certain curious details: from the head down I was paralyzed in symmetrical patches separated by a geography of weak tactility. When in the course of that first week my fingers 'awoke' (a circumstance that stupefied and even angered the Lecouchant sages, experts in dementia paralytica, to such a degree that they advised you to rush me off to some more exotic and broadminded institution – which you did) I derived much entertainment from mapping my sensitive spots which were always situated in exact opposition, e.g. on both sides of my forehead, on the jaws, orbital parts, breasts, testicles, knees, flanks. At an average stage of observation, the average size of each spot of life never exceeded that of Australia (I felt gigantic at times) and never dwindled (when I dwindled myself) below the diameter of a medal of medium merit, at which level I perceived my entire skin as that of a leopard painted by a meticulous lunatic from a broken home.

In some connection with those 'tactile symmetries' (about which I am still attempting to correspond with a not too responsive medical journal, swarming with Freudians), I would like to place the first pictorial compositions, flat, primitive images, which occurred in duplicate, right and left of my traveling body, on the opposite panels of my hallucinations. If, for example, Annette boarded a bus with her empty basket on the left of my being, she came out of that bus on my right with a load of vegetables, a royal cauliflower presiding over the cucumbers. As the days passed, the symmetries got replaced by more elaborate inter-responses, or reappeared in miniature within the limits of a given image. Picturesque episodes now accompanied my mysterious voyage. I glimpsed Bel rummaging after work amidst a heap of naked babies at the communal day-nursery, in frantic search for her own firstborn, now ten months old, and recognizable by the symmetrical blotches of red eczema on its sides and little legs. A glossy-haunched swimmer used one hand to brush away from her face wet strands of hair, and pushed with the other (on the *other* side of my mind) the raft on which I lay, a naked old man with a rag around his foremast, gliding supine into a full moon whose snaky reflections rippled among the water lilies. A long tunnel engulfed me, half-promised a circlet of light at its far end, half-kept the promise, revealing a publicity sunset, but I never reached it, the tunnel faded, and a familiar mist took over again. As was 'done' that season, groups of smart idlers visited my bed, which had slowed down in a display hall where Ivor Black in the role of a fashionable young doctor demonstrated me to three actresses playing society belles: their skirts ballooned as they settled down on white chairs, and one lady, indicating my groin, would have touched me with her cold fan, had not the learned Moor struck it aside with his ivory pointer, whereupon my raft resumed its lone glide.

Whoever charted my destiny had moments of triteness. At times my swift course became a celestial affair at an allegorical altitude that bore unpleasant religious connotations – unless simply reflecting transportation of cadavers by commercial aircraft. A certain notion of daytime and nighttime, in more or less regular alternation, gradually established itself in my mind as my grotesque adventure reached its final phase. Diurnal and nocturnal effects were rendered obliquely at first with nurses and other stagehands going to extreme lengths in the handling of movable properties, such as the bouncing of fake starlight from reflecting surfaces or the daubing of dawns here and there at suitable intervals. It had never occurred to me before that, historically, art, or at least artifacts, had preceded, not followed, nature; yet that is exactly what happened in my case. Thus, in the mute remoteness clouding around me, recognizable sounds were produced at first optically in the pale margin of the film track during the taking of the actual scene (say, the ceremony of scientific feeding); eventually something about the running ribbon tempted the ear to replace the eye; and finally hearing returned – with a vengeance. The first crisp nurse-rustle was a thunderclap; my first belly wamble, a crash of cymbals.

I owe thwarted obituarists, as well as all lovers of medical lore, some clinical elucidations. My lungs and my heart acted, or were induced to act, normally; so did my bowels, those buffoons in the cast of our private miracle plays. My frame lay flat as in an Old Master's Lesson of Anatomy. The prevention of bedsores, especially at the Lecouchant Hospital, was nothing short of a mania, explicable, maybe, by a desperate urge to substitute pillows and various mechanical devices for the rational treatment of an unfathomable disease. My body was 'sleeping' as a giant's foot might be 'sleeping'; more accurately, however, my condition was a horrible form of protracted (twenty nights!) insomnia with my mind as consistently alert as that of the Sleepless Slav in some circus show I once read about in *The Graphic*. I was not even a mummy; I was – in the beginning, at least – the longitudinal section of a mummy, or rather the abstraction of its thinnest possible cut. What about the head? – readers who are all head must be clamoring to be told. Well, my brow was like misty glass (before two lateral spots got cleared somehow or other); my mouth stayed mute and benumbed until I realized I could feel my tongue – feel it in the phantom form of the kind of air bladder that might help a fish with his respiration problems, but was useless to me. I had some sense of duration and direction – two things which a beloved creature seeking to help a poor madman with the whitest of lies, affirmed, in a later world, were quite separate phases of a single phenomenon. Most of my cerebral aqueduct (this is getting a little technical) seemed to descend wedgewise, after some derail-ment or inundation, into the structure housing its closest ally – which oddly enough is also our humblest sense, the easiest and sometimes the most gratifying to dispense with – and, oh, how I cursed it when

I could not close it to ether or excrements, and, oh (cheers for old 'oh'), how I thanked it for crying 'Coffee!' or *'Plage!'* (because an anonymous drug smelled like the cream Iris used to rub my back with in Cannice half a century ago!).

Now comes a snaggy bit: I do not know if my eyes remained always wide open 'in a glazed look of arrogant stupor' as imagined by a reporter who got as far as the corridor desk. But I doubt very much I could blink – and without the oil of blinking the motor of sight could hardly have run. Yet, somehow, during my glide down those illusory canals and cloudways, and right over another continent, I did glimpse off and on, through subpalpebral mirages, the shadow of a hand or the glint of an instrument. As to my world of sound, it remained solid fantasy. I heard strangers discuss in droning voices all the books I had written or thought I had written, for everything they mentioned, titles, the names of characters, every phrase they shouted was preposterously distorted by the delirium of demonic scholarship. Louise regaled the company with one of her good stories – those I called 'name hangers' because they only *seemed* to reach this or that point – a *quid pro quo*, say, at a party – but were really meant to introduce some high-born 'old friend' of hers, or a glamorous politician, or a cousin of that politician. Learned papers were read at fantastic symposiums. In the year of grace 1798, Gavrila Petrovich Kamenev, a gifted young poet, was heard chuckling as he composed his Ossianic pastiche *Slovo o polku Igoreve*. Somewhere in Abyssinia drunken Rimbaud was reciting to a surprised Russian traveler the poem *Le Tramway ivre* (. . . *En blouse rouge, à face en pis de vache, le bourreau me trancha la tête aussi* . . .). Or else I'd hear the pressed repeater hiss in a pocket of my brain and tell the time, the rime, the meter that who could dream I'd hear again?

I should also point out that my flesh was in fairly good shape: no ligaments torn, no muscles trapped; my spinal cord may have been slightly bruised during the absurd collapse that precipitated my voyage but it was still there, lining me, shading my being, as good as the primitive structure of some translucent aquatic creature. Yet the medical treatment I was subjected to (especially at the Lecouchant place) implied – insofar as now reconstructed – that my injuries were all physical, only physical, and could be only dealt with by physical means. I am not speaking of modern alchemy, of magic philtres injected into me – those did, perhaps, act somehow, not only on my body, but also on the divinity installed within me, as might the suggestions of ambitious shamans or quaking councilors upon a mad emperor; what I cannot get over are such imprinted images as the damned braces and belts that held me stretched on my back (preventing me from walking away with my rubber raft under my arm as I felt I could), or even worse the man-made electric leeches, which masked executioners attached to my head and limbs – until chased away by that saint in Catapult, Cal., Professor H. P. Sloan, who was on the brink of suspecting, just when I started to get well, that I might be cured – might have been cured! – in a trice by hypnosis and some sense of humor on the hypnotist's part.

3

To the best of my knowledge my Christian name was Vadim; so was my father's. The U.S.A. passport recently issued me – an elegant booklet with a golden design on its green cover perforated by the number 00678638 – did not mention my ancestral title; this had figured, though, on my British passport, throughout its several editions. Youth, Adulthood, Old Age, before the last one was mutilated beyond recognition by friendly forgers, practical jokers at heart. All this I re-gleaned one night, as certain brain cells, which had been frozen, now bloomed anew. Others, however, still puckered like retarded buds, and although I could freely twiddle (for the first time since I collapsed) my toes under the bedclothes, I just could not make out in that darker corner of my mind what surname came after my Russian patronymic. I felt it began with an *N*, as did the term for the beautifully spontaneous arrangement of words at moments of inspiration like the rouleaux of red corpuscles in freshly drawn blood under the microscope – a word I once used in *See under Real*, but could not remember either, something to do with a roll of coins, capitalistic metaphor, eh, Marxy? Yes, I definitely felt my family name began with an *N* and bore an odious resemblance to the surname or pseudonym of a presumably notorious (Notorov? No) Bulgarian, or Babylonian, or, maybe, Betelgeusian writer with whom scatterbrained *émigrés* from some other galaxy constantly confused me; but whether it was something on the lines of Nebesnyy or Nabedrin or Nablidze (Nablidze? Funny) I simply could not tell. I preferred not to overtax my willpower (go away, Naborcroft) and so gave up trying – or perhaps it began with a *B* and the *n* just clung to it like some desperate parasite? (Bonidze? Blonsky? – No, that belonged to the BINT business.) Did I have some princely

Caucasian blood? Why had allusions to a Mr. Nabarro, a British politician, cropped up among the clippings I received from England concerning the London edition of *A Kingdom by the Sea* (lovely lilting title)? Why did Ivor call me 'MacNab'?

Without a name I remained unreal in regained consciousness. Poor Vivian, poor Vadim Vadimovich, was but a figment of somebody's – not even my own – imagination. One dire detail: in rapid Russian speech longish name-and-patronymic combinations undergo familiar slurrings: thus 'Pavel Pavlovich,' Paul, son of Paul, when casually interpellated is made to sound like 'Pahlpahlych' and the hardly utterable, tapeworm-long 'Vladimir Vladimirovich' becomes colloquially similar to 'Vadim Vadimych.'

I gave up. And when I gave up for good my sonorous surname crept up from behind, like a prankish child that makes a nodding old nurse jump at his sudden shout.

There remained other problems. Where was I? What about a little light? How did one tell by touch a lamp's button from a bell's button in the dark. What was, apart from my own identity, that other person, promised to me, belonging to me? I could locate the bluish blinds of twin windows. Why not uncurtain them?

> *Tak, vdol' naklónnogo luchá*
> *Ya výshel iz paralichá.*
>
> *Along a slanting ray, like this*
> *I slipped out of paralysis.*

– if 'paralysis' is not too strong a word for the condition that mimicked it (with some obscure help from the patient): a rather quaint but not too serious psychological disorder – or at least so it seemed in lighthearted retrospect.

I was prepared by certain indices for spells of dizziness and nausea but I did not expect my legs to misbehave as they did, when – unbuckled and alone – I blithely stepped out of bed on that first night of recovery. Beastly gravity humiliated me at once: my legs telescoped under me. The crash brought in the night nurse, and she helped me back into bed. After that I slept. Never before or since did I sleep more deliciously.

One of the windows was wide open when I woke up. My mind and my eye were by now sufficiently keen to make out the medicaments on my bedside table. Amidst its miserable population I noticed a few stranded travelers from another world: a transparent envelope with a non-masculine handkerchief found and laundered by the staff; a diminutive golden pencil belonging to the eyelet of a congeric agenda in a vanity bag; a pair of harlequin sunglasses, which for some reason suggested not protection from a harsh light but the masking of tear-swollen lids. The combination of those ingredients resulted in a dazzling pyrotechny of sense; and next moment (coincidence was still on my side) the door of my room moved: a small soundless move that came to a brief soundless stop and then was continued in a slow, infinitely slow sequence of suspension dots in diamond type. I emitted a bellow of joy, and Reality entered.

4

With the following gentle scene I propose to conclude this autobiography. I had been wheeled into the rose-twined gallery for Special
Convalescents in the second and last of my hospitals. You were
reclining in a lounge chair beside me, in much the same attitude in
which I had left you on June 15, at Gandora. You complained gaily
that a woman in the room next to yours on the ground floor of the
annex had a phonograph playing bird-call records, by means of which
she hoped to make the mockingbirds of the hospital park imitate the
nightingales and thrushes of her place in Devon or Dorset. You knew
very well I wished to find out something. We both hedged. I drew
your attention to the beauty of the climbing roses. You said: 'Everything is beautiful against the sky (*na fone neba*)' and apologized for
the 'aphorism.' At last, in the most casual of tones I asked how you
had liked the fragment of *Ardis* I gave you to read just before taking
the little walk from which I had returned only now, three weeks later,
in Catapult, California.

You looked away. You considered the mauve mountains. You
cleared your throat and bravely replied that you had not liked it at all.

Meaning she would not marry a madman?

Meaning she would marry a sane man who could tell the difference
between time and space.

Explain.

She was awfully eager to read the rest of the manuscript, but *that*
fragment ought to be scrapped. It was written as nicely as everything
I wrote but happened to be marred by a fatal philosophical flaw.

Young, graceful, tremendously charming, hopelessly homely Mary
Middle came to say I would have to be back when the bell tinkled for

tea. In five minutes. Another nurse signaled to her from the sun-striped end of the gallery, and she fluttered away.

The place (you said) was full of dying American bankers and perfectly healthy Englishmen. I had described a person in the act of imagining his recent evening stroll. A stroll from point H (Home, Hotel) to point P (Parapet, Pinewood). Imagining fluently the sequence of wayside events – child swinging in villa garden, lawn sprinkler rotating, dog chasing a wet ball. The narrator reaches point P in his mind, stops – and is puzzled and upset (quite unreasonably as we shall see) by being unable to execute mentally the about-face that would turn direction HP into direction PH.

'His mistake,' she continued, 'his morbid mistake is quite simple. He has confused direction and duration. He speaks of space but he means time. His impressions along the HP route (dog overtakes ball, car pulls up at next villa) refer to a series of time events, and not to blocks of painted space that a child can rearrange in any old way. It has taken him time – even if only a few moments – to cover distance HP in thought. By the time he reaches P he has accumulated duration, he is saddled with it! Why then is it so extraordinary that he cannot imagine himself turning on his heel? Nobody can imagine in physical terms the act of reversing the order of time. Time is not reversible. Reverse motion is used in films only for comic effects – the resurrection of a smashed bottle of beer –'

'Or rum,' I put in, and here the bell tinkled.

'That's all very well,' I said, as I groped for the levers of my wheelchair, and you helped me to roll back to my room. 'And I'm grateful, I'm touched, I'm cured! Your explanation, however, is merely an exquisite quibble – and you know it; but never mind, the notion of trying to twirl time is a *trouvaille*; it resembles (kissing the hand resting on my sleeve) the neat formula a physicist finds to keep people happy until (yawning, crawling back into bed) until the next chap snatches the chalk. I had been promised some rum with my tea – Ceylon and Jamaica, the sibling islands (mumbling comfortably, dropping off, mumble dying away) –'

Contemporary ... Provocative ... Outrageous ...
Prophetic ... Groundbreaking ... Funny ... Disturbing ...
Different ... Moving ... Revolutionary ... Inspiring ...
Subversive ... Life-changing ...

What makes a modern classic?

At Penguin Classics our mission has always been to make the best
books ever written available to everyone. And that also means
constantly redefining and refreshing exactly what makes a 'classic'.
That's where Modern Classics come in. Since 1961 they have been an
organic, ever-growing and ever-evolving list of books from the last
hundred (or so) years that we believe will continue to be read over and
over again.

They could be books that have inspired political dissent, such as
Animal Farm. Some, like *Lolita* or *A Clockwork Orange*, may have
caused shock and outrage. Many have led to great films, from *In Cold
Blood* to *One Flew Over the Cuckoo's Nest*. They have broken down
barriers – whether social, sexual, or, in the case of *Ulysses*, the
boundaries of language itself. And they might – like *Goldfinger* or
Scoop – just be pure classic escapism. Whatever the reason, Penguin
Modern Classics continue to inspire, entertain and enlighten millions
of readers everywhere.

'No publisher has had more influence on reading habits than Penguin'
Independent

'Penguins provided a crash course in world literature'
Guardian

The best books ever written

PENGUIN  CLASSICS

SINCE 1946

Find out more at www.penguinclassics.com